Make time for frien...

DEBBIE
MACOMBER

DEBBIE MACOMBER

A Mother's Wish

HARLEQUIN®MIRA®

This edition published in Great Britain 2015
by Harlequin MIRA, an imprint of Harlequin (UK) Limited,
Eton House, 18-24 Paradise Road,
Richmond, Surrey, TW9 1SR

ISBN 978-0-263-91558-7

22-0215

Harlequin (UK) Limited's policy is to use papers that are natural, renewable and recyclable products and made from wood grown in sustainable forests. The logging and manufacturing processes conform to the legal environmental regulations of the country of origin.

Printed and bound by
CPI Group (UK) Ltd, Croydon, CR0 4YY

Debbie Macomber is a number one *New York Times* bestselling author. Her recent books include *44 Cranberry Point*, *50 Harbor Way*, *6 Rainier Drive*, and *Hannah's List*. She has become a leading voice in women's fiction worldwide and her work has appeared on every major bestseller list. There are more than one hundred million copies of her books in print. For more information on Debbie and her books, visit www.Debbie Macomber.com.

Wanted: Perfect Partner

For Arlene Tresness, a grandma like me,
a lover of books, a devoted reader of mine.
Thank you for your unfailing support and enthusiasm.
(Your grandchildren think the world of you!)

Prologue

"Is our ad there?" Fifteen-year-old Lindsey Remington whispered to her best friend. She glanced nervously at her bedroom door. Lindsey's biggest fear was that her mother would find her and Brenda scanning the Dateline section of the Wednesday paper and discover what they'd done.

Okay, so it was a bit…dishonest to write an ad on Meg Remington's behalf, but it was clear to Lindsey that her mom needed help. She was convinced that Meg *wanted* to remarry, whether she knew it or not.

It wasn't as if Lindsey could pull a potential husband out of nowhere. So she wrote the ad, with her best friend advising her.

"Here," Brenda said excitedly, pointing to the middle

of the page. "It's here. Oh, my goodness! It's really here, just the way we wrote it."

Lindsey found the ad. She read aloud:

"Wanted: Perfect partner. I'm dating-shy, divorced and seeking a man with marriage in mind. I look like a beauty queen, cook like a mom, kiss like a woman in love. Box 1234."

"It sounds even better in print," Brenda said.

"Do you think anyone will actually respond?" Lindsey asked.

"I bet we get lots of letters."

"I still think we should've said her kisses taste better than chocolate."

"It didn't fit. Remember?" They'd worked long and hard on the wording. Lindsey had wanted to describe her mother as "stunning," and Brenda was afraid it might not meet the truth-in-advertising rules.

All right, so her mother wasn't fashion model material, but she was very pretty. Or she could be, with a little assistance from the magazines Lindsey had been reading lately. Luckily Meg had a daughter who knew the ropes.

"Don't worry, Linds," Brenda said with a romantic sigh. "This is the best thing you could ever have done for your mother."

Lindsey hoped her mom appreciated her efforts. "Just remember, this guy has to be *perfect*. We'll need to be careful who we pick."

"No problem. If we don't like the sound of one guy, we'll choose someone else," Brenda said, as if they were guaranteed to have tons of applicants. "That's the beauty of our plan. We'll screen all the applicants before your mother has a chance to date them. How many teenagers get to choose their own stepfathers? Not many, I bet."

Lindsey returned her attention to the ad, gnawing on the corner of her lip. She was experiencing a twinge of pride along with a mild case of guilt.

Her mother wasn't going to like this. When Meg learned what she and Brenda had done, she'd probably get all bent out of shape.

As for the ad, Lindsey figured if she were a man inclined to read the Dateline section, the ad would intrigue her.

"Some men will write just because your mom's pretty, but it's the part about her being a good cook that'll really work," Brenda assured her. "My grandma says Grandpa married her because her German potato salad was so good. Can you believe it?"

Brenda brought up a good point. "How will we know if a man is marrying her for her looks or her meat loaf or 'cause he loves her?"

"We won't," Brenda said, "but by then we'll be out of the picture. Your mother will be on her own."

Lindsey wished she knew more about men. Unfortunately her experience was limited. She'd only gone on two real dates, both times to school dances. And her mother had been a chaperone.

"The day will come when Mom will appreciate what we've done for her," Lindsey said. "She's the one who's always saying how important it is to go after your dreams. Well, this is my dream for her. She wants a man. She just doesn't know it yet."

"All she needs is a little help from us."

"And she's got it," Lindsey said, smiling broadly.

One

Those girls were up to something. Meg Remington peeked in her fifteen-year-old daughter's bedroom to see Lindsey and her best friend, Brenda, crouched on the floor beside the bed. They were speaking in heated whispers.

Meg cleared her throat and instantly both girls were silent.

"Hi, Mom," Lindsey said, her bright blue eyes flashing.

Meg knew the look, which generally spelled trouble. "What are you two doing?"

"Nothing."

"Nothing," Brenda echoed with angelic innocence.

Meg crossed her arms and leaned her shoulder against the doorjamb. She had all the time in the world, and she wanted them to know it. "Tell me why I don't believe that. You two have the *look*."

"What look?" Lindsey repeated, turning to Brenda.

"The one every mother recognizes. You're up to something, and I want to know what." She crossed her ankles, indicating that she'd make herself comfortable until they were ready to let her in on their little secret. She could outwait them if need be.

"All right, if you *must* know," Lindsey said with a shrug of defeat. She leapt to her feet and Brenda followed suit. "But we haven't finished planning everything yet."

"I must know." Meg was struck by how beautiful her daughter had become over the past few years. She'd gone from the gangly, awkward, big-teeth stage to real beauty almost overnight. Meg's ex-husband, Dave, had commented on the changes in Lindsey when she'd flown from Seattle to Los Angeles to visit over spring break. Their little girl was growing up.

"We've been doing some heavy-duty planning," Brenda explained.

"And exactly what are the two of you working on? I haven't seen you all evening." Generally, when Brenda stayed over, which was at least one night of every weekend, the two of them were up until all hours playing music, watching television or DVDs. The house had been suspiciously quiet all evening. Come to think of it, they'd been spending a lot of time in Lindsey's bedroom of late. Far too much time.

The girls glanced at each other before answering.

"You tell her," Brenda urged, "she's your mother."

"I know." Lindsey brushed back the long strands of hair. "But it might be a little easier coming from you."

"Lindsey?" Meg was more curious than ever now.

"You'd better sit down, Mom." Lindsey took Meg by the hand and guided her to the bed.

Meg sat on the edge. Both girls stood in front of her and each seemed to be waiting for the other to speak first.

"You're such an attractive woman," Lindsey began.

Meg frowned. This sounded like a setup to her, and the best way to handle that was to get straight to the point. "You need money? How much, and for what?"

With her usual flair for the dramatic, Lindsey rolled her eyes. "I don't need any money. I meant what I said— you're beautiful."

"It's true," Brenda piped up. "And you're only thirty-seven."

"I am?" Meg had to think about that. "Yeah, I guess I am."

"You're still so young."

"I wouldn't go that far…"

"You've still got it, Mrs. Remington," Brenda cut in, her voice intense. "You're young and pretty and single, and you've got *it*." Her fist flew through the air and punctuated the comment.

"Got what?" Meg was beginning to feel a bit confused.

"You're not in bad shape, either," Lindsey commented, resting her chin on one hand.

Meg sucked in her stomach, feeling pleased with the girls' assessment.

"Of course you'd look even better if you lost ten pounds," her daughter said thoughtfully.

Ten pounds. Meg breathed again and her stomach pouched out. Those ten pounds had first made their appearance when Meg was pregnant with Lindsey nearly sixteen years earlier. She was downright proud of having maintained her post-pregnancy weight for all these years.

"Ten pounds isn't too much to lose," Brenda said confidently.

"It won't be hard at all—especially with the two of us helping you."

Meg stared into their eager, expectant faces. "Why is it so important for me to lose ten pounds? I happen to like the way I look."

"There's more."

Meg glanced from one girl to the other. "More? What is that supposed to mean?"

"You need to be physically fit. Think about it, Mom. When's the last time you ran an eight-minute mile?"

Meg didn't need to consider that at all—she already

knew the answer. "Never." She'd jogged around the track during high school, only because it was required of her. The lowest grade she'd ever received was in phys ed.

"See?" Lindsey said to Brenda.

"We'll work with her," Brenda answered. "But we'll have to start soon."

Lindsey crossed her arms and carefully scrutinized Meg. "About your clothes, Mom."

"My clothes?" Meg cried, still astonished that her daughter wanted her to run an eight-minute mile. She owned a bookstore, for heaven's sake. In the eight years since she'd bought out Mr. Olsen, not once had she been required to run for anything.

"I want to know what's going on here," Meg said. "Now."

"I promise we'll answer all your questions in a minute," Brenda explained. "Please be patient, Mrs. Remington."

Lindsey sighed. "Mom, I don't mean to be rude or anything, but when it comes to your clothes, well…you need help."

"Help?" And to think Meg had been dressing herself for the past thirty-some years. Until now, no one had bothered to tell her what a poor job she'd done.

"I'm here to see you don't ever wear high-waisted jeans again," Lindsey said, as though pledging her life to a crusade. "They're called mom jeans," she whispered.

"So you two are official members of the fashion

police?" Meg asked. Apparently they'd issued an APB on her!

Lindsey and Brenda giggled.

"That's what it sounds like."

"We're here to help you," Brenda said in loving tones.

"We're here to keep you from committing those fashion sins."

"What sins?" Meg should've known. "Do you mind telling me what this little heart-to-heart is all about?"

"*You,* Mom," Lindsey said, in a voice that suggested the answer should've been obvious.

"Why now? Why me?"

"Why not?" Lindsey responded.

Meg started to get up, but Lindsey directed her back onto the bed. "We aren't finished yet. We're just getting to the good part."

"Honey, I appreciate what you're doing, but…"

"Sit down, Mom," Lindsey said in stern tones. "I haven't told you the most important thing yet."

Meg held up both hands. "Okay, okay."

"Like we already said, you're still young," Brenda began.

Lindsey smiled sweetly. "You could have more children if you wanted and—"

"Now wait a minute!" Meg cried.

"What we're really saying is that you're quite attractive."

"Or I could be," Meg amended, "with a little assistance from the two of you."

"Not all that much," Brenda added sympathetically. "We just want to get you started on the right track."

"I see," Meg muttered.

"Together," Lindsey said, slipping her arm around Brenda's waist and beaming a proud smile, "we're going to find you a husband."

"A husband." Meg's feet went out from under her and she slipped off the bed and landed with a solid whack on the carpet.

Lindsey and Brenda each grabbed one arm and pulled her off the floor. "Are you all right?" Lindsey asked, sounding genuinely concerned.

"You should've been more subtle," Brenda said accusingly. "There was no need to blurt it out like that."

Meg rubbed her rear end and sat back down on the bed. "What makes either of you think I want a husband?" she demanded angrily. She'd already been through one bad marriage and she wasn't eager to repeat the experience.

"When's the last time you went out on a date?" Lindsey asked.

"I don't remember," Meg snapped. "What does it matter, anyway?"

"Mother, it's clear to me you aren't thinking about the future."

"The future? What are you talking about?"

"Do you realize that in three years I'll be in college?"

"Three years," Meg repeated. "No-o, I guess I hadn't given it much thought." Although at the moment sending her daughter away actually seemed appealing.

"You'll be all alone."

"Alone isn't such a bad thing," Meg told them.

"At forty it is," Lindsey said dramatically. "I'll worry myself sick about you," she continued.

"She will," Brenda confirmed, nodding twice.

Meg figured it was a good thing she was sitting down.

"Tell me, Mother," Lindsey said, "what would it hurt to start dating again?"

"Honey, has it ever occurred to you that I'm happy just the way I am?"

"No," Lindsey returned. "You aren't happy. You're letting life pass you by. It's time to take action. I don't know what went wrong between you and Dad, but whatever it was must've been traumatic. You haven't had a relationship since—have you?"

Meg didn't answer that question, but wanted to reassure Lindsey about the break-up of her marriage. "It was a friendly divorce." In fact, Meg got along better with Dave now than she had when they were married.

Brenda shook her head. "There's no such thing as a friendly divorce. My dad's an attorney and he should know."

"I don't want to talk about the divorce," Meg said in her

sternest voice. "It happened a long time ago and bringing it up now isn't going to help anyone."

"It might help *you*," Lindsey said, her eyes intense, "but I can understand why you don't want to talk about it. Don't worry," she said, and a bright smile transformed her face, "because you're going to get all the help you need from Brenda and me."

"That's what I was afraid of." Meg stood up and moved toward the door.

"Your diet starts tomorrow," Lindsey called after her.

"And your exercise regime," Brenda added. "You haven't got a thing to worry about, Mrs. Remington. We're going to find you a man before you know it."

Meg closed her eyes. If thirty-seven was so young, why didn't she have the energy to stand up to these two? She wasn't going on any diet, nor did she have time for exercising.

As for having Lindsey as a wardrobe consultant... That was ridiculous, and Meg intended to tell her daughter and Brenda exactly that.

First thing in the morning.

Meg soon learned exactly how serious Lindsey and Brenda were about finding her a husband. She woke Saturday morning to the sound of a workout DVD playing loudly on the television in her bedroom.

She lay facedown, awakened from a pleasant dream

about a sunny beach. Her arm hung over the side of the bed, her fingertips dangling an inch or so above the carpet.

"You ready, Mrs. Remington?" Brenda called from the doorway.

She tried to ignore the girl, but that didn't work.

"You ready?" Brenda called a second time. She seemed to be jogging in place. "Don't worry, we'll go nice and slow in the beginning."

"I'm not doing anything without speaking to my attorney first," Meg muttered. She stuck out her arm and searched blindly for the phone.

"Forget it, Mom. That isn't going to work." Lindsey walked into the bedroom and set a coffee mug on the nightstand.

"Bless you, my child," Meg said. "Ah, coffee." She'd struggled into a sitting position before she realized caffeine had nothing to do with whatever Lindsey had brought her. "What *is* this?" she barked.

"It's a protein supplement. The lady at the health food store recommends it for toning skin in women over thirty."

"Are you sure you're supposed to drink it?" Meg asked.

Lindsey and Brenda looked at each other blankly.

"I'd better check the instructions again," Lindsey said and carried it away.

"Don't worry, Mrs. Remington, we'll have you whipped into shape in no time."

"Coffee," she pleaded. She couldn't be expected to do anything, let alone exercise, without caffeine.

"You can have your coffee," Brenda promised her, "but first..."

Meg didn't bother to listen to the rest. She slithered back under the covers and pulled a pillow over her head. Although it did block out some of the noise, she had no trouble hearing the girls. They weren't accepting defeat lightly. They launched into a lively discussion about the pros and cons of allowing Meg to drink coffee. She had news for these two dictators. Let either one of them try to stand between her and her first cup of coffee.

The conversation moved to the topic of the divorce; Brenda apparently believed Meg had suffered psychological damage that had prevented her from pursuing another relationship.

It was all Meg could do not to shove the pillow aside and put in her two cents' worth. What she should've done was order them out of the bedroom, but she was actually curious to hear what they had to say.

Her divorce hadn't been as bad as all that. She and Dave had made the mistake of marrying far too young. Meg had been twenty-two when she'd had Lindsey, and Dave was fresh out of college. In the five years of their marriage there hadn't been any ugly fights or bitter disagreements. Maybe it would've helped if there had been.

By the time Lindsey was four, Dave had decided

he didn't love Meg anymore and wanted a divorce. It shouldn't have come as a surprise, but it did—and it hurt. Meg suspected he'd found someone else.

She was right.

For a long time after the divorce was final, Meg tried to convince herself that her failed marriage didn't matter. She and her husband had parted on friendly terms. For Lindsey's sake, Meg had made sure they maintained an amicable relationship.

Dave had hurt her, though, and Meg had denied that pain for too long. Eventually she'd recovered. It was over now, and she was perfectly content with her life.

She'd started working at Book Ends, an independent bookstore, and then, with a loan from her parents she'd managed to buy it.

Between the bookstore and a fifteen-year-old daughter, Meg had little time for seeking out new relationships. The first few years after the divorce she'd had a number of opportunities to get involved with other men. She hadn't. At the time, Meg simply wasn't interested, and as the years went on, she'd stopped thinking about it.

"Mother, would you please get out of this bed," Lindsey said, standing over her. Then in enticing tones, she murmured, "I have coffee."

"You tricked me before."

"This one's real coffee. The other stuff, well, I apologize about that. I guess I misunderstood the lady at the health food store. You were right. According to the directions, you're supposed to use it in the bath, not drink it. Sorry about that."

Meg could see it wasn't going to do the least bit of good to hide her face under a pillow. "I can't buy my way out of this?" she asked.

"Nope."

"You'll feel much better after you exercise," Brenda promised her. "Really, you will."

An hour later, Meg didn't feel any such thing. She couldn't move without some part of her anatomy protesting.

"You did great, Mrs. Remington," Brenda praised.

Meg limped into her kitchen and slowly lowered herself into a chair. Who would've believed a workout DVD, followed by a short—this was the term the girls used—one-mile run, would reduce her to this. In the past hour she'd been poked, prodded, pushed and punished.

"I've got your meals all planned out for you," Lindsey informed her. She opened the refrigerator door and took out a sandwich bag. She held it up for Meg's inspection. "This is your lunch."

Meg would've asked her about the meager contents if she'd had the breath to do so. All she could see was one radish, a square of cheese—low-fat, she presumed—and a small bunch of seedless grapes.

"Don't have any more than the nonfat yogurt for breakfast, okay?"

Meg nodded, rather than dredge up the energy to argue.

"Are you going to tell her about dinner?" Brenda asked.

"Oh, yeah. Listen, Mom, you've been a real trooper about this and we thought we should reward you. Tonight for dinner you can have a baked potato."

She managed a weak smile. Visions of butter and sour cream waltzed through her head.

"With fresh grilled fish."

"You like fish don't you, Mrs. Remington?"

Meg nodded. At this point she would've agreed to anything just to get the girls out of her kitchen, so she could recover enough to cook herself a decent breakfast.

"Brenda and I are going shopping," Lindsey announced. "We're going to pick out a whole new wardrobe for you, Mom."

"It's the craziest thing," Meg told her best friend, Laura Harrison, that same afternoon. They were unpacking boxes of books in the back room. "All of a sudden, Lindsey said she wants me to remarry."

"Really?"

Laura found this far too humorous to suit Meg. "But she wants me to lose ten pounds and run an eight-minute mile first."

"Oh, I get it now," Laura muttered, taking paperbacks from the shipping carton and placing them on a cart.

"What?"

"Lindsey was in the store a couple of weeks ago looking for a book that explained carbs and fat grams."

"I'm allowed thirty fat grams a day," Meg informed her. "And one hundred grams of carbohydrates." Not that her fifteen-year-old daughter was going to dictate what she did and didn't eat.

"I hope Lindsey doesn't find out about that submarine sandwich you had for lunch."

"I couldn't help it," Meg said. "I haven't been that hungry in years. I don't think anyone bothered to tell Lindsey and Brenda that one of the effects of a workout is a voracious appetite."

"What was that phone call about earlier?" Laura asked.

Meg frowned as she moved books onto the cart. "Lindsey wanted my credit card number for a slinky black dress with a scoop neckline." Lindsey had sounded rapturous over the dress, describing it in detail, especially the deep cuts up the sides that would reveal plenty of thigh. "She said she found it on sale—and it was a deal too good to pass up." She paused. "Needless to say, I told her no."

"What would Lindsey want with a slinky black dress?"

"She wanted it for me," Meg said, under her breath.

"You?"

"Apparently once I fit the proper image, they plan to dress me up and escort me around town."

Laura laughed.

"I'm beginning to think you might not be such a good friend after all," Meg told her employee. "I expected sympathy and advice, not laughter."

"I'm sorry, Meg. Really."

She sounded far more amused than she did sorry.

Meg cast her a disgruntled look. "You know what your problem is, don't you?"

"Yes," Laura was quick to tell her. "I'm married, with college-age children. I don't have to put up with any of this nonsense and you do. Wait, my dear, until Lindsey gets her driver's license. *Then* you'll know what real fear is."

"One disaster at a time, thank you." Meg sat on a stool and reached for her coffee cup. "I don't mind telling you I'm worried about all this."

"Why?" Laura straightened and picked up her own cup, refilling it from the freshly brewed pot. "It's a stage Lindsey's going through. Trust me, it'll pass."

"Lindsey keeps insisting I'll be lonely when she leaves for college, which she reminded me is in three years."

"Will you be?"

Meg had to think about that. "I don't know. I suppose in some ways I will be. The house will feel empty without her." The two weeks Lindsey spent with her father every year seemed interminable. Meg wandered around the house like a lost puppy.

"So, why *not* get involved in another relationship?" Laura asked.

"With whom?" was Meg's first question. "I don't know any single men."

"Sure you do," Laura countered. "There's Ed, who has the insurance office two doors down."

"Ed's single?" She rather liked Ed. He seemed like a decent guy, but she'd never thought of him in terms of dating.

"The fact that you didn't know Ed was single says a lot. You've got to keep your eyes and ears open."

"Who else?"

"Buck's divorced."

Buck was a regular customer, and although she couldn't quite understand why, Meg had never cared for him. "I wouldn't go out with Buck."

"I didn't say you had to go out with him, I just said he was single."

Meg couldn't see herself kissing either man. "Anyone else?"

"There are lots of men out there."

"Oh, really, and I'm blind?"

"Yes," Laura said. "If you want the truth, I don't think Lindsey's idea is so bad. True, she may be going about it the wrong way, but it wouldn't hurt you to test the waters. You might be surprised at what you find."

Meg sighed. She'd expected support from her best friend, and instead Laura had turned traitor.

By the time Meg had closed the bookstore and headed home, she was exhausted. So much for all those claims about exercise generating energy. In her experience, it did the reverse.

"Lindsey," she called out, "are you home?"

"I'm in my room," came the muffled reply from the bedroom at the top of the stairs.

Something she couldn't put her finger on prompted Meg to hurry upstairs to her daughter's bedroom despite her aching muscles. She knocked once and opened the door to see Lindsey and Brenda sitting on the bed, leafing through a stack of letters.

Lindsey hid the one she was reading behind her back. "Mom?" she said, her eyes wide. "Hi."

"Hello."

"Hello, Mrs. Remington," Brenda said, looking decidedly guilty.

It was then that Meg saw the black dress hanging from the closet door. It was the most provocative thing she'd seen in years.

"How'd you get the dress?" Meg demanded, angry that Lindsey had gone against her wishes and wondering how she'd managed to do it.

The two girls stared at each other, neither one eager to give her an answer. "Brenda phoned her mother and she put it on her credit card," Lindsey said at last.

"What?" Meg felt ready to explode.

"It was only a small lie," Brenda said quickly. "I told my mom it was perfect and on sale and too cheap to resist. What I didn't tell her was that the dress wasn't for me."

"It's going back right this minute, and then the three of us are paying Brenda's parents a visit."

"Mom!" Lindsey flew off the bed. "Wait, please." She had a panicked look in her eyes. "What we did was wrong, but when you wouldn't agree to buy the dress yourself, we didn't know what to do. You just don't have anything appropriate for Chez Michelle."

Chez Michelle was one of the most exclusive restaurants in Seattle, with a reputation for excellent French cuisine. Meg had never eaten there herself, but Laura and her husband had celebrated their silver wedding anniversary at Chez Michelle and raved about it for weeks afterward.

"You're not making any sense," Meg told her daughter.

Lindsey bit her lip and nodded.

"You have to tell her," Brenda insisted.

"Tell me what?"

"You're the one who wrote the last letter," Lindsey said. "The least you could've done was get the dates right."

"It's tonight."

"I know," Lindsey snapped.

"Would someone tell me what's going on here?" Meg asked, her patience at its end.

"You need that dress, Mom," Lindsey said in a voice so low Meg had to strain to hear her.

"And why would that be?"

"You have a dinner date."

"I do? And just who am I going out with?" She assumed this had something to do with Chez Michelle.

"Steve Conlan."

"Steve Conlan?" Meg repeated. She said it again, looking for something remotely familiar about the name and finding nothing,

"You don't know him," Lindsey told her. "But he's really nice. Brenda and I both like him." She glanced at her friend for confirmation and Brenda nodded eagerly.

"You've met him?" Meg didn't like the sound of this.

"Not really. We exchanged a couple of letters and then we e-mailed back and forth and he seems like a really great guy." The last part was said with forced enthusiasm.

"You've been writing a strange man."

"He's not so strange, Mom, not really. He sounds just like one of us."

"He wants to meet you," Brenda put in.

"Me?" Meg brought her hand to her throat. "Why would he want to do that?"

The girls shared a look, reminiscent of the one she'd caught the night before.

"Lindsey?" Meg asked. "Why would this man want to meet me?"

Her daughter lowered her eyes, refusing to meet Meg's. "Because when we wrote Steve…"

"Yes?"

"Brenda and I told him we were you."

Two

Steve Conlan glanced at his watch. The time hadn't changed since he'd looked before. He could tell it was going to be one of those nights. He had the distinct feeling it would drag by, one interminable minute after another.

He still hadn't figured how he'd gotten himself into this mess. He was minding his own business and the next thing he knew… He didn't want to think about it, because whenever he did his blood pressure rose.

Nancy was going to pay for this.

He was early, not because he was so eager for tonight. No, he was only eager to get it over with.

He tried not to check the time and failed. A minute had passed. Or was it a lifetime?

His necktie felt as if it would strangle him. A tie. He

couldn't believe he'd let Nancy talk him into wearing a stupid tie.

Because he needed something to occupy his time, he took the snapshot out of his shirt pocket.

Meg Remington.

She had a nice face, he decided. Nothing spectacular. She certainly wasn't drop-dead gorgeous, but she wasn't plain, either. Her eyes were her best feature. Clear. Bright. Expressive. She had a cute mouth, too. Very kissable. Sensuous.

What was he supposed to say to the woman? The hell if he knew. He'd read her letters and e-mails a dozen times. She sounded—he hated to say it—immature, as if she felt the need to impress him. She seemed to think that because she ran an eight-minute mile it qualified her for the Olympics. Frankly, he wondered what their dinner would be like, with her being so food conscious and all. She'd actually bragged about how few fat grams and carbs she consumed. Clearly she wasn't familiar with the menu at Chez Michelle. He couldn't see a single low-fat or low-carb entrée.

That was another thing. The woman had expensive tastes. Dinner at Chez Michelle would set him back three hundred bucks—if he was lucky. So far he'd been anything but...

Involuntarily his gaze fell to his watch again, and he groaned inwardly. His sister owed him for this.

Big time.

* * *

"I refuse to meet a strange man for dinner," Meg insisted coldly. There were some things even a mother wouldn't do.

"But you have to," Brenda pleaded. "I'm sorry, Mrs. Remington, I feel really bad springing this on you, but Steve didn't do anything wrong. You've just *got* to show up. You have to…otherwise he might lose faith in all women."

"So?"

"But he's your date," Lindsey said. "It would've worked out great if…" she paused and scowled at her best friend "…if one of us hadn't gotten the days mixed up."

"Exactly when did you plan on telling me you've been communicating with a strange man, using *my* name?"

"Soon," Lindsey said with conviction. "We had to… He started asking about meeting you almost right away. We did everything we could to hold him off. Oh, by the way, if he asks about your appendix, you've made a full recovery."

Meg groaned. The time frame of their deception wasn't what interested her. She was stalling, looking for a way out of this. She could leave a message for Steve at the restaurant, explaining that she couldn't make it, but that seemed like such a cowardly thing to do.

Unfortunately no escape plan presented itself. Brenda was right; it wasn't Steve's fault that he'd been duped by a pair of teenagers. It wasn't her fault, either, but then Lindsey was her daughter.

"He's very nice-looking," Brenda said. She reached behind her and pulled out a picture from one of the envelopes scattered across Lindsey's bed. "Here, see what I mean?" Meg swore she heard the girl sigh. "He's got blue eyes and check out his smile."

Meg took the photo from Brenda and studied it. Her daughter's friend was right. Steve Conlan was pleasant-looking. His hair was a little long, but that didn't bother her. He wore a cowboy hat and boots and had his thumbs tucked into his hip pockets as he stared into the camera.

"He's tall, dark and *lonesome,*" Lindsey said wistfully.

"Has he ever been married?" Meg asked, curiosity getting the better of her.

"Nope." This time it was Brenda who supplied the information. "He's got his own business, same as you, Mrs. Remington. He owns a body shop and he's been sinking every penny into it."

"What made him place the ad?" she asked the girls. A sudden thought came to her. "He *is* the one who advertised, isn't he?"

Both girls looked away and Meg's heart froze. "You mean to say you two advertised for a husband for me?" She spoke slowly, each word distinct.

"We got lots of letters, too," Brenda said proudly. "We went through them all and chose Steve Conlan."

"Don't you want to know why?" Lindsey prodded.

Meg gestured weakly, still too shocked to react.

"Steve says he decided to answer your ad because one day he woke up and realized life was passing him by. All his friends were married, and he felt like something important was missing in his life. Then he knew it wasn't *something* but someone."

"What about female friends?" Meg asked, thinking he didn't look like a man who'd have to find companionship in the classifieds.

"He said in his letter that…" Lindsey paused and rustled through a sheaf of papers, searching for the right envelope. "Here it is," she muttered. "He doesn't have much opportunity to meet single women unless they've been in an accident, and generally they're not in the mood for romance when they're dealing with a body shop and an insurance company." Lindsey grinned. "He's kind of witty. I like that about him."

"He said a lot of women his age have already been married and divorced and had a passel of kids."

This didn't sound too promising to Meg. "You did happen to mention that I'm divorced, too, didn't you?"

"Of course," Lindsey insisted. "We'd never lie."

Meg bit her tongue to keep from saying the obvious.

"Just think," Brenda said, "out of all the women who advertised, Steve chose you and we chose him. It's destiny."

The girls thought she'd feel complimented, but Meg was suspicious. "Surely there was someone younger and prettier, without children, who interested him."

The two girls exchanged a smile. "He liked the fact that you count carbs and fat grams," Brenda said proudly.

So much for their unwillingness to stretch the truth. "You actually told him that?" She closed her eyes and groaned. "What else did you say?"

"Just that you're really wonderful."

"Heroic," Brenda added. "And you are."

Oh, great. They'd made her sound like a thin Joan of Arc.

"You will meet him, won't you?" Lindsey's dark eyes pleaded with Meg.

"What I should do is march the two of you down to that fancy restaurant and have you personally apologize to him. You both deserve to be grounded until you're forty."

The girls blinked in unison. "But, Mom…"

"Mrs. Remington…"

Meg raised her hand and stopped them. "I won't take you to Chez Michelle, and as for the grounding part… we'll discuss it later."

Two pairs of shoulders sagged with relief.

"But I won't have dinner with Steve Conlan," she said emphatically. "I'll go to the restaurant, introduce myself and explain what happened. I'm sure he'll agree that the best thing to do is skip dinner altogether."

"You'll wear the dress, won't you?" Lindsey asked, eyeing the slinky black concoction hanging outside her closet door.

"Absolutely not," Meg said. She refused to even consider it.

"But you don't have anything special enough for Chez Michelle. Just try it on, Mom."

"No. Well…"

"Come on, Mom. Brenda and I want to see how it looks."

An hour later Meg pulled up at Chez Michelle in the very dress she'd sworn she'd never wear. It fit as if it'd been designed just for her, enhancing her figure and camouflaging those stubborn ten pounds. At least that was what Lindsey and Brenda told her.

"Hello." The hostess greeted her with a wide smile. "Table for one?"

"I'm…meeting someone," Meg said, glancing around the waiting area looking for a man who resembled "tall, dark and lonesome" in the photo. No one did. Nor was there a single male wearing a cowboy hat.

The only man who looked vaguely like the one in the photograph stood in the corner of the room, leaning indolently against the wall as if he had all the time in the world.

He straightened and stared at her.

Meg stared back.

He reached inside his suit pocket and took out a picture.

Meg opened the clasp of her purse and removed the photo the girls had given her. She looked down at it and then up again.

He appeared to be doing the same thing.

"Meg Remington?" he asked uncertainly.

She nodded. "Steve Conlan?"

He nodded, too.

He wore a suit and tie. A suit and tie. The guy had really gone all out for her. Meg swallowed uncomfortably. He'd invited her to this ultrafancy restaurant expecting to meet the woman who'd exchanged those letters and messages with him. Meg felt her heart settle somewhere in the vicinity of her knees. She couldn't very well introduce herself and immediately say it had all been a mistake and cancel dinner. Not when he'd gone to so much trouble.

"I believe our table is ready," Steve said, holding out his arm to her. His hand touched her elbow and he addressed the hostess. "We can be seated now."

The woman gave him an odd look, then picked up two huge menus. "This way."

Meg might've been wrong, but she thought she heard some reluctance in his voice. Perhaps she was a disappointment to Steve Conlan. After the fitness drill Lindsey and Brenda had put her through, Meg was feeling her advancing age.

Pride stiffened Meg's shoulders. So she hadn't signed

any modeling contracts lately. What did he expect from a thirty-seven-year-old woman? If he wanted to date a woman in her twenties, he shouldn't have answered her ad. Lindsey's ad, she corrected. It was all Meg could do not to stop Steve Conlan right then and there and tell him this was as good as it got.

Especially in this dress. It was simply gorgeous. Meg knew now the girls had made the perfect choice. She was glad she'd given in to them on this one. Besides, Lindsey was right; she didn't own anything fancy enough for Chez Michelle. Before she could stop herself she'd agreed to wear it. Soon both girls were offering her fashion advice.

They were escorted to a linen-covered table next to the window, which overlooked Elliot Bay and Puget Sound. The moon's reflection on the water sent gilded light across the surface, and the restaurant's interior was dimly lit.

Meg squinted, barely able to read her menu. She wondered if Steve was having the same problem. Originally she hadn't intended to have dinner with him. Wouldn't even now, if he hadn't gone to so much trouble on her behalf. It seemed crass to drop in, announce it had all been a misguided attempt by her daughter to play match-maker, ask his forgiveness and speedily disappear.

"I believe I'll have the chicken cordon bleu," she said, deciding on the least expensive item on the menu. "And please, I insist on paying for my own meal." It would be unforgivable to gouge him for that as well.

"Dinner's on me," Steve insisted, setting his menu aside. He smiled for the first time and it transformed his face. He studied her, as if he wasn't sure what to make of her.

"But…" Meg lowered her gaze and closed her mouth. She didn't know where to start and yet she didn't know how much longer she could maintain the pretense. "This is all very elegant…."

"Yes," he agreed, spinning the stem of his water glass between his thumb and index finger.

"You look different than your picture." Meg had no idea why she'd told him that. What she *should* be doing was explaining about Lindsey and Brenda.

"How's that?"

"Your eyes are much bluer and you've cut your hair."

He gave a slight grin. "And your picture didn't do you justice."

Meg hadn't thought to ask Lindsey which one she'd mailed Steve. "Can I see?"

"Sure." He pulled it out of his pocket and handed it over.

Meg took one look and rolled her eyes. She couldn't believe Lindsey had sent this particular photograph to anyone. It'd been taken just before Christmas a year earlier. She was standing in front of the Christmas tree wearing a white dress that drained all the color from her face.

The flash from the camera made her eyes appear red. She looked like she was recovering from a serious ailment.

"This is one of the worst pictures ever taken of me," she said impatiently. "The one of me at the bookstore is *much* better."

Steve's brow creased with a frown. "I see. You should've sent that one."

Meg realized what she'd said too late. "You're right, I should have…. How silly of me."

The waitress came and they placed their orders, both declining a drink, Meg to keep down the cost and Steve, no doubt, to hurry the meal along.

Once the server had left the table, Meg carefully smoothed the napkin across her lap. "Listen, Steve…"

"Meg…"

They both stopped.

"You go first," he said, gesturing toward her.

"All right." She cocked her head to one side and then the other, going over the words in her mind. "This isn't easy…."

Steve frowned. "It's been a pleasure to meet me, but the chemistry just isn't there and you'd like to let me down gently and be done with it."

"No!" she hurried to assure him.

"Oh."

The disappointment in his tone came as a mild shock.

Then she understood. "You…expected a different kind of woman and—"

"Not in the least. If the truth be known, I'm pleasantly surprised."

She swallowed. "I wish you hadn't said that."

"Why not?"

"Because…" She dragged in a deep breath. "Because I'm not the person you think I am. I mean…" This was proving even more difficult than it should have. "I didn't write those letters."

Steve's eyes narrowed. "Then who did?"

"My daughter and her friend."

"I…see."

Meg's fingers crushed the linen napkin in her lap. "You have every reason to be upset. It was an underhanded thing to do to us both."

"You didn't know anything about this?"

"I swear I didn't. I would've put a stop to it immediately if I had."

Steve reached for his water and drank thirstily. "I would have, too."

"I want you to know I intend to discipline Lindsey for this. I can only apologize…" She stopped midsentence when she saw his shoulders moving with suppressed laughter. "Steve?"

"I didn't write those letters, either. The ones from me."

"What?" Disbelief settled over Meg. "You mean to say you didn't respond to the ad in Dateline?"

"Nope. My romantic little sister did. Nancy's on this kick about seeing me married. I don't understand it, but—"

"Just a minute," Meg said, raising her hand. "Let me see if I've got this straight. You didn't place the ad in Dateline."

"You've got it."

"Then why are you here?"

He shrugged. "Probably for the same reason you are. I figured you were some lonely heart seeking companionship and frankly I felt bad that Nancy had led you on like this. It isn't your fault my crazy sister thinks it's time I got married."

He paused when their meals were delivered.

Meg dug into her chicken with gusto. Irritation usually made her hungry. She stabbed a carrot slice with her fork.

"So you felt sorry for me?" she said, chewing the carrot vigorously.

He looked up, apparently sensing her irritation. "No sorrier than you felt for me."

He had her there.

"It's the reason you showed up, isn't it?" he pressed.

She agreed with a nod. "When did you find out about this dinner date?"

"This morning. You?"

She glanced at her watch. "About two hours ago."

Steve chuckled. "They didn't give you much opportunity to object, did they?"

"Actually they got the days mixed up and went into a panic. I don't suppose you happened to read any of the letters or e-mails they wrote?"

"As a matter of fact I did. Interesting stuff."

"I'll bet." She stabbed one of the potato pieces with her fork. "You should know that not everything they said was the truth." She put the potato in her mouth and chewed.

"So you don't actually run an eight-minute mile."

"No…"

"Nine minutes?"

"I don't exactly run, and before you ask me about carbs and fat grams, you can forget everything Lindsey told you about those, too. And for the record, my appendix is in great shape."

Steve chuckled. "What did Nancy tell you about me?"

"Since I've only read tidbits of your letters and e-mails, I can't really say."

"Oh?" His voice fell noticeably.

"As I recall, your sister did suggest that your life's quite empty and you're looking for something to fill your lonely nights—" she paused for effect "—until you realized it wasn't *something* you were searching for but *someone*."

His jaw tightened. "She said that?"

"Yup." Meg took some pleasure in telling him that.

"Well, that's a crock of bull. I certainly hope you didn't believe it."

Meg smiled. "Not really. Lindsey didn't mean any harm, you know."

"Nancy, either, although I'd like to throttle her. The kid's nineteen and she's got romance and marriage on her mind. Unfortunately, it's me she's trying to marry off."

"Lindsey thinks I'm lost and lonely, but I'm perfectly content with my life."

"Me, too."

"Why ruin everything now?"

"Exactly," Steve agreed with conviction. "A woman would want to change everything about me."

"A man would string me along until he found someone prettier and sexier. Besides," Meg added, "I have no intention of becoming a pawn in some ploy of my daughter's."

"Nancy can take a flying leap into Green Lake before I'll let her arrange my love life," Steve told her adamantly. "I certainly intend to marry, but on *my* time—not when my kid sister ropes me into a lonely-hearts-club relationship."

"I feel the same way."

"Great." Steve grinned at her, and Meg had to admit he had a wonderful smile. It lit up his eyes and softened his features. "Shall we drink to our agreement?"

"Definitely."

Steve attracted the waitress's attention and ordered a bottle of wine.

Meg was astonished by the ease with which they could talk, once all the pretense between them had been resolved. She told him about her bookstore and liked hearing about his body shop. They lingered over coffee and dessert, and not until it became apparent that the restaurant was about to close did they get up to leave.

"I enjoyed myself," Meg said as they strolled to the door.

"Don't sound so surprised."

"Frankly, I am."

He laughed. "I guess I am, too."

The valet brought her Ford Escort to the front of the restaurant and held open her door.

"Thank you for a lovely dinner," she said, suddenly feeling shy and awkward.

"The pleasure was all mine."

Neither of them made an effort to move. The valet checked his watch and Meg glanced at him guiltily. Steve ignored him and eventually so did Meg.

"I guess this is goodbye," she said, wishing now that she hadn't made such a big issue about not being her daughter's pawn.

"Looks that way."

She lowered her eyes, fighting the enticement she read in his. "Thanks again."

Steve traced his finger along her jaw. His work-calloused fingertip felt warm against her skin. If they hadn't been standing under the lights of a fancy French restaurant with a valet looking on, Meg wondered if he would've kissed her. She wanted to think he might have.

On the drive home, she dismissed the idea as fanciful. It had been a long time since she'd been wined and dined, that was all. And an even longer time since she'd been kissed…

Sensation after sensation traveled across her face where he'd touched her. Smile after smile flirted with her mouth at the memory of his lips so close to hers. She wouldn't forget the date or the man anytime soon. That was for sure.

"Well, how'd it go?" Nancy demanded. His teenage sister met Steve at the door. Her eyes were wide with curiosity as she followed him inside.

Steve looked at his watch and frowned. "What are you still doing up?"

Nancy's face fell. "You asked me to wait for you, so we could talk."

Steve slid his fingers through his hair. "I did, didn't I?"

"You're much later than you thought you'd be."

He didn't respond, unwilling to let his sister know how much he'd enjoyed himself. "I'm furious with you for what you did," he said, forcing his voice to sound gruff with irritation.

"I don't blame you," she agreed readily enough.

"Haven't you got an exam to study for or something?" he asked, although he knew very well she didn't. Nancy attended the nearby University of Washington. She was staying with Steve for the summer, since their parents were now living in Montana.

"You liked her, didn't you?"

Nancy sounded much too smug to suit Steve.

"And no, I don't have any exams to study for, and you know it. They ended two weeks ago." Since then, she'd taken a summer job at the university library.

"So you've decided to stay in Seattle and make my life miserable."

"No, I've decided to stay in Seattle and see you married. Come on, Steve, you're thirty-eight! That's getting up there." She flopped down on the sofa and sat with her legs underneath her, as if she planned to plant herself right there until he announced his engagement.

The problem, Steve decided, was that Nancy was the product of parents who'd never expected a second child and had spoiled her senseless. He was partially to blame, as well, but he'd never thought she'd pull something like this.

"You work too hard," she said. "Loosen up and enjoy life a little."

"You're going to write Meg Remington a formal letter of apology." He refused to back down on this.

"Okay, I'll write her." All at once she was on her feet. "When are you seeing her again?"

"I'm not."

Nancy fell back onto the sofa. "Why not?"

Darned if Steve could give her an answer. He and Meg had made that decision early on in their conversation, and for the life of him he couldn't remember why.

"Because," he growled. "Now leave me alone."

Nancy threw back her head and laughed. "You like her. You really, really like her."

Meg sat in the back storeroom and rubbed her aching feet. The new shoes pinched her toes, but this was what she got for buying them half a size too small. They were on sale and she loved them, although the store had been out of size eights. Even knowing her feet would pay the penalty later, Meg had chosen to wear them today.

Laura stuck her head through the door and smiled when she saw her. "A beautiful bouquet of flowers just arrived for you," she said.

"For me?"

"That's what the envelope said."

"Who from?"

"I didn't read the card, if that's what you're asking, but

Lindsey's here and she grabbed it and let out a holler. My guess is the flowers are from Steve."

"Steve." Pain or no pain, Meg was on her feet. She hobbled to the front of the store and found her fifteen-year-old daughter grinning triumphantly.

"Steve Conlan sent flowers," she crowed.

"So I see." Meg's fingers shook as she removed the card from the small envelope.

"He said, and I quote, 'You're one special woman, Meg Remington. Love, Steve.'"

The bouquet was huge, with at least ten different varieties of flowers all arranged in a white wicker basket. It must have cost him easily a hundred dollars.

"We agreed," she whispered.

"Agreed to what?" Lindsey prodded.

"That we weren't going to see each other again."

"Obviously he changed his mind," Lindsey said, as excited as if she'd just discovered a twenty-dollar bill in the bottom of her purse.

Unwilling to trust her daughter's assessment of the situation, Meg stared at her best friend.

"Don't look at me," Laura said.

"I'm sure you're wrong," Meg said to Lindsey, her heart still beating a little too fast.

"Why else would he send flowers?" Lindsey asked calmly.

"He wanted to say he was glad we met, that's all. I don't

think we should make something out of this," she said. "It's just…a courtesy."

"Call him," Lindsey pleaded.

"I most certainly will not!"

"But, Mom, don't you see? Steve's saying he likes you, but he doesn't want to pressure you into anything unless you like him, too."

"He is?" Whatever confidence she'd felt a moment earlier vanished like ice cream at a Fourth of July picnic.

"The next move is yours."

"Laura?"

"I wouldn't know," her fickle friend said. "I've been married to the same man for twenty-six years. All this intrigue is beyond me."

"I agree with your daughter," a shy voice said from the other side of the counter. "You should call him."

It was Meg's customer, Judith Wilson. Meg wasn't sure she should listen to the older woman who faithfully purchased romance novels twice a month. Judith was a real romantic and would undoubtedly read more into the gesture than Steve had intended.

"See?" Lindsey said excitedly. "The ball's in your court. Steve made his move and now he's waiting for yours."

Meg didn't know what to do.

"It's been three days," Lindsey reminded her. "He's had time to think over the situation, and so have you."

"Call him," Laura suggested. "If for nothing more than to thank him for the flowers."

"Yes, call him," Judith echoed, clutching her bag of books.

"It's the least you can do." Once more it was her daughter offering advice.

"All right," Meg said reluctantly. The flowers were gorgeous, and thanking him would be the proper thing to do.

"I'll get his work number for you," Lindsey volunteered, pulling the Yellow Pages from behind the cash register.

The kid had Steve's shop number faster than directory assistance could have located it.

"I'll use the phone in the back room," Meg said. She didn't need several pairs of ears listening in on her conversation.

She felt everyone's eyes on her as she hurried into the storeroom. Her hand actually shook as she punched out the telephone number.

"Emerald City," a gruff male voice answered.

"Hello, this is Meg Remington calling for Steve Conlan."

"Hold on a minute."

"Of course."

A moment later, Steve was on the line. "Meg?"

"Hello, Steve. I know you're busy, so I won't take up

much of your time. I'm calling to thank you for the flowers."

A long pause followed her words. "Flowers? What
flowers?"

Three

"You mean you don't know anything about these flowers?" Meg cried, her voice raised. Steve could see that he hadn't done a very good job of breaking the news, but he was as shocked as she was.

"If you didn't send them, who did?" Meg demanded.

It wasn't difficult to figure that one out. "I can make a wild guess," he said with heavy sarcasm. He jerked his fingers through his hair, then glanced at the wall clock. It was close to quitting time. "Can you meet me?"

"Why?"

Her blatant lack of enthusiasm irritated him. He'd been thinking about her for three days. Nancy was right—he liked Meg Remington. She was a bit eccentric and a little on the hysterical side, but he was willing to overlook that.

During their time together, he'd been struck by her intelligence and her warmth. He'd wished more than once that they'd decided to ignore the way they'd been thrown together and continue to see each other. Apparently Meg suffered no such regrets and was pleased to be rid of him.

"Why do you want to meet?" she repeated, lowering her voice.

"We need to talk."

"Where?"

"How about a drink? Can you get away from the store in the next hour or so?"

She hesitated. "I'll try."

Steve mentioned a popular sports bar in Kent, and she agreed to meet him there at five-thirty. His spirits lifted considerably at the prospect of seeing her again. He must've been smiling as he hung up because his foreman, Gary Wilcox, cast him a puzzled look.

"I didn't know you had yourself a new girlfriend," Gary said. "When did this happen?"

"It hasn't." The last thing Steve needed was Gary feeding false information to his sister. Nancy and her outrageous ideas about marrying him off was enough of a problem, without Gary encouraging it.

"It hasn't happened *yet,* you mean," Gary said, making a notation in the appointment schedule.

Steve glanced over his shoulder, to be sure Gary wasn't making notes about the conversation he'd had with Meg.

He was getting paranoid already. A woman did that to a man, made him jumpy and insecure; he knew that much from past experience.

An hour later Steve sat in the bar, facing a big-screen television with a frosty mug of beer in his hand. The table he'd chosen was in the far corner of the room, where he could easily watch the front door.

Meg walked in ten minutes after him. At least Steve thought it was Meg. The woman carried a tennis racket and wore one of those cute little pleated-skirt outfits. He hadn't realized Meg played tennis. He knew she didn't run and disliked exercise, but...

Steve squinted and stared, unsure. After all, he'd only seen her the one time, and in the slinky black dress she'd looked a whole lot different.

Meg solved his problem when she apparently recognized him. She walked across the room, and he noticed that she was limping. She slid into the chair beside him, then set the tennis racket on the table.

"Lindsey knows," she announced.

Steve's head went back to study her. "I beg your pardon?"

"My daughter figured it out."

"Figured what out?"

"That I was meeting you," she said in exasperated tones. "First, I called you from the back room at the store, so our conversation could be private."

"So?"

She glared at him. "Then I made up this ridiculous story about a tennis game I'd forgotten. I haven't played tennis in years and Lindsey knows that. She immediately had all these questions. She saw straight through me." She pulled the sweatband from her hair and stuffed it in her purse. "She's probably home right now laughing her head off. I can't do this…. I could never lie convincingly."

"Why didn't you just tell your daughter the truth?" He was puzzled by the need to lie at all.

Meg's look of consternation said that would've been impossible. "Well…because Lindsey would think the two of us meeting meant something."

"Why? You told her I didn't write those letters and e-mails, didn't you?"

"No."

"Why not?"

Meg played with the worn strings of the tennis racket as her eyes avoided his. "I should have…. I mean, this is crazy."

"You can say that again." He tried to sound nonchalant and wondered if he'd managed it. He didn't think so. He was actually rather amused by the whole setup. Her daughter and his sister. The girls were close in age and obviously spoke the same language.

"Lindsey's still got romantic ideas when it comes to

men and marriage, but…" Meg paused and chanced a look at him. "She really stepped over the line with this stunt."

"What did you say about our date?"

Meg's hands returned to the tennis racket. "Not much."

Steve hadn't been willing to discuss the details of their evening together with Nancy, either. Nothing had surprised him more than discovering how attractive he'd found Meg Remington. It wasn't solely a sexual attraction, although she certainly appealed to him.

Whenever he'd thought about her in the past three days, he'd remember how they'd talked nonstop over wine and dessert. He remembered how absorbed she'd been in what he was saying; at one point she'd leaned forward and then realized her dress revealed a fair bit of cleavage. Red-faced, she'd pulled back and attempted to adjust her bodice.

Steve liked the way her eyes brightened when she spoke about her bookstore and her daughter, and the way she had of holding her breath when she was excited about something, as if she'd forgotten to breathe.

"Your sister—the one who wrote the letters—is the same one who sent the flowers?" Meg asked, breaking into his thoughts.

Steve nodded. "I'd bet on it."

Meg fiddled with the clasp of her purse and brought out a small card, which she handed him.

Steve raised his arm to attract the cocktail waitress's attention and indicate he wanted another beer for Meg.

"I shouldn't," she said, reaching for a pretzel. "If I come home with beer on my breath, Lindsey will know for sure I wasn't playing tennis."

"According to you, she's already figured it out."

She slid the bowl of pretzels closer and grabbed another handful. "That's true."

Steve opened the card that had come with the flowers and rolled his eyes. "This is from Nancy, all right," he muttered. "I'd never write anything this hokey."

The waitress came with another mug of beer and Steve paid for it. "Do you want more pretzels?" he asked Meg.

"Please." Then in a lower voice, she added, "This type of situation always makes me hungry."

She licked the salt from her fingertips. "Has my daughter, Lindsey, been in contact with you?"

"No, but then I wouldn't know, would I?"

Meg was holding the pretzel in front of her mouth. "Why wouldn't you?"

"Because Lindsey would be writing to Nancy."

Meg's head dropped in a gesture of defeat. "You're right. Much more of this craziness and heaven only knows what they could do to our lives."

"We need to take control," Steve said.

"I totally agree with you," was her response. She took a sip of her beer and set the mug down. "I shouldn't be drinking this on an empty stomach—it'll go straight to my head."

"The bar's got great sandwiches."

"Pretzels are fine." Apparently she'd realized that she was holding the bowl, and she shoved it back to the center of the table. "Sorry," she muttered.

"No problem."

He saw her wince and recalled that she'd been limping earlier. "Is there something wrong with your foot?"

"The shoes I wore to work were too tight," she said, speaking so quietly he had to strain to hear.

"Here," he said, reaching under the table for her feet and setting them on his lap.

"What are you doing?" she asked in a shocked voice.

"I thought I'd rub them for you."

"You'd do that?"

"Yes." It didn't seem so odd to him. The fact was, he hated to see her in pain. "Besides, we need to talk over how we're going to handle this situation. I have a feeling that we'll have to be in top mental form to deal with these kids."

"You're right." She closed her eyes and purred like a well-fed kitten when he removed her tennis shoes and kneaded her aching feet.

"Feel better?" he asked after a couple of minutes.

She nodded, her eyes still closed. "I think you should stop," she said, sounding completely unconvincing.

"Why?" He asked the question, but he stopped and bent down to pick up her shoes, which he'd placed on the floor.

"Thank you," Meg said. She looked around a little self-consciously as she slipped her shoes back on and tied the laces.

Feeling somewhat embarrassed by his uncharacteristic response to her, Steve cleared his throat and picked up his beer. "Do you have any ideas?" he asked.

She stared at him as if she didn't know what he was talking about, then straightened abruptly. "Oh, you mean for dealing with the kids. No, not really. What about you? Any suggestions?"

"Well, we're agreed that we've got to stop letting them run our lives."

"Exactly. We can't allow them to force us into a relationship."

He nodded. But if that was the case, he wondered, why did he experience the almost overwhelming desire to kiss her? All of a sudden, it bothered him that they were discussing strategies that would ensure the end of any contact between them.

He imagined leaning toward her, touching his lips to hers....

There's something wrong with this picture, Conlan, he said to himself, but he couldn't keep from studying her—and picturing their kiss.

He'd been wrong about her face, he decided. She was

beautiful, with classic features, large eyes, a full mouth. He'd trailed his finger down the curve of her cheek the first time they'd met, and now he did so a second time, mentally.

She knew what he was thinking. Steve swore she did. The pulse in her throat hammered wildly and she looked away.

Steve did, too. He didn't know what was happening, didn't want to know. He reached for his beer and gulped down two deep swallows.

What on earth was he doing? Rubbing her feet, thinking about kissing her. He didn't need a woman messing up his life!

Especially a woman like Meg Remington.

"So you met Steve again," Laura said. They sat on a bench in Lincoln Park enjoying huge ice-cream cones. A ferry eased toward the dock at Fauntleroy.

"Who told you that?" Meg answered, deciding to play dumb.

"Lindsey, who else? You really didn't think you fooled her, did you?"

"No." Clearly she had no talent for subterfuge.

"So tell me how your meeting went."

Meg didn't answer. She couldn't. She wasn't sure what, if anything, she and Steve had accomplished during their meeting at the bar. They'd come up with a plan to dissuade his sister and her daughter, but the more hours that passed, the more ridiculous it seemed. And Meg's willingness, indeed her eagerness, to see Steve again was disturbing.

In retrospect she saw that it'd been a mistake for them to get together. All she could think about was how he'd lifted her legs onto his lap and rubbed the tired achiness away. There'd been a sudden explosion of awareness between them. A living, breathing, throbbing awareness.

Rarely had Meg wanted a man to kiss her more. Right in the middle of a sports bar, for heaven's sake! It was the craziest thing to happen to her in years. That of itself was distressing, but what happened afterward baffled her even more.

Melting ice cream dripped onto her hand and Meg hurriedly licked it away.

"Meg?" Laura said, studying her. "What's wrong?"

"Nothing," she said, laughing off her friend's concern. "What could possibly be wrong?"

"You haven't been yourself the last couple of days."

"Sure I have," she said, then deciding it was pointless to go on lying, she blurted out the truth. "I'm afraid I could really fall for this guy."

Laura laughed. "What's so awful about that?"

"For one thing, he isn't interested in me."

This time Laura eyed her suspiciously. "What makes you think that?"

"Several things."

Laura bit into her waffle cone. "Name one."

"Well, he wanted to meet so we could figure out a way to keep the kids from manipulating our lives."

"That sounds suspiciously like an excuse to see you again," Laura murmured.

"Trust me, it wasn't. Steve did everything but come right out and say he's not interested in me."

"You're sure about this?"

"Of course I am! There was ample opportunity for him to suggest we get to know each other better, and he didn't." She'd assumed Steve had experienced the same physical attraction she had, but maybe she'd been wrong.

Lindsey and Brenda had insisted she still had it. All Meg could say was that recent experience had proven otherwise. Whatever *it* was had long since deserted her.

"Did it occur to you that he might've been waiting for *you* to suggest something?" Laura asked.

"No," Meg told her frankly. Steve wasn't a man who took his cues from a woman. If he wanted something or someone, he'd make it known. If he wanted to continue to see her, he would've said so.

"There's got to be more than that."

"There is." Meg took a deep breath. "I was just getting ready to tell you. Steve came up with the idea originally, but I agreed."

"To what?"

Meg stood and found the closest garbage receptacle to dump what remained of her ice cream. "Before I tell you, remember I'd been drinking beer on an empty stomach." Okay, she'd had the pretzels.

"This doesn't sound promising," Laura said.

"It isn't." Drawing in another deep breath, she sat down on the park bench again. "We realized that the louder we protested and the more often we said we weren't attracted to each other, the less likely either Lindsey or Nancy will believe us."

"There's a problem with this scenario," Laura muttered.

"There is?"

"Yes. You *are* interested in Steve. Very interested." Laura gave her a look that said Meg hadn't fooled her.

Meg glanced away. "I don't want to confuse the issue with that."

"All right, go on," Laura said with a wave of her hand.

"Steve thinks the only possible way we have of convincing Lindsey that he's not the right person for me is if he starts dating me and—"

"See?" Laura said triumphantly. "He's interested. Don't you get it? This idea of his is just an excuse."

"I doubt it." Meg could see no reason for him to play games if he truly wanted a relationship with her. "You can come over this evening if you want and see for yourself."

"See what?"

"Steve's coming to meet Lindsey."

"To your house?"

"Yes."

Laura grinned widely. "R-e-a-l-l-y," she said, dragging out the word.

"Really. But it isn't what you think." Because if Laura did believe Steve wanted to pursue something with Meg, her friend was in for a major disappointment.

Meg got home an hour later. Lindsey had taken Steve's visit seriously. She'd cleaned the house, baked cookies and wore her best jeans. A dress would've been asking too much.

"Hello, sweetheart."

"Mom," Lindsey said, frowning at her watch. "Do you have any idea what time it is?"

"Yeah."

"Don't you think you should shower and change clothes? Steve will be here in an hour and a half."

"I know." She supposed she should reveal more enthusiasm, if only for show, but she couldn't make herself do it. This had been Steve's idea and she'd agreed, but she still wasn't convinced.

"I was thinking you should wear that sundress we bought last year with the pretty red-rose print," Lindsey suggested. "That and your white sandals." She studied her mother critically. "I wish you had one of those broad-brimmed sun hats. A pretty white one would be perfect. Very romantic."

"We'll just have to make do with the sombrero Grandpa bought you in Mexico," Meg teased.

"Mother," Lindsey cried, appalled. "That would look stupid!"

Meg sighed dramatically, for effect. "I don't know how I managed to dress myself all these years without you."

She thought—or hoped—that her daughter would laugh. Lindsey didn't. "That might be the reason you're still single. Have you considered that?"

This kid was no help when it came to boosting her confidence.

"You're a great mother," Lindsey said, redeeming herself somewhat, "but promise me you'll never go clothes-shopping without me again."

Rather than make rash pledges she had no intention of keeping, Meg hurried up the stairs and got into the shower. The hot water pulsating against her skin refreshed her and renewed her sense of humor. She could hardly wait to see Lindsey's face when she met Steve.

With a towel tucked around her, Meg wandered into her bedroom and examined the contents of her closet. In this case, Lindsey was right; the sundress was her best choice. She wore it, Meg told herself, because it looked good on her and *not* because Lindsey had suggested it.

Her daughter was waiting for her in the living room. The floral arrangement Steve, or rather Nancy, had sent was displayed in the middle of the coffee table.

Lindsey had polished the silver tea set until it gleamed. The previous time Meg had used it was when Pastor Delany came for a visit shortly after Meg's father died.

The doorbell chimed. Lindsey turned to her mother with a grin. "We're ready," she said, and gave her a thumbs-up sign.

Meg had assumed she knew what to expect, but when she opened the front door her mouth sagged open.

"Steve?" she whispered to the man dressed in a black leather jacket, tight blue jeans and a white T-shirt. "Is that you?"

He winked at her. "You expecting someone else?"

"N-no," she stammered.

"Invite me in," he said in a low voice. As she stepped aside, he walked past her and placed his index finger under her chin, closing her mouth.

He stood in the archway between the entry and her living room, feet braced apart. "You must be Lindsey," he said gruffly. "I'm Steve."

"You're Steve?" Lindsey sounded uncharacteristically meek.

"Lindsey, this is Steve Conlan," Meg said, standing next to him.

Steve slid his arm around Meg's waist and planted a noisy kiss on her cheek. He glanced at Lindsey. "I understand you're the one who got us together. Thanks."

"You're welcome." Lindsey's eyes didn't so much as

flicker. She certainly wasn't about to let them read her thoughts. "You, uh, don't look anything like your picture."

Steve refused to take his eyes off Meg. He squeezed her waist again. "The one I sent was taken a while back," he said. "Before I went to prison."

Lindsey gasped. "Prison?"

"Don't worry, sweetheart. It wasn't a violent crime."

"What…were you in for?" Lindsey asked, her voice shaking.

Steve rubbed the side of his jaw, shadowed by a dark growth of beard. "If you don't mind, I'd rather not say."

"Sit down, Steve," Meg said from between gritted teeth. Talk about overkill. Any more of this and everything would be ruined.

"Would you care for coffee?" Lindsey asked. Her young voice continued to tremble.

"You got a beer?"

"It's not a good idea to be drinking this early in the afternoon, is it?" Meg asked sweetly.

Steve sat down on the sofa, balancing his ankle on the opposite knee. He looked around as if he were casing the joint.

Meg moved to the silver service. "Coffee or tea?"

"Coffee, but add a little something that'll give it some kick."

Meg poured coffee for him and added a generous

dollop of half-and-half. He frowned at the delicate bone china cup as though he wasn't sure how to hold it.

Lindsey sat down on the ottoman, her eyes huge. "I... you never said anything about prison."

"Don't like to mention it until people have a chance to meet me for themselves. Some of 'em tend to think the worst of a person when they hear he's had a felony conviction."

"A...felony." Lindsey snapped her mouth shut, inhaled deeply, then said in a subdued tone, "I see."

"The flowers are lovely." Meg fingered a rosebud from the bouquet.

Steve grinned. "My probation officer told me women like that sort of thing. Glad to know he was right." He sipped his coffee and made a slurping sound. "By the way, you'll be glad to hear I told him about you and me, and he did a background check on you and said it was fine for us to see each other."

"That's wonderful," Meg said with enthusiasm that wasn't *entirely* faked.

Steve set aside the delicate cup and leaned forward, his elbows on his knees. He stared at Lindsey and smiled. "Yup, I got to thank you," he said. "I realize your mother's upset with you placing that ad and everything. It's usually not a good idea to fool someone like that, but I wasn't being completely honest with you, either, so I guess we're even."

Lindsey nodded.

"Your mother's one special woman. There aren't a lot of females who'd be willing to overlook my past. Most women don't care that I've got a heart of gold. Your mama did. We sat down in that fancy restaurant and I took one look at her pretty face and I knew she was the woman for me." He rubbed the side of his unshaven jaw and laughed. "I do have to tell you, though, that when you suggested Chez Michelle, I was afraid Meg might be too high maintenance for someone like me."

"I'm sorry..." Lindsey floundered with the apology. "I didn't know."

"Don't you worry. Your mama was worth every penny of that fancy dinner. Just getting to know her and love her—why, a man couldn't ask for a prettier gal." He eyed her as if she were a Thanksgiving feast, then moistened his lips, implying it was all he could do to keep from grabbing her right then and there and kissing her.

"Steve..." Meg muttered.

"Sorry," he said, and seemed to pull himself together. "Earl Markham, my probation officer, says I've gotta be careful not to rush things. But I look at your beautiful eyes and I can't help myself."

"Yes, well..."

"You didn't tell me how good-looking your daughter is," he said, as though Meg had purposely been holding out on him.

"Lindsey's my pride and joy," Meg said, beaming her daughter a smile.

"I got plenty of friends who wouldn't mind meeting a good-looking girl like you." He winked at Lindsey, suggesting that all he needed was one word from her and he'd make the arrangements immediately.

"Absolutely not!" Meg said, forgetting this was just a game. "I won't have you introducing my daughter to your friends."

Steve's eyes widened with surprise and he held up his right hand, as if taking an oath. "Sorry, I didn't mean to offend. You don't want Lindsey dating any of my buddies, fine, I'll see it never happens."

"Good." Meg had to acknowledge that Steve was an excellent actor. He almost had *her* believing him. She suspected that was because he'd turned himself into the man she'd half expected to meet that night.

Steve smacked his lips. "I gotta tell you when I first saw Meg in that pretty black dress, my heart went all the way to the floor. She's the most beautiful woman I've seen since I was released." His eyes softened as his gaze fell on Meg.

"Released?" Lindsey squeaked.

"From prison," Steve clarified, his gaze immediately returning to Meg.

It would help considerably if he didn't look so sincere, Meg thought.

"Yes, well…" she said, standing. But once she was on her feet, she wasn't sure what to do.

"I'll bet you want me to take you on that motorcycle ride I been promising you," Steve said, downing the last of his coffee.

"Mom's going on a motorcycle with you?" Lindsey asked, swallowing visibly.

"I'd better change clothes," Meg said, eager to escape so she could speak to Steve alone.

"No need," Steve said. "You can ride sidesaddle if you want. I brought my Hog. There's plenty of room, although I gotta tell you, I been dreaming about you sitting behind me, wrapping your arms around my waist. You'll need to hold on tight, honey, real tight." His eyes didn't waver from hers, and the sexual innuendo was unmistakable.

"Yes, well…" Either the room had grown considerably warmer or Meg was in deep trouble.

Judging by the look of disgust Lindsey cast her, she could see it was the latter.

"I think I'll change into a pair of jeans, if it's all the same to you."

"Sure," Steve said, wiping the back of his hand across his mouth. "Just don't keep me waiting long, you hear?"

"I won't," she promised.

Meg rushed toward the stairs, anxious to get away.

Steve reached out to stop her. His hand closed over her shoulder and he brought her into his arms. She gasped in shock. Without giving her time to recover, he lowered his mouth to hers.

It was all for show, but that didn't keep her heart from fluttering wildly. Her stomach muscles tightened at the unexpectedness of his kiss.

Her lips parted and she slid her arms tightly around his narrow waist.

Steve groaned and Meg was afraid the hunger she felt in him was a reflection of her own. By the time he dragged his lips from hers they were both panting. Speechless, they stared at each other.

"I'll…I'll be right back," she managed to whisper. Then she raced up the stairs as if demons were in hot pursuit. On the way she caught a glimpse of Lindsey staring after her, open-mouthed.

Four

The minute they were alone outside, Meg hit Steve across his upper arm, hurting her hand in the process. Biting her lip, she shook her fingers several times, then clutched her aching hand protectively with the other.

"What was that for?" Steve demanded, glaring at her.

"You overdid it," she snapped, barely understanding her own outrage.

"I had to convince her I was unsuitable, didn't I?"

Meg bristled. "Yes, but you went above and beyond what we discussed. All that business about me being so beautiful," she muttered as she walked to the driveway where he'd parked the Harley-Davidson. She climbed onto the leather seat without thinking.

"I thought I did a great job," Steve argued. A smile raised the edges of his mouth.

"That's another thing," she said, unable to stop looking at him. "Was that kiss really necessary?"

"Yes," he said calmly, but Meg could tell that he didn't take kindly to her rebuke. "Lindsey needed to see me in action," he insisted.

"You frightened my daughter half out of her wits as it was. There was no need to…"

Steve's eyes widened, then softened into a smile. "You liked the kiss," he said flatly. "You liked it and that scared you."

"Don't be ridiculous! It…it was disgusting."

"No, it wasn't." His smile was cocky. He laughed, the timbre low and mildly threatening. "Maybe I should prove how wrong you are."

Meg shifted uncomfortably on the seat. "Let's get this over with," she said, feigning boredom. "You're going to take me out for an hour or so and then drive me back. Right? By the way, where did you get the motorcycle?"

He advanced a step toward her. "It's mine."

"Yours?" He was exactly the kind of man her mother had warned her about, and here she was flirting with danger. He moved a step closer and she held herself rigid.

"You don't know much about men, do you?" he asked, his voice low and husky.

"I was married for nearly six years," she informed

him primly. He was close now, too close. She kept her spine stiff and her eyes straight ahead. If the motorcycle was his, it was reasonable to assume the leather jacket belonged to him as well. The persona he'd taken on, the criminal element, might not be too far from the truth.

"You haven't been with a man since, have you?"

She felt his breath against her flushed face. "I refuse to answer questions of a personal nature," she returned, her voice hoarse and low.

"You haven't," he said confidently. "Look at me, Meg."

"No. Let's get this ride over with."

"Look at me," he repeated.

She tried to resist, but the words were warm and hypnotic. Against her better judgment, she twisted toward him. "Yes?" she asked, her heart pounding so hard she thought it might leap right through her chest.

He wove his hands into her hair and tilted her head back so that she couldn't avoid staring up at him. His gaze bored relentlessly into hers.

"Admit it," he whispered. "You enjoyed the kiss." His eyes were compelling, she admitted reluctantly, resisting him every step.

"How like a man—everything's about ego," she said in an effort to make light of what had happened. "Even a silly little kiss."

Steve frowned.

There was a fluttery feeling in the pit of her stomach,

the same feeling that had attacked her when he'd kissed her by the staircase. She felt vulnerable and helpless.

"It wasn't little and it wasn't silly. But it was what we both wanted," he said in a deceptively normal voice.

"You're crazy," she murmured, hurrying to assure him that he'd been wrong. Very wrong. She lowered her eyes, but this proved to be a tactical error. Before she realized what he intended, he was kissing her again.

Meg wanted to protest. If she'd fought him, struggled, he might have released her. But her one weak objection came in the form of a moan, and it appeared to encourage rather than dissuade him.

All at once it was important to get closer. A moment later she was kneeling on the leather cushion and Steve had slipped his arms around her middle. They didn't stay there long. He glided his hands along her back, urging her more tightly against him.

Meg didn't require much inducement. Her body willfully molded itself to his. Then, abruptly, her eyes fluttered open and with a determined effort she broke free. Steve's arms tightened before he relaxed and finally released her.

The look on his face was one of shock.

For her own part, Meg was having a difficult time breathing. Sensations swarmed through her. Unwanted sensations. Steve made her feel as if she'd never been kissed before, never been held or loved. Never been married or shared intimacies with a man.

She blinked, and Steve backed away. He frowned and raked his fingers through his hair, apparently sorting out his own troubled emotions.

"I suppose you expect me to admit I enjoyed that," she said with more than a hint of belligerence. These feelings frightened her. The fact that she'd reacted to him could easily be explained. Good grief, she was a normal woman—but this giddy, end-of-the-world sensation wasn't anything she'd ever experienced.

"You don't have to admit to a damned thing," he said. He climbed onto the Hog and revved the engine aggressively.

"Stop," she cried, shouting above the noise. She waved a hand to clear away the exhaust.

"What's wrong now?" he snapped, twisting around to look at her.

"Nothing…. Just go slow, all right?"

Separated by only a couple of inches, Meg felt him tense. "I'm not exactly in a slow mood."

"I guessed as much."

She didn't know what he intended as he expertly maneuvered the motorcycle out of her driveway. Mortified, Meg glanced up and down the street, wondering how many of her neighbors had witnessed the exchange between her and Steve. Fortunately Lindsey wasn't at the front window watching as Meg had half feared.

"Hang on," he shouted.

She placed her hands lightly on either side of his waist, hoping to keep the contact as impersonal as possible—until they turned the first corner. From that moment on, she wrapped her arms around him as tightly as she could.

Meg was grateful that he chose not to drive far. He stopped at a park less than a mile from her house. After he'd eased into a parking space, he switched off the engine and sat motionless for a couple of minutes.

"You okay?" he asked after a while.

"I'm fine. Great. That was...fun." She was astonished at her new talent for telling white lies. She was far from fine. Her insides were a mess, although that had almost nothing to do with the motorcycle ride. Her heart refused to settle down to a normal pace, and she couldn't stop thinking about their kisses. The first time had been traumatic, but it didn't compare to her nearly suffocating reaction to his second kiss.

Steve checked his watch. "We'll give it another five minutes and then I'll take you back to the house. That should give Lindsey enough time to worry about you without sending her into a panic."

"Perfect," she said brightly—a little too brightly.

"Then tomorrow afternoon I'll pick you up after work and you can do your thing with my sister."

Although he couldn't see her, she nodded. Meg only hoped her act for Nancy would be as convincing as Steve's had been with Lindsey.

"After that, we won't need to see each other again," Steve said. "As far as I'm concerned, it isn't a minute too soon."

Meg felt much the same way. She was just as eager to get him out of her life.

Wasn't she?

It hadn't been a good day. Steve would've liked to blame his foul mood on work-related problems, but everything at Emerald City Body Shop had run like clockwork. The one reason that presented itself was Meg Remington.

He'd known from the first night that getting involved with her would mean trouble. Sure enough, he was waist-deep in quicksand, and all because he hadn't wanted to hurt the woman's feelings.

Okay, that accounted for their dinner date, but afterward…what happened was no one's fault except his own. Donning his leather jacket and jeans and playing the role of the disgruntled ex-con had been fun. But then he had to go and do something stupid.

The stupid part was because of the kiss. He'd been a fool to force Meg to admit how good it had been. This was what he got for allowing his pride to stand in the way.

Well, Steve had learned his lesson. The next time he

was tempted to kiss Meg, he'd go stand in the middle of the freeway. Man, oh man, she could kiss. Only she didn't seem to realize it. Much more of that kissing and he would've been renting a hotel room.

Not Meg, though. Oh, no. She acted as outraged as a nun. Apparently she'd forgotten that men and women did that sort of thing. Enjoyed it, too. Looked forward to doing it again.

The woman was insane, and the sooner he could extract her from his life, the better. He didn't need this. Who did?

One more night, he assured himself. He was taking Meg to meet Nancy this evening, and when they were finished, it would be over and they'd never have to see each other again. If she played her cards right. He'd done his part.

Despite his sour mood, Steve grinned. He'd never forget the look of shock and horror in Lindsey's eyes when he walked into the house. Her jaw had nearly hit the carpet when he put his arms around Meg's waist and announced that he was an ex-con. He wouldn't forget the look in Meg's eyes, either.

Steve laughed outright.

"Something funny?" Gary Wilcox asked.

Steve glared at his foreman. "Not a thing. Now get back to work."

At six o'clock, Steve pulled into the parking space in the alley behind Meg's bookstore. He didn't like the idea of sneaking around and going to her back door, but that was what Meg wanted and far be it from him to argue. He'd be well rid of the woman—at least that was what he kept trying to tell himself.

He knocked and waited a few minutes, growing impatient.

The door opened and a woman in black mesh nylons and the shortest miniskirt he'd seen in years stood in front of him. She vaguely resembled Tina Turner. She wore tons of makeup and she'd certainly had her hair done at the same salon as Tina.

"I'm here for Meg Remington," he said, annoyed that Meg had made such a fuss about his coming to the back door and then sent someone else to answer it.

"Steve," Meg whispered, "it's me."

"What the hell?" He jerked his head back and examined her more thoroughly. "We're meeting my sister," he reminded her stiffly, "not going to some costume party."

"I took my cue from you," she said. "Good grief! You arrived at my door looking like a Hell's Angel—what did you expect *me* to do?"

Steve rubbed his face. Darned if he knew anymore. All he wanted was to get this over with. "Fine. Let's get out of here."

"Just a minute. I need to change shoes."

She slipped out of a perfectly fine pair of flats and into spiky high heels that added a good five inches to her height. Steve wondered how she'd manage to walk in those things. She might as well have been on stilts.

He led her around to his car and opened the door. He noticed that she sighed with what sounded like relief once she was inside the car.

"I didn't know what I was going to do if you brought that motorcycle again." She tugged down her miniskirt self-consciously.

"For the record, I don't often take it out."

She looked relieved, but why it should matter to her one way or the other, he had no idea.

"Just remember," he said, feeling obliged to caution her. "Nancy's a few years older than Lindsey. She won't be as easily fooled."

"I'll be careful about overkill," she mumbled, "unlike certain people I know."

The drive took an eternity, and it wasn't due to heavy traffic, either. In fact, when Steve looked at his watch he was surprised at what good time they'd made. What made the drive so troublesome—he hated to admit this— was Meg's legs. She'd crossed them, exposing plenty of smooth, shapely thigh. Her high heels dangled from the ends of her toes.

Steve appreciated women as a whole—some more than others, of course. He didn't focus on body parts. But it was torture to sit with Meg in the close confines of his car and keep his eyes off her legs. The woman looked incredible. If only she'd keep her mouth shut!

Nancy was standing on the porch when Steve pulled into the driveway.

"This is where your sister lives?" Meg asked.

"It's my home," Steve answered, certain she was about to find something wrong with it.

"Your home?" She sounded impressed. "It's very nice."

"Thanks." He turned off the engine. "Nancy's quite a bit younger than I am—a surprise for my mom and dad. She attends college at the University of Washington nine months out of the year. Our parents retired to Montana a couple of years back."

"I see. Does Nancy live with you?"

"Not on your life," he said, climbing out of the car. "She's in residence during the school year. She got a job here this summer and I agreed to let her stay with me a few months. A mistake I don't plan to repeat anytime soon."

Steve was watching for his sister's reaction when he helped Meg out of the car. To her credit, the nineteen-year-old didn't reveal much, but Steve knew her well enough to realize she was shocked by Meg's appearance.

"You must be Nancy," Meg said in a low, sultry voice.

"And you must be Meg," Nancy said, coming down the steps to greet her. "I've been dying to meet you."

"I hope I'm not a disappointment." This was said in a

soft, cooing tone, as if she couldn't have tolerated disillu-sioning Steve's little sister. She clasped Steve's arm and he noticed for the first time that her nails—now two inches long—were painted a brilliant fire engine red.

Nancy held open the door and smiled in welcome. "Please, come inside."

Meg's high heels clattered against the tile entryway. Steve looked around, pleased to note that his sister had cleaned up the house a bit.

"Oh, Stevie," Meg whined, "you never told me what a beautiful home you have." She trailed one finger along the underside of his jaw. "But then, we haven't had time to discuss much of anything, have we?"

"Make yourself comfortable," Steve said and watched as Meg chose to sit on the sofa. She sat, crossing her legs with great ceremony. Then she patted the empty space beside her, silently requesting Steve to join her there. He glanced longingly at his favorite chair, but moved across the room and sat down next to Meg.

The minute he was comfortable, Meg placed her hand possessively on his knee and flexed her nails into his thigh. Inch by provocative inch she raked her nails up his leg until it was all Steve could do not to pop straight off the sofa. He caught her hand and stopped her from reach-ing what seemed to be her ultimate destination.

Her expression was mildly repentant when she looked

at him, but Steve knew her well enough to know the action had been deliberate.

"I thought you might be hungry before Steve takes you to dinner, so I made a few hors d'oeuvres," Nancy said and excused herself.

"What are you doing?" Steve whispered the minute his sister was out of the room.

"Doing? What do you mean?" She had wide-eyed innocence down to an art.

"Never mind," he muttered as Nancy returned from the kitchen carrying a small silver platter.

"Those look wonderful," Meg said sweetly when his sister put the tray on the coffee table in front of them. "But I couldn't eat a thing."

To the best of his knowledge it was the first time his sister had cooked from the moment she'd moved in with him, and he wasn't about to let it go to waste. He chose a tiny wiener wrapped in some kind of crispy dough and tossed it in his mouth.

"You shouldn't have gone to all this trouble," Meg told his sister.

Nancy sat across the room from them, apparently at a complete loss for words.

"I suspect you're wondering about all these letters and e-mails I wrote," Meg said, getting the conversation going. "I hope you aren't unhappy with me."

"No, no, not at all," Nancy said, rushing the words together.

"It's just that I've come to know what people *really* want from me by the things they say." She turned, and with the tip of her index finger wiped a crumb from the corner of his mouth. Her tongue moistened her lips and Steve's insides turned to mush.

"I learned a long time ago what men want from a woman," Meg continued after a moment, "especially when I went to work for a phone sex line. Most of the guys are just looking for a woman to talk dirty to them."

"I see." Nancy folded her hands primly in her lap.

"There was the occasional guy who was looking for a good girl to shock, of course. I got very talented at acting horrified." She made a soft, gasping sound, then laughed demurely.

"Why…why would someone like you place an ad in Dateline?" Nancy asked, nervously brushing the hair from her face.

"Well, first," Meg said, holding his sister's gaze, "it's just about the only way someone like me can meet anyone decent. But it wasn't your brother who answered the ad, now, was it?"

"No, but—"

"Not that it matters," Meg said, cutting her off. "I was tired of my job and all those guys asking me to say those nasty things, and I didn't want to start working on my back again."

"On your...back," Nancy repeated.

"I'm sorry, sugar. I didn't mean to shock you. I've got a colorful past—but that doesn't mean I'm a bad girl. I've got a heart just brimming with love. All I need is the right man." Her gaze wandered to Steve and was long and deliberate. "Your brother's given me a reason to dream again," Meg said softly. "Lots of people think women like me don't have feelings, but they're wrong."

"I'm sure that's true," Nancy said tentatively.

"I knew I chose right when I found out your brother has his own business."

"He's struggled financially for years," Nancy was quick to tell her. "It's still touch and go. He lives from one month to the next." Nancy glared at him pointedly. "Don't you, Steve?"

"Not anymore. I'm more than solvent now," Steve tossed in for good measure, struggling not to laugh. He was enjoying this.

Meg tightened her arm around his. "I can see how well Stevie's doing for himself. He's wonderful," she said, refusing to look away. The adoration on her face embarrassed him.

"Why, Steve here could make enough money to keep me in the lifestyle to which I'd like to become accustomed." She laughed coyly.

"Ah…" It sounded to Steve as if his sister was close to hyperventilating.

"Of course, I wouldn't take anything from him without giving in return. That wouldn't be fair." She snuggled closer to his side and gave him a look so purely sexual Steve was convinced he'd embarrass them all.

"There are things I could teach your brother," Meg said in a husky voice full of sexual innuendo. She acted as though she was eager to get started right that moment and the only thing holding her back was propriety. Her breathing grew heavy—and if he didn't know better he'd think she actually *had* worked for one of those disreputable phone services.

Soon he was having a problem controlling his own breathing.

"Steve!" Nancy snapped.

He turned his attention back to his sister, staring at her blankly.

"Didn't you hear Meg?" she asked.

He shrugged. He knew the two women were talking, but he'd barely noticed their conversation.

"Meg's talking about moving in with you," Nancy said through clenched teeth.

"I don't mean to rush you, darling'," Meg whispered. Leaning forward, she licked his earlobe with the tip of her tongue.

Hot sensation shot down his spine.

Meg threw back her head and laughed softly, then whispered just loudly enough for Nancy to hear, "I have an incredibly talented tongue."

Nancy closed her eyes as if she couldn't bear to watch another minute of this. Frankly, Steve didn't know how much more he could take himself.

"I think it's time we left for dinner," he said. Otherwise he was going to start believing all the promises Meg was making. Heaven knew, he *wanted* to believe them. The demure bookseller had turned into something completely different. All traces of innocence had disappeared and in their place was the most sexually provocative female he'd ever met. Just being in the same room with her made his blood sizzle.

"You want to leave already?" Meg gave the impression that she was terribly disappointed.

"That's probably best," Nancy muttered, and then realizing what she'd said, hurried to add, "I mean, you two don't want to waste your evening with me, do you?" She frowned at Steve. "You won't be late, will you?"

"No."

"Unfortunately, I'm still working for the phone people," Meg said, "so I won't keep him too long, but I can't promise he'll have much kick left in him when I'm finished." Apparently thinking herself exceptionally clever, Meg laughed at her own joke.

It wasn't until they were back in the car and on the freeway that Steve recognized how angry he was. It made no sense, but he wasn't exactly rational just then.

"Why are you so mad?" Meg asked about halfway back to the bookstore. They hadn't spoken a word from the time they'd left his house.

"Talk about overkill," he muttered.

"I thought I did a good job," she said.

"You came off like a—"

"I know. That's what I wanted. After meeting me, do you honestly think your sister's going to encourage our relationship?"

"No," he growled.

"I can guarantee you that Lindsey doesn't want me to see you, either. I thought that's what this whole scheme of yours was about."

"It sounded like a good idea at the time." He tightened his hands on the steering wheel. "It seemed like a surefire way to convince your daughter that I was the wrong man for you."

"And your sister that I was equally wrong for you."

Silence settled over them like nightfall. Neither of them seemed inclined to talk again.

Steve edged his car into the alley behind Meg's store and parked his car behind hers.

"I'm not so sure anymore," he said without looking at her.

"About what?"

"The two of us. Somewhere in the middle of all this, I

decided I kind of like you." It hadn't been easy to admit, and he hoped she appreciated what it had cost his pride. "It probably wouldn't have been as obvious if you hadn't made yourself out to be so cheap. That isn't you any more than the rebel without a cause is me."

He wished she'd say something. When she did speak, her voice was timid and small. "Then there was the kiss."

"Kisses," he corrected. "They were pretty great and we both know it," he said with confidence. He knew what his own reaction had been, and she hadn't fooled him with hers.

"Yes," she said softly.

"Especially the one on the motorcycle," he said, prompting her to continue.

"Especially the one on the motorcycle," she mimicked. "Honestly, Steve, you must've known."

His smile was full blown. "I did."

"I…I didn't do a very good job of disguising what I was feeling."

She hadn't, but he was in a gracious mood.

"How about dinner?" he suggested. He was eager to have the real Meg Remington back. Eager to experiment with a few more kisses—see if they were anything close to what his memory kept insisting they'd been.

She hesitated. "I want to, but I can't," she eventually said.

He bristled and turned in the driver's seat to face her. "Why not?"

"I promised Lindsey I'd be home by seven and it's nearly that now."

"Call her and tell her you're going out to dinner with me."

She dragged in a deep breath and seemed to hold it. "I can't do that, either."

"Why not?"

"After meeting you, I promised her we'd talk. She wanted to last evening, and we didn't…. That was my fault. You kissed me," she said, "and I didn't feel like a heart-to-heart with my daughter after that."

"And it's all my fault?"

"Yes," she insisted.

"Do you know what Lindsey wants to discuss?"

"Of course, I know. You. She doesn't want me seeing you again, which is exactly the point of the entire charade. Remember?"

"Yeah," Steve said, scowling.

"Are…are you telling me you've changed your mind?" she asked.

"Yes." He hated to be the one to say it first, but one of them had to. "What about you?"

"I think so."

Steve flattened his hand against the steering wheel. "I

swear you're about the worst thing that's ever happened to my ego."

She laughed and rested her hand on his shoulder. The wig she had on tilted sideways and she righted it. "That does sound terrible, doesn't it?"

He smiled. "Yeah. The least you could do is show some enthusiasm."

"I haven't dated much in the last ten years. But if I was going to choose any man, it would be you."

"That's better," he said. He wanted to kiss her. He'd been thinking about it from the moment he'd picked her up.

"Only…" Meg said sadly.

"Only what?" he repeated, lowering his mouth to hers.

Their lips met and it was heaven, just the way he'd known it would be. By the time the kiss ended, Steve was leaning his head against the window of the car door, his eyes closed. It was even more wonderful than he'd remembered, and that seemed impossible.

Meg's head was on his chest, tucked beneath his chin.

"It's too late," she whispered.

"What's too late?"

"We've gone to all this trouble to convince Lindsey that you're all wrong for me."

"I know, but…"

"Do you think Nancy will believe this was all a silly joke?"

"No."

"I think we should end everything right here and now, don't you?" she asked.

Steve stiffened. "If that's what you want."

She moved away from him. "I guess it is," she said, with just a hint of regret.

Five

Lindsey was pacing the living room, waiting for Meg when she walked in the front door.

"Hi, honey," Meg said, trying to sound cheerful yet exhausted—since she'd led Lindsey to believe she was taking inventory at the bookstore and that was why she'd come home so late.

"It's way after seven!" her daughter cried, rushing toward her. "You weren't with Steve, were you?"

"Ah…" Meg wasn't willing to lie outright. Half truths and innuendos were about as far as she wanted to stretch this.

Lindsey closed her eyes and waved her hands vaguely. "Forget it. Don't answer that."

"Honey, what's wrong?" Meg asked as calmly as she

could. Unfortunately, she didn't think she sounded all that reassuring. She'd left Steve only moments earlier and was already feeling some regret. After following through with this ridiculous charade, Steve wanted to change his mind and continue seeing Meg. She'd quickly put an end to *that* idea. Now she wasn't sure she'd made the right decision.

"Mom," Lindsey said, her dark eyes challenging, "we need to talk."

"Of course." Meg walked into the kitchen and took the china teapot from the hutch. "My mother always made tea when we had something to discuss." Somehow, the ritual of drinking tea together put everything in perspective. Meg missed those times with her mother.

Lindsey helped her assemble everything they needed and carried it into the dining room. Meg poured them each a cup, once the tea had steeped, and they sat across from each other at the polished mahogany table.

Meg waited, and when Lindsey wasn't immediately forthcoming she decided to get the conversation started. "You wanted to talk to me about Steve, right?"

Lindsey clasped the delicate china cup with one hand and lowered her gaze. "Do you really, really like him?" she asked anxiously.

Meg answered before she took time to censor the question. "Yes."

"But why? I mean, he's nothing like what I thought he'd be." She hesitated. "I suppose this is what Brenda and I get for pretending we were you," she mumbled. "Maybe if you'd read his stuff, you would've been able to tell what kind of guy he really is."

"Steve is actually a fine person." And he was. Or at least the Steve Meg knew.

Lindsey risked a glance at her. "You've said hundreds of times that you don't want me to judge others by outward appearances, but sometimes that's all there is."

"You're worried about me and Steve, aren't you?" Meg said gently.

Lindsey rubbed her finger along the edge of the teacup. "I realize now that what Brenda and I did was really stupid. We linked you up with a guy who has a prison record. We sure were easy to fool," Lindsey said with a scowl. "We're only fifteen years old!"

"But I like Steve," Meg felt obliged to tell her.

Lindsey looked as if she didn't know how to account for that. "I'm afraid he's going to hurt you."

"Steve wouldn't do that," Meg assured her, "but I understand your concern, honey, and I promise you I won't let the situation get out of hand."

Lindsey frowned, stiffened her shoulders and blurted out, "I don't want you to see him again."

"But…"

"I mean it, Mom. This guy is trouble."

Talk about role reversal!

"I want you to *promise* me you won't see Steve Conlan again."

"Lindsey..."

"This is important. You may not understand it now, but I promise you will in the future. There are plenty of other men, law-abiding citizens, who'd give their right arms to meet a woman like you."

Meg stared. She couldn't be hearing this. This sounded exactly like something her mother had said back when Meg was in high school.

The intense look in Lindsey's eyes softened and she gestured weakly. "The time will come when you'll thank me for this."

"Really?" Meg couldn't resist raising her eyebrows.

"There'll be a boy in my life that you'll disapprove of and I won't understand why," Lindsey went on. "When that happens, I want you to remind me of now."

Meg shook her head—in bafflement and disbelief. "Are you telling me you'd break up with a boy simply because I didn't like him?"

"No," Lindsey said carefully. "But I'd consider it because I know how I feel about you seeing Steve, and I'd understand how you might feel about someone I was dating. Don't get me wrong," she hurried to add, "I don't dislike Steve.... He's kind of cute. It's just that I feel you could do a whole lot better."

"I'll think about it," Meg promised.

Lindsey nodded. "I can't ask for more than that."

Her daughter had behaved just as Meg had predicted. This had gone precisely according to plan. But Meg didn't feel good about it. If anything, she felt more depressed following their conversation than before.

She didn't have any talent when it came to relationships, Meg decided, as she finished putting away the dinner dishes later that evening. Steve had come right out and told her he'd had a change of heart, and she'd bungled everything. Instead of admitting that she felt the same way he did, she'd trampled all over his ego.

Meg turned to the kitchen phone, tempted to call him. It couldn't end like this, with such confusion, such uncertainty about what she really wanted. What *they* wanted.

Never had an evening passed more slowly. It seemed to take Lindsey hours to go to bed, and by then Meg was yawning herself.

As soon as Meg could be reasonably sure that her daughter was asleep, she tiptoed toward the kitchen phone and dialed Steve's number, her heart pounding. Finally she heard his groggy voice.

"Steve?" she whispered. "Thank goodness it's you. I didn't know what I was going to do if Nancy answered."

"Meg? Is that you?" He sounded surprised to hear from her, and none too pleased.

She bristled. "How many other women do you have phoning you at eleven o'clock at night?"

He didn't respond right away, and when he spoke his voice definitely lacked welcome. "I thought you said it wasn't a good idea for us to see each other."

"I...I don't know what I want."

"Do you expect me to make your decisions for you?"

"Of course not." This wasn't going well. In fact, it was going very badly. She probably should've waited until she'd had time to figure this out a little more clearly.

"Is there a reason you called?" he asked gruffly.

"Yes," she said, sorry now that she'd phoned him. "I wanted to apologize for being abrupt earlier. I...can see now that I shouldn't have called."

Having said that, she carefully replaced the receiver. For a long moment she stared at the phone, feeling like an idiot.

She'd turned away to head up the stairs when the phone rang, jolting her. Quickly she grabbed it before the noise could wake Lindsey.

"Hello," she whispered.

"Meet me." It was Steve.

"I can't leave Lindsey."

"Why not? She's in bed, isn't she?"

"Yes, but..."

"Write her a note. Tell her you're going to the grocery store."

How reasonable he made it sound—as if she usually did her shopping in the middle of the night.

"She won't even know you're gone," Steve said.

Meg closed her eyes. They'd been together only a few hours earlier, and yet it felt as if they'd been apart for weeks.

Her stomach twisted. Then—before she could change her mind—she blurted out, "All right, but I can't stay long."

"Fair enough."

They agreed to meet in the Albertson's parking lot. The huge store was open twenty-four hours a day. Meg had been shopping there for years. The note she left Lindsey said she'd gone to pick up some milk—that classic excuse—but it was exactly what she intended to do.

She sat in her car until she saw Steve pull into the nearly empty lot. Uncertain she was doing the right thing, she got out and waited for him.

Steve parked in the spot next to hers. They stood facing each other for a moment, neither speaking.

"I can't believe we're doing this," she said.

It appeared she wasn't the only one with doubts. Steve's face was blank, emotionless. "Me neither."

They walked into the store together and reached for grocery carts. Meg's had a squeaky wheel. The sound echoed through the cavernous store.

The deli was closed, but Steve was able to get them each a cup of coffee from the friendly night manager.

They parked their empty carts and sat at a small white table in the deli section. Neither seemed inclined to speak.

She felt encouraged that Steve had phoned her back, but she suspected he regretted it now.

"You know what you said earlier?" she began.

"I said lots of things earlier. Which particular thing are you referring to?"

Meg guessed his sarcasm was warranted. After all, she'd wounded his ego, and he wasn't giving her the chance to do it again. "About the two of us, you know, dating."

"You said Lindsey wouldn't like it."

"She doesn't," Meg said. "She asked me not to see you again."

His gaze pinned hers. "Did you agree?"

"Not...entirely."

His eyes narrowed with a frown. "You'd better explain."

"Well, as you've already surmised, Lindsey isn't keen on me seeing you. Which is exactly the reason you stopped by the house and did your biker routine, right? Well, it worked. She's worried that you're the wrong man for me." It would've helped if he hadn't bragged about his prison record and mentioned his parole officer's name. But now didn't seem to be the time to bring that up.

"Did you or did you not promise her you wouldn't see me again?"

"Neither." Meg sipped from the disposable cup and grimaced at the taste of burned coffee.

"Then what *did* you say to her?"

Meg lifted one shoulder in a shrug. "That I'd think about it."

"Have you?"

Propping her elbows on the table's edge, Meg swirled the black liquid around the cup and avoided looking at Steve. "I called you, didn't I?"

"I still haven't figured out why."

That was the problem: she hadn't, either. Not really. "I guess it's because you have a point about seeing each other again."

"Oh, yeah?" He gave her a cocky grin.

Her anger flared. "Would you stop it?"

"Stop what?" he asked innocently.

"The next thing I know, you're going to ask me how much I enjoyed kissing you."

Steve smiled for the first time. "It wouldn't hurt to know."

"All right, since it means so much to you, I'll admit it. No man's ever kissed me the way you do. It scares me— but at the same time I wish it could go on forever." Having admitted this much, she supposed she might as well say it all. "My marriage left me wondering if I was…if I was capable of those kinds of feelings…." She paused and lowered her eyes. "I was afraid I was, you know, frigid," she said in a choked whisper.

She stared down at her coffee, then took a sip, followed by several more, as if the vile stuff were the antidote to some dreaded illness.

The last thing she expected her small confession to provoke in Steve was a laugh. "You're joking!"

She shook her head forcefully. "Don't laugh. Please."

His hand reached for hers and their fingers entwined. "I wasn't laughing at you, Meg," he said gently. "You're one of the most sensual women I've ever met. Trust me, if you're frigid—and there's a word I haven't heard in years—then I'm a monk."

Meg looked up and offered him a fragile smile. It astonished her that this man who'd known her for only a few days could chase away the doubts that had hounded her through the years after her divorce.

He cleared his throat. "I, uh, don't think you should look at me like that."

"Like what?"

"Like you want me to kiss you."

Her eyes drifted shut. "Maybe I do…. That's what makes everything so complicated. I'm really attracted to you. I haven't felt like this before—not ever, not even with my ex-husband, and like I said, that scares me."

He stood up, still holding Meg's hand, and tugged her to her feet.

"Where are we going?" she asked.

"Someplace private," he said, scanning the store. He led her through the frozen food section, past the bakery and into a small alcove where the wine was kept. With her back to the domestic beer, he brought her into his arms and covered her mouth with his.

Their kiss was rough with need, but she wasn't sure whose need was greater. Meg could feel Steve's heart racing as hard as her own. She supposed she should've pulled away, ended the kiss, stepped out of his arms. But Meg didn't want that.

Steve yawned. He was *so* tired. With good reason. It'd been almost three before he'd gone to bed and four before he'd been able to fall asleep. His alarm had gone off at six.

He arrived at the shop and made a pot of coffee. He mumbled a greeting when Gary got in.

"I hope you're in a better mood than you were yesterday," his foreman told him. "What's wrong with you, anyway?"

Steve checked over the job orders for the day. "Women," he muttered in explanation and apology.

"I should've guessed. What's going on?"

"You don't want to hear this," he said and headed for the garage.

"Sure I do," Gary said, following him. "I don't suppose this has anything to do with Nancy, does it?"

Steve glared at him. "What do you know about my sister?"

"Not much," Gary said and held up both hands. "Just what you said about her fixing you up with some woman. It's none of my business, but you and this woman seem to be hitting it off just fine."

Steve continued to glare at him. "What makes you say that?"

Gary laughed. "I haven't seen you this miserable in years. Which probably means you've fallen for her. Why don't you put yourself out of your misery? Shoot yourself and be done with it."

Frowning, Steve turned away. The kid was a smartass, although now that Steve thought about it, Gary might have come up with the perfect solution.

It was noon before Steve had a chance to go into his office. He made sure no one was looking, then closed the door and reached for the phone.

"Book Ends, Laura speaking," a woman said in a friendly voice.

"Is Meg available?" he asked, sounding as businesslike as possible.

"May I ask who's calling?"

Steve hesitated. "Steve Conlan."

"One minute, please."

It took longer than that for Meg to get on the line. "Steve, hi." She seemed tired but happy to hear from him. That helped.

"How are you?" he asked, struggling to hold back a yawn.

"Dead on my feet. I'm not as young as I used to be."

"Does Lindsey know you slipped out of the house last night?"

"No, but I should never have stayed out that late."

Steve didn't have any argument there. They'd left the Albertson's store when a stock boy stumbled upon them in the wine section, embarrassing Meg no end—although Steve had rather enjoyed the way her blush had brightened her cheeks.

With no other idea of where to take her at that hour, Steve had driven down to Alki Point in west Seattle, where they sat on the beach and talked.

They hadn't discussed anything of earth-shattering importance, but he discovered that they had a great deal in common. Mostly, he discovered that he liked Meg. He was already well aware of what Meg, the sensuous and beautiful woman, was capable of doing to him physically. Last night, he learned about Meg, the person.

They hadn't kissed again. Steve was convinced they both knew how dangerous kissing had become. It wouldn't take much for their kisses to lead to more…a *lot* more.

And when that happened, he didn't plan to have it take place on a public beach.

He didn't know where the time had gone, but when he'd looked at his watch he'd been shocked. Meg, too. It was after three in the morning. They'd rushed their farewells without making arrangements to see each other again.

"When can we get together?" he asked.

"I don't know...."

Was this how it was going to be? Would they have to start over each and every time they met? "Would you rather we didn't meet again?" he asked.

"No," she said immediately.

"We've got to make some decisions," he said, angry with himself for not saying anything about it on that moonlit beach. They'd discussed so many different things, from politics to movies to lifelong dreams, yet hadn't talked about their own relationship.

"I know."

"Would tonight work?" he asked. "Same time?"

She hesitated and he gritted his teeth with impatience.

"Okay." The longing in her voice reassured him.

"Fine," he said, relieved. "I'll pick you up at your house at eleven."

"I have to go now."

"Yeah. Me, too."

Steve replaced the receiver and glanced up to find

Nancy standing in his office doorway, her arms folded in disapproval.

"Was that Meg?" she demanded.

"That's none of your business," Steve said sharply.

"We need to talk about her and I'm tired of you putting me off."

"I'm not discussing Meg Remington with you."

"How could you date someone like her?" Nancy asked, her face wrinkled in disgust.

"Might I remind you that you were the one who introduced us?"

"Yes, but she deceived me. Steve, be serious! Can you honestly imagine introducing her to Mom and Dad?"

"Yes," he answered calmly.

Nancy threw her arms in the air. "This is your problem. You're thinking with your you-know-what."

"Nancy!"

"It's true!"

"Stay out of my business. Understand?"

"But…"

"I make my own decisions," Steve said forcefully.

"And your own mistakes," Nancy muttered, walking out of the room.

"We're both crazy," Meg said, sitting next to Steve in his car. She sipped from a can of cold soda, enjoying the sweet taste of it.

"Candidates for the loony bin," he agreed.

"I wasn't sure I'd be able to get away," Meg confessed. "Brenda's spending the night with Lindsey, and those two are going to be up half the night."

"Did you tell them you were leaving the house?"

"No," she said, "but I left them a note. Just in case... Although I'm hoping they won't come downstairs. Oh, and this time I should remember to bring home some milk."

"I was thinking Lindsey and I should have another meeting," Steve began. "Only this time I want you to bring her to the shop. I'll show her around and explain that the whole biker, ex-con routine was a joke." He waited, then looked at Meg. "What do you think?"

"I'm afraid hell hath no fury like a teenager fooled."

"That's what I was afraid you were going to say." Steve finished his drink and placed his arm around her shoulder. "One thing's for sure. I'm through with sneaking around in the middle of the night."

Meg covered her mouth as she yawned. "I'm too old for this."

"You and me both."

Meg finished her soda, too, and leaned back against Steve, his chest supporting her back. She didn't dare close her eyes for fear she'd fall asleep.

"Nancy isn't any too happy about me seeing you, either."

"I'll talk to her, explain everything." Except that, like Lindsey, Steve's sister probably wouldn't be too pleased.

"It's settled, then," Steve said. "I'll talk to Lindsey and you'll talk to Nancy. Neither one of them is going to enjoy being the butt of a joke, but it wasn't like we planned this. Besides, it serves them right for manipulating us like they did."

"You'd think they'd be pleased," Meg inserted. "Their plan worked—not the way they wanted, mind you, but we're seeing each other and that's the whole point. Right?"

Steve chuckled and stroked her hair. "Right."

"I wish it wasn't like this," Meg whispered.

Steve kissed the top of her head. "So do I."

Meg smiled, twisting in his arms so they faced each other.

Steve's hands lingered on her face. His mouth was so close she could feel his breath against her cheek. A shiver of awareness skittered down her spine.

Meg closed her eyes and lifted her mouth to Steve's. He hesitated for a fraction of a second, as if he had second thoughts about what might happen next.

His kiss was warm and gentle. But his gentleness didn't last long. There was a hunger in Steve, a hunger in Meg that flared to life like a fire stoked.

"Meg…"

"I know…I know."

"Tomorrow," he said and drew in a deep, even breath.

"Tomorrow," she repeated, but she had no idea what she was agreeing to. She opened her eyes and leaned back. "What about tomorrow?"

"We'll talk to Lindsey and Nancy."

"Okay."

Fifteen minutes later, Steve dropped her off at the house.

It wasn't until he drove away that she realized she'd left her purse in his car. Her purse with the key to her house…

"Damn," she muttered, hurrying into the backyard, hoping Lindsey had forgotten to lock the sliding glass door. She hadn't; it was locked tight.

No help for it—she searched until she found the spare key, hidden under one of the flowerpots on her porch. It'd been there for so many years she wasn't sure it would work.

Luckily it did. As quietly as she could, Meg slipped into the house.

She climbed the stairs and tiptoed into her room. She undressed without turning on the light and was in bed minutes later.

The neighbor's German shepherd barked, obviously from inside their house, and Lindsey looked up from painting her toenails. "There it is again," she said.

"I heard it, too," Brenda said.

"Wolf doesn't bark without a reason."

Ever curious, Brenda walked over to the bedroom window and peered into the yard below. After a moment, she whirled around. "There's someone in your backyard," she whispered, wide-eyed.

"This isn't the time for jokes," Lindsey said, continuing to paint her toenails a bright shade of pink. "We were discussing my mother, remember?"

Brenda didn't move away from the window. "There *is* someone there."

"Who?"

"It's a man.... Oh, my goodness, come and look."

The panic in her friend's voice made Lindsey catapult to a standing position. Walking on her heels to keep her freshly painted toenails off the carpet, she hobbled toward the window.

Brenda was right; she *did* see someone in the yard. "Turn the lights off," she hissed.

Lindsey's heart lodged in her throat as she recognized the dark form. "It's Steve Conlan!" She saw him clearly in the moonlight; he wasn't even making any attempt to hide.

"What's that in his hand?"

Lindsey focused her attention on the object Steve was carrying. It looked like a purse. Gasping, she twisted away from the window and placed her back against the wall. She gestured wildly toward the phone.

"What's wrong?" Brenda cried. "Are you having an asthma attack?"

Lindsey shook her head. "He broke in to the house and stole my mother's purse." Brenda handed her the phone and Lindsey dialed 911 as fast as her nervous fingers would let her.

She barely gave the operator time to answer. "There's a man in our backyard," she whispered frantically. "He took my mother's purse."

The emergency operator seemed to have a thousand questions she wanted Lindsey to answer. Lindsey did the best she could.

"He's a convicted felon.... I can give you the name of his probation officer if you want. Just hurry!" she pleaded.

"Officers have been dispatched."

"Please, please hurry." Lindsey was afraid that unless the police arrived within the next minute Steve would make a clean getaway.

Steve debated whether he should leave Meg's purse on the front porch. It would be easy enough to tuck it inside the mailbox, but then she might not find it until much later the next day.

He walked around the house to the backyard, thinking there might be someplace he could put it where she'd find it in the morning.

There wasn't.

The only thing he'd managed to do was rouse the neighbor's dog. He would've rung the doorbell and given her the silly thing if there'd been any lights on, but apparently she'd gone to bed. He wasn't especially eager to confront Lindsey, either. Not yet.

He still hadn't made up his mind, when he heard a noise from behind him.

"Police! Freeze!"

Was this a joke? Maybe not—whoever it was sounded serious. He froze.

"Put the purse down and turn around slowly."

Once more Steve did as instructed. With his arms raised, he turned to find two police officers with their weapons drawn and pointed at him.

"Looks like we caught ourselves a burglar," one of them said, switching on a huge flashlight.

"Caught him redhanded," the other agreed.

Six

"If you'd let me explain," Steve said, squinting against the light at the two officers. A dog barked ferociously in the next-door neighbor's yard. A man in pajamas had let the dog out and joined the audience.

"Do you always carry a woman's purse?"

"It belongs to—"

"My mother."

Although Steve couldn't see her face, he recognized the righteous tones as belonging to Meg's daughter. Lindsey and her friend stood beside the two officers and looked as if they'd gladly provide the rope for a hanging.

"Wolf." The neighbour silenced the German shepherd, but made no move to go inside.

"My name's Steve Conlan," Steve said, striving to come

across as sane and reasonable. This was, after all, merely
a misunderstanding.

"I wouldn't believe him if I were you," Lindsey advised
the officers. "It might not be his real name." Then in lower
tones she added, "He has a criminal record. I happen to
know for a fact that he's a convicted felon."

"I'm not a felon," Steve growled. "And it *is* my real
name. Officers, if you'd give me the opportunity to—"

"His parole officer's name is Earl Markham." Lindsey
cut him off, her voice indignant. "He told me himself!"

"I know Earl Markham," the younger of the two police-
men said. "And he is a parole officer."

"I know him, too," Steve barked impatiently. "We went
to high school together."

"Yeah, right."

The scorn in Lindsey's voice reminded Steve of Meg
when she was furious with him. Like mother, like daughter, it seemed.

"If you'd let me explain." Steve tried again, struggling
to stay calm. It wasn't easy with two guns aimed at him
and a man in pajamas clutching the collar of a huge dog—
thank goodness for the fence. Not to mention a couple of
teenage girls accusing him of who knew what.

"Don't listen to him," the other girl was saying. "He
lies! He had us believing all kinds of things, and all because he thought we were Lindsey's mother."

A short silence followed her announcement. "Say that

again?" the older officer muttered. "How well do you know this man?"

"My name's Steve Conlan." Steve tried yet again.

"Which may or may not be his real name." This, too, came from Lindsey's friend.

"If you'll let me get my wallet, I'll prove who I am," Steve assured them. He made an effort to sound vaguely amused by the whole situation. He lowered one arm and started to move his hand toward his back pocket.

"Keep your hands up where I can see them," the older cop snapped.

"What's going on?" The voice drifted down from the upstairs area of the house. A sweetly feminine, slightly groggy voice.

Steve glanced up, and to his great relief saw Meg's face framed in the second-floor window.

"Meg," Steve shouted, grateful that she'd finally heard the commotion. "Tell these men who I am, so they can put their weapons away."

"Steve?" she cried, shocked. "What are you doing at my house?"

"Do you know this man?" the cop asked, tilting his head back and shouting up at Meg.

"Ma'am, would you mind stepping outside?" the second officer asked. He mumbled something Steve couldn't hear under his breath.

"I'll be right down," Meg told them, and Steve watched her turn away from the window.

"Have you been sneaking around seeing my mother?"

"Lindsey, it's not like it seems," Steve said, experiencing a twinge of guilt at the way he'd misled the girl. He'd planned to talk to Meg's daughter soon, but he hadn't intended to do it in front of the police.

"I'd be more interested to find out why he has your mother's purse, if I were you," the second teenager said.

"I already know why he's got Mom's purse," Lindsey said loudly. "He stole it."

"No, I didn't!" Steve rolled his eyes. "I was trying to return it."

"You have my purse?" This was from Meg. "Oh, hello, Mr. Robinson. Hi, Wolf. I think everything's under control here." Man and dog went back inside a moment later.

"My purse!" she said again.

Steve relaxed and lowered his arms. "You left it in my car," he said.

"Thank goodness you found it." Meg, at least, displayed the appropriate amount of appreciation. "I didn't know when I'd get it back."

Now that the flashlight wasn't blinding him and the officers had returned the guns to their holsters, Steve saw Meg for the first time. In fact, he couldn't take his eyes off her. She'd thrown a flimsy cotton robe over her baby-doll pajamas but despite that, they revealed a length of sleek, smooth thigh whenever she moved. The top was low-cut and the robe gaped open and… Meg grabbed the lapels and held them together with both hands. It didn't help much.

Steve was afraid he wasn't the only one who'd noticed Meg's attire. Both officers looked approvingly in her direction. Steve was about to ask the younger of the two to wipe the grin off his face, but he held his breath and counted backward from ten.

He got to five. "Lindsey, go get your mother a coat."

"I don't have to take orders from you," the girl snapped.

Meg blinked and seemed to realize that despite the robe, such as it was, her nightwear left little to the imagination.

In an apparent effort to deflect a shouting match, one officer asked Lindsey a few questions, while the other engaged Steve and Meg in conversation.

"You know this man?" he asked Meg.

"Yes, of course. His name's Steve Conlan."

"Steve Conlan." The officer made note of it on a small pad. "That's what he said earlier."

Steve pulled out his wallet and flipped it open, silently thrusting it out. The cop glanced at it and nodded.

"He didn't steal my purse, either," Meg went on.

Steve cast the other man an I-told-you-so look, but said nothing.

"You went out with Steve behind my back?" Lindsey

cried, peering around the second policeman. Her eyes narrowed. "I can't *believe* you'd do something like that— after our talk and everything."

Meg cast her a guilty look. "We'll discuss this later."

But Lindsey wasn't going to be so easily dissuaded. "After our talk, I really, really thought I was getting through to you. Now I see how wrong I was."

"If you'd give me a chance to explain…" Steve began, wanting to avoid an argument between Meg and her daughter.

Static from the police officer's walkie-talkie was followed by a muffled voice. The two men were obviously being dispatched to another location.

"Everything okay here?" the policeman asked Meg.

"It's fine."

"Young lady?"

Lindsey folded her arms and pointed her nose toward the night sky. "All I can say is that my mother's a serious disappointment to me."

"I'm afraid I can't help you there."

"I didn't think you could," she said, shaking her head. "I thought better of her than this—sneaking out at night to see a man of…of low moral fiber."

"Lindsey!"

"Why don't we all go inside and discuss this," Steve suggested. He felt more than a little ridiculous standing in Meg's yard, and he was eager to clear the air between Lindsey and him.

"I have nothing to say to either of you," Lindsey said. She marched into the house, with Brenda scurrying behind.

Steve watched them stomp off in single file and released a deep breath. He was about to apologize for having made such a mess of things, when Meg whirled around to face him.

"I can't believe you!"

Steve ran his fingers through his hair. Meg didn't seem to grasp that this ordeal hadn't exactly been a pleasure for him, either.

"I apologize, Meg." He did feel bad about all the trouble he'd caused, but he'd only been trying to help. When he'd found her purse, returning it had seemed the best thing to do. He didn't want her wondering where it was, and he'd honestly thought he could do it without ending up in jail.

"How dare you tell my daughter to get me a coat."

Steve's head jerked up. His throat tightened with the strength of his anger. "I nearly got myself arrested— thanks to your daughter, I might add—and *you're* upset because I objected to you traipsing around in front of the neighborhood half-naked?"

Meg opened her mouth and then closed it.

"Okay," he amended, "you are wearing a robe, although

it's not much of one. Neither of those cops could take their eyes off you. I supposed you enjoyed the attention."

"Don't be ridiculous! I came downstairs as fast as I could, in order to help you."

"You call parading in front of those men like that *helping* me? All I needed was for you to identify me so I could leave. That's all." His words grew louder. He was close to losing his cool and he knew it.

"I think you'd better go," Meg said, pointing in the direction of the street. Steve noticed with satisfaction that her finger shook.

"I'm out of here," he told her, "and not a minute too soon. You might have appreciated the embarrassment I endured trying to do you a favor, but I can see you don't. Which is fine by me."

"Like *you* didn't embarrass *me?*" she shouted.

"You weren't the one who had a gun pointed at you and a kid claiming you were a menace to society."

"Lindsey was only repeating what you'd told her." Meg pushed the hair away from her face, using both hands. "This isn't working."

"Wrong," he said sharply. "It's working all too well. You make me crazy, and I don't like it."

"But…"

"If I'm going to get arrested, I want it to be for someone who's willing to acknowledge the trouble I've gone through for her." Certain he was making no sense whatsoever, Steve stalked over to his car and drove away.

Meg squared her shoulders and drew her flimsy robe more tightly around her as she opened the screen door and walked back inside. The exhaust from Steve's car lingered in the yard, reminding her how angry he'd been when he left.

She was angry, too. And confused.

It didn't help to find Lindsey and Brenda sitting in the darkened living room waiting for her.

"You should both be in bed," Meg told them.

"We want to talk to you first," Lindsey announced, her hands folded on her knees.

"Not tonight," she said shortly. "I'm tired and upset."

"You!" Lindsey cried. "Brenda and I are exhausted, but that doesn't matter. What does is that you broke your word."

"I didn't promise not to see Steve again," Meg told her. She'd been careful about that.

Meg went back to the door and stood in front of the screen, half hoping Steve would return—not knowing what she'd say or do if he did.

"You've been sneaking out of the house to see him, haven't you?"

Meg lifted one shoulder in a shrug.

"You have!" Lindsey was outraged. "When?"

Meg lifted the other shoulder.

"Can't I trust you anymore?"

"Lindsey, Steve's not exactly what he said he was."

"I'll just bet," she muttered. "He's got you fooled, hasn't he? You'd believe anything he says because that's what you *want* to believe. You're so crazy about this guy you can't even see what's right in front of your face."

If she'd been a little less upset herself, Meg might've been willing to set the record straight then and there. "We want to talk to you," Meg told her daughter. "Steve and I, together, and explain everything."

"Never!"

"Mrs. Remington, don't let him fool you," Brenda threw in dramatically.

"Let's not worry about this now," she said as defeat settled over her. "It's late and I have to be at the store early in the morning."

Lindsey stood, her hands clenched at her sides. "I want you to promise me you won't see him again."

"Lindsey, please."

"If you don't, Mom, I'll never be able to trust you again."

"It's time we had a little talk," Nancy said, bringing a steaming cup of coffee to the breakfast table. After the night he'd had, the last thing Steve wanted was a tête-à-tête with his troublesome younger sister.

"No, thanks."

Nancy left the table, taking the coffee with her.

"Hey, I want the coffee."

"Oh." She brought it back and slipped into the chair across from him. "Something's bothering you."

"Nothing gets past you, does it?" He almost scalded his mouth in his eagerness to get some caffeine into his system.

"Can you tell me what's wrong?" She stared at him with big brown eyes that suggested she could solve all his problems, if only he'd let her.

"No."

"It has to do with that Meg, doesn't it?"

Steve mumbled a noncommittal reply. He didn't care to discuss Meg Remington just then. What he'd told Meg was the simple truth—she made him crazy. No woman had ever affected him as powerfully as she did. After the way they'd parted, he doubted they'd see each other again, and damn it all, that wasn't what he wanted.

"She's not the woman for you," Nancy said, her eyes solemn.

"Nancy," he said in a low voice, "don't say any more. Okay?"

She closed her eyes, shaking her head. "You're falling in love with her."

"No, I'm not," he muttered. Cradling the mug in both

hands, he tried the coffee again, sipping from the edge to avoid burning his mouth.

"Thou protest too much," she told him, with a sanctimonious sigh. "I'm afraid you've made it necessary for me to take matters into my own hands. Someone's got to look out for your best interests."

Steve lowered the mug and glared at his sister. "What did you do *this* time?"

"Nothing yet. There's this woman, a widow I met on campus, and I'd like you to get to know her. She's nothing like Meg, but as far as I'm concerned..."

"No!" He wasn't listening to another word. The last time his sister had roped him into her schemes he'd met a crazy woman with an even crazier daughter. No more.

"But Steve..."

"You heard me." The chair made a scraping sound against the tile floor as he stood. "I won't be home for dinner."

Nancy stood, too. "When will you be back?"

Steve regarded her suspiciously. "I don't know. Why?"

"Because the least you can do is meet Sandy."

Steve gritted his teeth. "You invited her to the house?"

"Don't worry—I didn't mention you. I wanted the two of you to meet casually. She's nervous about dating again, and I was afraid if I told her about my big, bad brother she'd run in the opposite direction."

"That's what I'm going to do. If you want to work on anyone's love life, you might try your own."

"All right, all right," Nancy said, sounding defeated. "Just stay away from Meg, okay? The woman's bad news."

Steve's laugh was humorless. "You're telling me?"

A week passed. Steve refused to dwell on his confrontation with Meg. He didn't call her and she didn't phone him, either.

He hated to end it all, but he didn't see any other option.

He missed her, though. He tried to tell himself otherwise. Tried to convince himself a man has his pride. Tried not to think about her.

And failed.

Early one afternoon, Nancy came by the shop with a friend. They were on their way to a movie, or so Nancy claimed.

Nancy smiled a little-sister smile and cheerfully asked Steve if he'd give Sandy an estimate on repairing her fender.

Sandy was petite. Cute. A little fragile.

It didn't take Steve long to figure out that this Sandy was the same one Nancy had wanted him to meet. The widow. The woman who'd save him from Meg's clutches.

"Pleased to meet you," Steve said, wiping his greasy hands on the pink cloth he had tucked in his hip pocket.

Nancy smiled innocently, looking pleased with herself.

"I'll have a written estimate for you by the time you two get back here."

"You don't have to work late again, do you?" Nancy asked, not even attempting to be coy.

Steve could already see what was coming. His conniving sister was about to wrangle a dinner invitation out of him. One that meant he'd be stuck entertaining Sandy.

"I'm afraid I'm tied up this evening," he said stiffly.

"Oh, darn. I was hoping you could take Sandy and me to dinner."

"Sorry," he said. "Now, if you'll excuse me…"

"It was a pleasure to meet you, Mr. Conlan."

"The pleasure was mine," he said and turned away.

Unfortunately, it didn't end with Sandy. His sister had several other friends with dented fenders or cracked windshields. They all seemed to need estimates in the days that followed.

"The next time a woman comes in and asks for me, I'm unavailable," he told his crew. Steve made sure that on her next visit Nancy would know he didn't have time for her matchmaking games. He told her as much when she stopped by—alone—a couple of days later.

"I was only trying to help."

"Thanks, but no thanks." He sat at his desk, making his way through the piles of paperwork stacked in front of him.

Nancy expelled a sigh. "You aren't seeing Meg again, are you?"

His hand tightened around the pen. "That's none of your business."

"Yes, it is! A woman like that could ruin your life."

In some ways she already had, but Nancy wouldn't understand. Whenever he met another woman, Steve found himself comparing her to Meg. Invariably everyone else fell short. Far short. He was miserable without her.

Nancy left, and Steve leaned back in his chair, studying the phone. All it would take was one call. He wouldn't have to mention the incident with the police. He could even make a joke of it, maybe buy her a pair of flannel pajamas. The kind that went from her neck to her feet. They'd both laugh, say how sorry they were and put an end to this stalemate.

Then he'd take her in his arms, hold her and kiss her. This was the part he dwelled on most. The reconciliation.

"Steve." Gary Wilcox stuck his head in the office door.

Steve jerked his attention away from the phone.

"There's someone here to see you. A woman."

Impatience made Steve's blood boil. "What did I say earlier? I gave specific instructions to tell any of my sister's friends that I'm unavailable."

"But—"

"Is that so hard to understand?"

"Nope," Gary said without emotion. "I don't have

a problem doing that, if it's what you really want, but I kinda had the feeling this one's special."

Knowing his foreman had cast an appreciative eye at the widow, Steve suspected it was Sandy who'd dropped by unannounced. "You talk to her."

"Me?"

"Yeah, you."

"What am I supposed to say?"

Steve rubbed a hand down his tired face. Did he have to do everything himself? "I don't know, just say whatever seems appropriate. I promise you Nancy won't be sending any more eligible women to the shop."

"Nancy didn't send this one."

The pen slipped from Steve's hands and rolled across the desk. "Who did?"

"She didn't say. All I got was her name. Meg Remington. I seem to recall hearing it mentioned a time or two—generally when you were upset."

Steve pushed back his chair and slowly stood. His heart reacted with a swift, furious pace. "Meg's here?"

"That's what I've been trying to tell you for the last five minutes."

Steve sank back into the chair. "Send her in."

A mischievous grin danced across Gary's mouth. "That's what I thought you'd say."

Steve stood, then sat back down and busied himself with things on his desk. He wanted Meg to think he was busy. The minute she walked into the room, he'd set everything aside.

A full five minutes passed and still she didn't show up. Steve came out of his office and ran into Gary, who frowned and shook his head. "She's gone."

"Gone?"

Gary nodded. "The only thing I can figure out is that she must've overheard you say you weren't available and left."

Steve muttered a four-letter word and hurried out. He wasn't sure where he'd find her, but he wasn't going to let her walk out of his life.

She wasn't at the bookstore and he didn't see her car at home. He tried the grocery store, too, for good measure. Without success.

It wasn't until nearly seven that he drove to her house again. That he was willing to confront her daughter was a sign of how desperate he'd become.

He stood on her front porch and rang the doorbell. Waiting for someone to answer, he buried his hands deep in his pockets. A preventive action, he realized, to keep from reaching for her the instant she appeared.

"Just a minute," he heard her call.

Then the door opened and Meg was standing there.

His gaze drifted over her. He'd planned to play it cool, casually mention that he was in the neighborhood and heard she'd stopped by the office. Their eyes met, held, and Steve forgot about hiding his feelings. She wore a pretty pale blue summer dress.

"Hello, Steve."

"Hello."

The screen door stood between them.

They continued to stare at each other.

"Can I come in?" he asked. Pride be damned. It'd been cold comfort in the past two weeks. If he had to apologize, or grovel or beg forgiveness, then so be it. He wanted her back in his life.

"Of course." She unlatched the door and pushed it open.

Steve stepped inside. He could barely breathe, never mind think. Pulling her into his arms didn't seem appropriate, but that was all he wanted to do.

"Where's Lindsey?" he managed to ask.

Meg's voice was breathy and uneven. "She's out for the evening."

He needed to touch her. Reaching up, he cupped her cheek in his rough palm. Slowly, Meg closed her eyes and leaned her head into his hand.

"I had to come here," he whispered.

"I'm so sorry. About everything."

"Me, too."

Unable to wait a second longer, Steve folded her in his arms and brought her mouth to his. Gentleness was beyond him, his hunger as great as any he'd ever known.

Meg grabbed his shirt as if she needed an anchor, something to secure her during the wild, sensual storm. He backed her against the door.

Meg gasped, and Steve moved a few inches away. With his hands framing her cheeks, he studied her beautiful face. Her shoulders were heaving, and he realized his own breathing was just as labored.

He rubbed the pad of his thumb across her moist, swollen lips. The action was unhurried—an apology for his roughness, his eagerness.

She moaned softly and he kissed her again. Gently. With restraint. Her arms were around his neck, and Steve had never tasted a sweeter kiss.

"I was going to call," he told her, burying his face in the slope of her neck. "A thousand times I told myself I'd call. Every minute apart from you was torture."

"I wanted to call you, too."

"I'm glad…."

"You were right," Meg confessed. "I should've been wearing something more…discreet."

"I was jealous, pure and simple." He felt her smile against the side of his face and smiled, too.

"I would've been jealous if the situation had been reversed."

"Don't worry. I didn't date a single one of the women Nancy arranged for me to meet."

Meg jerked back. "What women?"

"Ah…it's not important."

"It is to me."

He knew it would've been to him, as well, so he explained. "Nancy felt it was necessary to save me from a loose woman, so she introduced me to some of her friends."

"And you refused to go out with them." Meg sounded pleased.

"All I want to do is talk to Lindsey. Get things straightened out."

"Me, too. But we can't right now."

"So I see."

"Hold me," she said, nestling in his arms. "I don't want you to leave for a long, long time."

Steve planted tiny kisses along the side of her neck, marking his way back to her lips. "When will Lindsey be back?" he whispered.

"She's spending the night at Brenda's."

His hold tightened. "Meg," he said, then kissed her with a hunger he couldn't deny. "I want to make love to you. There's a lot we have to discuss before we make that kind of commitment, but we have an opportunity to do that now, don't we?"

"Mmm."

He kissed her again, pacing himself. "Thank God you

dropped in at the office. I don't know how long it would've taken me to come to my senses otherwise."

"The office?" Meg repeated, breaking away from him. "I was never at your office."

Seven

"It doesn't matter if you were at my office or not," Steve said, kissing Meg again. Slowly. Thoroughly.

She couldn't manage even a token resistance, although her mind whirled with questions.

She was starved for the taste of him. Starved for his touch. Starved for *him*. The loneliness had been suffocating. Before she'd met Steve, her life had seemed just fine. Then within a matter of weeks she'd realized how empty everything was without him.

"I've missed you so much," she told him between deep kisses.

"Me, too."

"You should've phoned," she whispered.

"You, too."

"I know."

"I'm crazy about you."

She was so tempted to throw caution to the wind and make love with this man who excited her so much. Who made her feel alive.

If ever the moment was right it was now, with Lindsey gone until morning.

But...

The questions returned. There'd only been one man in her life, her ex-husband, Lindsey's father, and by the time they'd divorced Meg had felt like a failure as a wife. Inadequate. Unresponsive.

"Steve...Steve." Her fingers were in Steve's hair as his mouth roamed over her throat. "Stop, please."

He went still, his lips pressed against the hollow of her throat. "You want me to stop? Now?"

"Please...for just a minute. Did you say you thought I'd been to your office?" She wanted that confusion cleared up first.

"It's what Gary told me." He raised his head, eyes clouded with passion. "It doesn't matter—I'm here now. I've missed you so much. I can't believe either of us let this go on so long."

"But it does matter," she argued. "Because I wasn't there."

Steve shut his eyes and seemed to be fighting something in himself. Finally, he straightened and eased away from her.

"I'm glad you're here," she whispered. "I've missed you, too. It's just that before we…" She felt as though her face was on fire. How she wished she was more experienced, more sophisticated. "You know."

"Make love," he finished for her.

"Yes… We should come to some sort of understanding. It's like you said—we should talk first."

Steve took her by the hand. He led her into the living room and chose the big overstuffed chair that was her favorite.

He sat and, reaching up, pulled her onto his lap. "So let's talk."

"Okay," she said, hating the way her voice trembled.

"First I want to clear something up. You say you *didn't* stop by my office this afternoon?"

"No. I was at the store until after six."

"I didn't see you there."

"I was in the back room, processing orders." Because she was afraid he'd think she was lying in order to save face, she added, "You can check with Laura if you want."

Steve frowned. "I believe you. Why wouldn't I?" He studied her. "But that isn't why you stopped us just now, is it?"

Meg lowered her gaze. "No," she whispered.

"I didn't think so. Are you going to tell me?"

"Tell you what?" Steve's arm went around her waist. It felt good to be this close to him.

"I suspect your reluctance has to do with your marriage."

"My marriage?"

"It doesn't take a detective to figure out that your ex-husband hurt you badly."

"No divorce is easy," Meg admitted, "but I'm not an emotional cripple, if that's what you mean."

"It isn't." He drew her even closer and kissed her again. She kissed him back, offering him her heart, her soul, her body...

"I can't seem to keep my hands off you," he murmured. "I wanted to talk to you about your marriage. Instead, I'm a second away from ravishing you."

And she was a second away from letting him.

"It was a friendly divorce," Meg insisted, returning to the subject he'd introduced. It wasn't a comfortable one—but it was safer than touching and kissing and where that would lead.

Steve eyed her suspiciously. "How friendly?" he asked.

"We parted amicably. It was a mutual decision."

"What caused the divorce?"

Meg closed her eyes and sighed. "He had a girlfriend," she said, trying not to reveal her bitterness. For years she'd kept the feelings of hurt and betrayal buried deep.

In the beginning, that had been for Lindsey's sake.

Later, she was afraid to face the anger for fear of what it would do to her. "Dave didn't love me anymore," she said, in an unemotional voice. As if it didn't matter. As if it had never mattered.

"What about Lindsey? He abandoned her, too?"

"He knew I'd always be there for her, and I will. He lives in California now."

"What about his commitment to you and his daughter? That wasn't important to him?"

"I don't know—you'd need to ask Dave about that."

"How long did this business with the girlfriend go on before he told you about her?"

"I don't know," she said again. She had her suspicions, plenty of them, but none she was willing to discuss with Steve. "I do know that when Dave got around to telling me he wanted a divorce, she was pregnant."

"In other words, you felt there was nothing you could do but step aside?"

"I had no problem doing that." Maybe if she'd loved Dave more, she would've been willing to fight for him. But by the time Dave told her about Brittany, she wanted out of the marriage. Just plain out.

"So you got divorced."

"Yes, with no fuss at all. He gave me what I wanted."

"And what was that?"

"He was willing to let me raise Lindsey." She shook her head. "It's not what you're thinking."

"And what am I thinking?"

She placed the back of her hand against her forehead and gave him a forlorn look, like the heroine of a silent movie. "That the divorce traumatized me."

"I wasn't thinking that at all," he assured her. "Your marriage had already taken care of that."

Meg dropped her hand, then raised it again to brush away her tears. How well Steve understood.

"It wasn't enough that your husband had an affair. When he walked out on you and Lindsey, he made sure you blamed yourself for his infidelity, didn't he?" She didn't respond, and he asked her a second time, his voice gentle. "Didn't he?"

Meg jerked her head away for fear he'd read the truth in her eyes. "It's over now…. It was all a long time ago."

"But it isn't over. If it was, we'd be upstairs making love instead of sitting here talking. You haven't been able to trust another man since Dave."

"No," she whispered, her head lowered.

"Oh, baby," he said tenderly, gathering her in his arms. "I'm so sorry."

She blinked rapidly in an effort to forestall more tears. "I trust you," she told him, and she knew instinctively that Steve would never betray his wife or walk away from his family.

"You do trust me," he said, "otherwise you wouldn't

have let me get this close to you. Just be warned. I intend to get a whole lot closer, and soon."

With anyone else Meg would have felt threatened, but with Steve it felt like a promise. A promise she wanted him to fulfill.

"It's better that we wait to make love," he surprised her by adding.

"It is?" Her head shot up.

"I want to clear the air with Lindsey first," he told her. "Get things settled between us. I'd much rather be her friend than her foe."

"And I'd like to be Nancy's friend, too," Meg said.

He smiled. "Those girls don't know what they started— or where it's going to end."

"Exactly where are we going?" Lindsey asked, staring out the car window.

"I already told you." Meg was losing patience with her daughter.

"To see Steve at work?"

"Yes."

"Work release, you mean."

"Lindsey!" Meg said emphatically. She'd never known her to be this difficult. "Steve has his own business. We both thought if you could see him at work, you'd know that what he told you about being an ex-con was all a farce."

Lindsey remained sullen for several minutes, then asked, "Why'd he say all those things if they weren't true?"

Her daughter had a valid point, but they'd gone over this same ground a dozen times. "We wanted you to dislike him."

Unfortunately Steve's plan had worked all too well. And Meg had obviously done an equally good job with Nancy, because his sister didn't want him continuing to see her, either. What a mess they'd created.

"Why wouldn't you and Steve want me to like him?" Lindsey asked.

"I've already explained, and I don't feel like repeating the story yet again," Meg said. "Suffice it to say I'm not especially proud of our behavior."

Lindsey pouted, but didn't ask any more questions.

Meg pulled into the parking lot at Steve's business and watched as Lindsey took in everything—the well-established body shop, the customers, the neat surroundings.

There were three large bays all filled with vehicles in various states of disrepair. Men dressed in blue-striped coveralls worked on the cars.

"They *all* look like they came straight from a prison yard," Lindsey mumbled under her breath.

"Lindsey," Meg pleaded, wanting this meeting to go well. "At least give Steve a chance."

"I did once, and according to you he lied."

Once more, Meg had no argument. "Just listen to him, okay?"

"All right, but I'm not making any promises."

The shop smelled of paint and grease; the scents weren't unpleasant. There was a small waiting area with a coffee-pot, paper cups and several outdated magazines.

"Hello," Meg said to the man standing behind the counter. "I'm Meg Remington. Steve is expecting me."

The man studied her. "*You're* Meg Remington?" he asked.

"Yes."

"You don't look like the Meg Remington who was in here last week."

"I beg your pardon?"

"Never mind, Gary," Steve said, walking out from the office. He smiled warmly when he saw Meg. Lindsey sat in the waiting area, reading a two-year-old issue of *Car and Driver* as if it contained the answers to life's questions.

"Hello, Lindsey," Steve said.

"Hello," she returned in starched tones.

"Would you and your mother care to come into my office?"

"Will we be safe?"

A hint of a smile cracked Steve's mouth, but otherwise he didn't let on that her question had amused him. "I don't think there'll be a problem."

"All right, fine, since you insist." She set aside the magazine and stood.

Steve ushered them into the spotlessly clean office and gestured at the two chairs on the other side of his desk. "Please, have a seat."

They did, with Lindsey perched stiffly on the edge of hers.

"Would you like something to drink?" he asked.

"No, thanks."

Meg didn't think she'd ever seen Lindsey less friendly. It wasn't like her to behave like this. Presumably she thought she was protecting her mother.

"I have a confession to make," Steve said, after an awkward moment. He leaned back in his chair.

"Shouldn't you be telling this to the police?" Lindsey asked.

"Not this time." His eyes connected with Meg's. She tried to tell him how sorry she was, but nothing she'd said had changed Lindsey's attitude.

"I did something I regret," Steve continued undaunted. "I lied to you. And as often happens when people lie, it came back to haunt me."

"I'm afraid I was a party to this falsehood myself," Meg added.

"How do you know it's really a lie?" Lindsey demanded of Meg. "Steve could actually be a convicted criminal. He might be sitting behind that desk, but how do we know if what he says is true?"

Meg rolled her eyes.

"Who are you *really,* Steve Conlan?" Lindsey leaned forward, planting both hands on the edge of his desk.

"I'm exactly who I appear to be. I'm thirty-eight years old. Unmarried. I own this shop and have ten full-time employees."

"Can you prove it?"

"Of course."

A knock sounded on the door.

"Come in," Steve called.

The man who'd greeted her when she first arrived stuck his head inside the door. He smiled apologetically. "Sorry to interrupt, but Sandy Janick's on the phone."

Steve frowned. "Are we working on Sandy's vehicle?" he wanted to know. "I don't remember seeing a work order."

"No, she's that friend your sister was trying to set you up with. Remember?"

"Tell her I'll call her back," Steve said without hesitating.

Meg bristled. He'd admitted that his sister had been playing matchmaker. So Nancy had set him up with another woman. Probably one without a troublesome teenager and a bunch of emotional garbage she was dragging around from a previous marriage. Meg tried to swallow the lump forming in her throat.

"Gary," Steve said, stopping the other man from leaving. "Would you kindly tell Lindsey who owns this shop?"

"Sure," the other man said with a grin. "Mostly the IRS."

"I'm serious," Steve said impatiently.

Gary chuckled. "Last I heard it was Walter Milton at Key Bank. Oops, there goes the phone again." He was gone an instant later.

"Walter Milton," Lindsey said skeptically. "So you really *don't* own this business."

"Walter Milton's my banker and a good friend."

"So is Earl Markham, your parole officer," Lindsey snapped. "A high school friend, correct?" She shook her head. "I'm afraid I can't believe you, Mr. Conlan. If you were trying to get me to change my mind about you seeing my mother, it didn't work." Then turning to Meg, she said, "I wouldn't trust him if I were you. He's got a look about him…."

"What look?" Meg and Steve asked simultaneously.

"You know—a criminal look. I'm sure I've seen his face before, and my guess is that it was in some post office."

Meg ground her teeth with frustration. "Lindsey, would you please stop being so difficult?"

"I don't think it's a good idea for you to date a man who lies."

"You're right," Steve surprised them both by saying. "I should never have made up that ridiculous story about being a felon. I've learned my lesson and I won't pull that stunt again. All I'm asking is that you give me a second chance to prove myself."

"I don't think so."

Meg resisted throwing her arms in the air.

"You know what really bothers me?" Lindsey went on. "That you'd involve my mother in this stupid scam of yours. That's really low."

"I don't blame you for being angry with me," Steve said, before Meg could respond. "But don't be upset with your mother—it was my idea, not hers."

"My mother wouldn't stoop to anything that underhanded on her own."

Meg's eyes met Steve's and she wanted to weep with frustration.

"I was hoping you'd find it in your heart to forgive me," Steve said contritely, returning his attention to Lindsey. "I'd like us to be friends."

"Even if we were, that doesn't mean I approve of you seeing my mother."

"Lindsey," Meg began. "I—"

"Mom, we can't trust this guy," Lindsey interrupted. "We know how willing he is to lie. And what about that phone call just now?" She pointed at Steve. "Another woman calls and he can hardly wait to get back to her. You saw the expression on his face."

"Don't be ridiculous," Steve snapped. "I'm crazy about your mother. I wouldn't hurt her for the world."

"Yeah, whatever. That's what they all say." Lindsey had perfected the world-weary tone so beloved of teenagers everywhere.

"I've had enough, Lindsey," Meg said sternly. "I think you'd better go wait in the car."

Lindsey leapt eagerly out of her chair and rushed from the office, leaving Steve and Meg alone.

"I'm sorry," she whispered, standing.

"I'll try to talk to her again." Steve walked around the desk and pulled her into his arms. "All she needs is a little time. Eventually she'll learn to trust me." He raised her hand to his mouth and kissed the knuckles. "But one thing's for sure...."

"What's that?"

"I'm through with sneaking around meeting you. I'm taking you to dinner tonight and I'm coming to the front door. Lindsey will just have to accept that we're dating. In fact, I'll ask her if she'd like to join us."

"She won't," Meg said with certainty.

"I'm still going to ask. She may not like me now, but in time I'll win her heart, just the way I intend to win her mother's."

What Steve didn't seem to understand was that he'd already won hers.

* * *

At seven that night, Meg was humming softly to herself and dabbing perfume on her wrists. Steve was due any minute.

The telephone rang, but Meg didn't bother to answer. There was no point. The call was almost guaranteed to be for Lindsey. She heard the girl racing at breakneck speed for the phone, as if reaching it before the second ring was some kind of personal goal.

"Mom!" Lindsey screeched from the kitchen downstairs, reaching her in the master bath.

"I'll be right there," she called back, checking her reflection in the bathroom mirror one last time.

Lindsey yelled something else that Meg couldn't hear.

"Who is it?" Meg asked, coming out of her bedroom and hurrying downstairs.

"I already told you it's Steve," Lindsey said indifferently as she passed her leaving the kitchen.

Meg glanced at her watch and reached for the phone. "Hello."

"Hi," he said, sounding discouraged. "I ran into a problem and it looks like I'm going to be late."

"What kind of problem?" It was already later than her normal dinnertime, and Meg was hungry.

"I'm not sure yet. Sandy Janick phoned and apparently she's got a flat tire…."

"Listen," Meg said with feigned cheerfulness, "why

don't we cancel dinner for this evening? It sounds like you've got your hands full."

"Yes, but…"

"I'm hungry right now. It's no big deal—we'll have dinner another night."

Steve hesitated. "You're sure?"

"Positive." She was trembling so badly it was difficult to remain standing. Steve and Sandy. She suspected Nancy had arranged the flat tire, but if Steve couldn't see through that, then it was obvious he didn't want to. "It's not a problem," Meg insisted.

"I'll give you a call tomorrow."

"Sure…. That would be great." She barely heard the rest of the conversation. He kept talking and Meg hoped she made the appropriate responses. She must have, because a couple of minutes later he hung up.

Closing her eyes, Meg exhaled and replaced the receiver.

"Mom?"

Meg turned to face her daughter.

"Is everything okay?"

She nodded, unable to chase away the burning pain that attacked the pit of her stomach and radiated out.

"Then how come you're so pale?"

"I'm fine, honey. Steve and I won't be going out to dinner after all." She tried to sound as if nothing was amiss, but her entire world seemed to be collapsing around her. "Why don't we get a pizza? Do you want to call? Order whatever you want. Okay?"

She was overreacting and knew it. If Steve was doing something underhanded, he wouldn't tell her he was meeting Sandy Janick. He'd do the same things Dave had done. He'd lie and cheat.

"I'm going to change my clothes," Meg said, heading blindly for the stairs.

She half expected Lindsey to follow her and announce that she'd been right all along, that Steve wasn't to be trusted. But to Meg's astonishment, her daughter said nothing.

"I knew if anyone could help Sandy with her flat tire it would be you," Nancy said, smiling benevolently at her older brother.

Steve glanced at his watch, frustrated and angry with his sister—and himself. She'd done it again. She'd manipulated him into doing something he didn't want to do. Instead of spending the evening with Meg, he'd been trapped into helping these two out of a fix.

Leave it to his sister. Not only had Nancy and Sandy managed to get a flat, but they'd been on the Mercer Island floating bridge in the middle of rush-hour traffic. Steve had to arrange for a tow truck and then meet them at his shop. From there, they'd all ended up back at the house, and Sandy had made it clear that she was looking for a little male companionship. There was a time Steve would've jumped at the chance to console the attractive widow. But no longer.

"I can't tell you how much I appreciate your help," Sandy told him now. "Thank you so much."

"You're welcome." He looked pointedly at his watch. It was just after nine, still early enough to steal away and visit Meg. Lindsey would disapprove, but that couldn't be avoided.

The girl was proving to be more of a problem than Steve had expected. She was downright stubborn and unwilling to give him the slightest bit of credit. Well, she was dealing with a pro, and Steve wasn't about to give up on either of the Remington women. Not without a fight.

"You're leaving?" Nancy asked as Steve marched to the front door.

"Yes," he said. "Is that a problem?"

"I guess not." His sister wore a downtrodden look, as if he'd disappointed her.

"I have to be going, too," Sandy Janick said. "Again, thank you."

Steve walked her to the door and said a polite goodbye, hoping it really *was* goodbye. He wished her well, but wasn't interested in becoming her knight in shining armor. Not when there was another damsel whose interest he coveted.

He closed the door as he went to retrieve his car keys from the hall table and grab his jacket.

Nancy got up and followed him as he prepared to leave. "Where are you going?" she asked.

Steve glared at his sister. "What makes you think it's any of your business?"

"Because I have a feeling that you're off to see that… that floozy."

"*Floozy?* What on earth have you been reading?" Shaking his head, he muttered, "Meg isn't a floozy or a woman of ill repute or a hussy or any other silly term you want to call her. She's a single mother and a businesswoman. She owns a bookstore. She—"

"That's not what she told me."

"Listen. I'm thirty-eight years old and I won't have my little sister running my love life. Now, I helped you and your friend, but I had to break a dinner date with Meg to do it."

"Then I'm glad Sandy got that flat tire," she said defiantly.

Steve had had enough. "Stay out of my life, Nancy. I'm warning you."

His sister raised her head dramatically, as if she'd come to some momentous decision. "I'm afraid I can't do that. I'm really sorry, Steve."

"What do you mean, you *can't?*"

"I can't stand idly by and watch the brother I've always

loved and admired make a complete fool of himself. Especially over a woman like *that*."

Steve's patience was gone. Vanished. But before he could say a word, Nancy threw herself in front of him.

"I won't let you do this!" she said, stretching her arms across the door.

The phone rang just then, and Steve knew he'd been saved by the bell. Nancy flew across the room to answer it.

Hoping to make a clean getaway, Steve opened the door and dashed outside. As he'd suspected, Nancy tore out after him.

"It's for you," she called from the front porch.

Steve was already in his car and he wasn't going to be waylaid by his sister a second time.

"Tell whoever it is I'll call back."

"It's a woman."

"What's her name?"

"Lindsey," she called at the top of her voice. "And she wants to talk to you."

Eight

The last person Steve expected to hear from was Meg's standoffish teenage daughter. He climbed out of his car and ran up the porch steps. He walked directly past his sister and without saying a word went straight to the phone.

"Lindsey? What's the problem?" he asked. He was in no mood for games and he wanted her to know it.

"Are you alone?" Lindsey asked him.

Steve noticed that her voice was lower than usual. He assumed that meant Meg wasn't aware of her daughter's call.

"My sister's here," he answered. Nancy stood with her arms folded, frowning at him with unconcealed disapproval.

"Anyone else?" Lindsey asked, then added snidely, "Especially someone named Sandy."

It sounded as if Lindsey was jealous on her mother's behalf, which was ridiculous. The kid would be glad of an excuse to get rid of him. "No. Sandy left a few minutes ago."

"So you *were* with her," she accused.

In light of the confrontation he'd just had with his sister, Steve's hold on his patience was already strained. "Is there a reason for your call?" he asked bluntly.

"Of course," Lindsey muttered with an undignified huff. "I want to know what you said that upset my mother."

"What I said?" Steve didn't understand.

"After you called, she told me to order pizza for dinner and then she said I could have anything on it I wanted. She knows I like anchovies and she can't stand 'em. Then," Lindsey said, after a short pause, "the pizza came and she looked at me like she didn't have a clue where it came from. Something's wrong and I want you to tell me what it is."

"I have no idea."

"Mom's just not herself." Another pause, a longer one this time. "You'd better come over and talk to her."

An invitation from the veritable dragon of a daughter herself? This was a stroke of luck. "You sure you can trust me?" he couldn't resist asking.

"Not really," she said with feeling. "But I don't think I have a choice. My mom likes you although I can't figure out why."

The kid was a definite hazard to his ego, but Steve decided to let the comment pass.

"You think your mother's upset because I broke our dinner date?" he asked. "Well, I've got news for you—she's the one who called it off. She said it was no big deal."

"And you believed her?"

"Shouldn't I?"

Steve could picture the girl rolling her eyes. "Either you aren't as smart as you look, or you've been in prison for so long you don't know anything about women."

Steve didn't find either possibility flattering. "All I did was phone to tell her I was going to be late. What's so awful about that?"

"You were late because you were meeting another woman!"

"Wrong," Steve protested. "I was *helping* another woman. Actually two women, one of whom was my sister."

"Don't you get it? My dad left my mother because of another woman. He made up all these lies about where he was and what he was doing so he could be with her."

"And you're worried that your mother assumes I'm

doing the same thing? Lindsey, isn't that a bit of a stretch?"

"Yes…no. I don't know," she said. "All I know is you canceled—"

"*She* canceled."

"Your dinner date because you were meeting another woman—"

"Helping another woman and my sister."

"Whatever. All I know is that Mom hasn't been the same since, and if you care about her the way you keep saying…"

"I do."

"Then I suggest you get over here, and fast." The line was abruptly disconnected.

Steve stared at the receiver, then replaced it, shaking his head as he did.

"What's wrong with Meg?" Nancy asked.

Steve shrugged. "Darned if I know. No one ever told me falling in love was so complicated." Having said that, he marched out the door.

Nancy ran after him. "You're in love with her?"

"I sure am."

A huge smile lit up his sister's face. Steve stood next to his car, wondering if he was seeing things. A smile was the last reaction he would've expected from Nancy.

He muttered to himself on the short drive to Meg's

house. He didn't stop muttering—about women and daughters and sisters—until he rang the doorbell.

The door was opened two seconds later by Lindsey. "It took you long enough," she said.

"Lindsey, who is it?" Meg asked, stepping out from the kitchen. She'd apparently been putting away dishes, because she had a plate and a coffee mug in her hand. "Steve," she whispered, "what are you doing here?"

"Have you had dinner yet?"

"Not really," Lindsey answered for her mother. "She nibbled on a slice of pizza, but that was only so I wouldn't bug her. I ordered her favorite kind, too." She paused and grimaced. "Vegetarian. Even though *I* like anchovies and pepperoni."

"Weren't you hungry?" Steve asked, silencing Lindsey with a look.

Meg raised one shoulder in a shrug. "Not really. What about you? Did you get anything to eat?"

"Nope."

"There's leftover pizza if you're interested."

"I'm interested," he said, moving toward her. Lindsey was right—Meg seemed upset.

"You're not going to *eat,* are you?" Lindsey demanded.

"Why not?" Steve asked.

The girl sighed loudly. "What my mother needs here is reassurance. If you had a romantic thought in that empty space between your ears, you'd take her in your arms and...and kiss her."

All Steve could do was stand there and stare. This was the same annoying girl who'd been a source of constant irritation from the moment they'd met. Something had changed, and he didn't know what or why.

"Lindsey?" Meg obviously had the same questions as Steve.

"What?" Lindsey asked. "Oh, you want to know why I changed my mind. Well, I've been thinking. If Steve really meant what he said about being friends, then I guess I'm willing to meet him halfway." This was said as if it had come at great personal sacrifice. She turned to Steve. "Actually, I can't see any way around it. It's clear to me that my mother's fallen in love with you."

"Lindsey!"

Steve enjoyed the way Meg's blush colored her pale cheeks.

"And it's equally clear to me that Steve feels the same, especially if he was willing to put up with all my insults. Frankly, I can't see fighting it any longer. What's the point? And really, I can't keep a constant eye on you two. I do have my own life."

Lindsey's change of heart was welcome news to Steve. The kid held the all-important key to Meg's heart. He'd never win her love, if he didn't gain Lindsey's approval first.

"Don't get the idea I *like* any of this," Lindsey added—to salvage her pride, he guessed. "But I can learn to live with it."

"Great," Steve said, offering her his hand. "Let's shake on it."

Lindsey studied his hand as if she wasn't sure she wanted to touch him. But once she did, her shake was firm and confident.

"You're nothing like you were supposed to be," she muttered under her breath.

"I apologize for being such a disappointment," he said out of the corner of his mouth.

"Can't do anything about that now. Mom's crazy about you."

"I think she's pretty terrific, too."

Lindsey sighed. "So I noticed."

"What are you two talking about?" Meg asked.

"Nothing," Lindsey answered with exaggerated innocence. She looked at Steve and winked.

He returned her wink, pleased to be on solid ground with the girl. "Did someone say something about pizza?"

"I did," Meg told him. "Come into the kitchen and I'll microwave the leftovers."

"Mother," Lindsey groaned. "I thought I could count on you to be a little more romantic. Or do I have to do everything myself?"

"What did I do wrong now?"

"Couldn't you make Steve something special?"

Meg took a moment to think this over. "I've got chicken I could make into a salad. If he doesn't like that, there's always peanut-butter-and-jelly sandwiches."

"I'd rather have the pizza," Steve interjected. He didn't want Meg wasting her time preparing a meal, all in the name of some romantic fantasy. He wanted her to talk—and to listen.

Before Lindsey could protest, Steve followed Meg into the kitchen. "Do you know what that was about?"

Meg smiled and opened the refrigerator. "Nope." She took out the pizza box and set it on the counter.

Steve climbed onto the stool. "So what happened earlier?" he asked.

Meg hesitated, separating a piece of the pizza. "I suppose Lindsey called you?"

"Yes, but I was already on my way over here."

He saw that she avoided his eyes, as she made busywork of setting two huge slices of pizza on a plate and heating them in the microwave. "After your phone call, I had kind of a panic attack."

"About?" he prompted.

"You… Us."

"And?"

"And I worked it out myself. I felt pretty foolish afterward. I realized you aren't the same kind of man Dave was…is. If you call to say you're helping another woman, then that's exactly what you're doing."

"You thought I was seeing someone else?" Lindsey had implied as much, but he hadn't taken it seriously.

"I feel silly now," she said, setting the sizzling pizza slices in front of him. She propped her elbows on the counter and rested her chin in her palms. "It was as if the craziness of my marriage was back. You see, at one time I tried to believe Dave. He'd make up the most outrageous stories to account for the huge periods of time he was away from home, and like a naive idiot, I'd believe him." She paused. "I guess because I wanted to. But Dave's not my problem anymore."

"A leopard doesn't change his spots," Steve said, finishing off the first slice. "If Dave cheated on you, he'll cheat on his present wife, too. It stands to reason."

"I know. From what Lindsey said after her last visit to California, Dave's marriage is on shaky ground. I'm sorry for him and for his wife."

Steve offered Meg the second slice, which she declined. He'd just taken a bite when the low strains of soulful violin music drifted toward them. Steve glanced at Meg and she shrugged, perplexed.

Lindsey appeared in the kitchen, looking thoroughly disgusted. "You two need my help, don't you?"

"Help?" Steve repeated. "With what?"

"Romance." She walked into the room and took Steve's

hand and then her mother's. She led them both into the living room. The furniture had been pushed to one side and the lights turned down low. Two crystal glasses and a bottle of red wine sat on the coffee table, ready to be put to good use.

"Now, I'll disappear into my room for a while," she said, "and you two can do all the things I've read about in novels."

Steve and Meg stared blankly at each other.

"Don't tell me you need help with that, too!"

"We can take it from here," Steve was quick to assure her.

"I should hope so," Lindsey muttered. With an air of superiority she headed up the stairs.

The music was sultry. Inviting. Once Lindsey was out of sight, Steve held his arms open to Meg. "Shall we dance?"

Steve could've sworn she blushed, very prettily, too, before she slipped into his embrace. He brought her close and sighed, reveling in the feel of her.

"I'm not very good at dancing," she murmured.

"Hey, don't worry. All we have to do is shift our feet a little." He laid his cheek next to hers.

He'd never had the time or the patience for romance. Or so he'd believed. Then he'd met Meg and his organized, safe, secure world had been turned upside down. Nothing had been the same since, and Steve suspected it never would be again.

Even Gary Wilcox seemed to recognize the difference between Steve's attitude toward Meg and his attitude to the other women he'd dated over the years. Steve didn't know how his foreman had figured it out, but he had. Of course, inviting Meg and Lindsey to the shop might have given Gary a clue. The idea of letting Lindsey see him at work had been an excuse; in reality he'd been trying to impress Meg, show her how successful he was. Prove to her that he was worthy of her attention.

Steve had always kept his personal life separate from the business. His personal life—that was a joke. He'd worked for years, dedicating his life to building a thriving business. He'd been successful, but that success had come at a price. There was very little room in his life for love.

But there was room for Meg and Lindsey.

Meg's lithe body moved with the music provocatively, seductively, against his. He wanted to hold her even tighter, kiss her, caress her...

They stopped moving, the pretense of dancing more than he could sustain. "I want you so badly," he whispered.

Meg sighed and raised her head so their eyes met in the dim light. "I want you, too. It frightens me how much..."

He ran his fingers up through her hair and held his breath as he slowly lowered his mouth to hers. "Oh, Meg." He kissed her over and over, unable to get enough of her.

The sound of a throat being cleared suddenly penetrated his brain.

Lindsey. Again.

Steve groaned inwardly. Slowly, reluctantly, he loosened his grip on Meg and eased his body away from hers.

She resisted. "Don't stop."

"Lindsey's back," he whispered.

Meg buried her face in his sweater.

"Hello, again," Lindsey said cheerfully from the stairs. "It looks like I returned in the nick of time." She pranced down the steps, walked over to the wine bottle and sadly shook her head. "You didn't even open the wine."

"We didn't get a chance," Steve muttered.

"I gave you twenty minutes," she said. "From what I can see, that was about five minutes longer than I should've waited. You're a fast worker."

"Lindsey," Meg said, in what was obviously meant to be her sternest voice. Unfortunately, the effect was more tentative than severe.

"I know I'm making a pest of myself—and I apologize, I really do. But we've been talking about this stuff in my sex-ed. class, and there's a case to be made for abstinence."

"What's that got to do with your mother and me?" Steve made the mistake of asking.

"You don't really want me to answer that, do you?" Lindsey asked. "Mom's flustered enough as it is."

"I guess not."

"We could discuss safe sex, if you want."

Steve watched in fascination as Meg's face turned a deep shade of red. "Lindsey!" This time her mother's voice was loud and clear. "You're embarrassing me."

"Sorry, Mom, but I figured we should raise the subject now instead of later." She dropped down on the sofa, then reached for the wine bottle and examined the label. "It's a good month, too. September. Brenda's uncle bought it for us. He said it wasn't a great wine, but it'd get the job done."

Steve's hand gripped Meg's shoulder. "It was, uh, thoughtful of you."

"Thanks." She smiled broadly. "But we were going for the romantic element."

"Now," Steve said, "would you mind if your mother and I talked? By ourselves? We didn't get much of a chance to do that earlier."

"I suppose that'd be all right—only I need to know something first." She set the wine bottle down and looked intently at Steve. "Are you going to marry my mother?"

Meg made a small mewling noise that suggested she

was mortified beyond words. She sank onto the ottoman and covered her face with both hands.

"Well, are you?" Lindsey pressed, ignoring her mother entirely.

Steve couldn't very well say he hadn't been thinking along those lines. There'd been little else on his mind for the past few days. He loved Meg. When he wasn't with her, it felt as if something was missing from his life. From his heart.

Steve had never imagined himself with a ready-made family, but he couldn't see himself without Meg and Lindsey. Not now.

"I believe that's a subject your mother and I need to discuss privately, but since you asked I'll tell you."

Lindsey got to her feet and Meg dropped her hands and looked up at him.

"You're going to marry us, aren't you." Lindsey's words were more statement than question. A satisfied smile lit up her face. "You're really going to do it."

"If your mother will have me."

"She will, trust me," Lindsey answered, looking gleeful. "I've known my mother forever and I've never seen her this gaga over a man."

"I can do my own talking, thank you very much," Meg said. "This is the most humiliating moment of my life—thanks to you, Lindsey Marie Remington." She stood, hands on her hips. "Go to your room and we'll talk when I've finished begging Steve to forgive you."

"What did I do that was so terrible?" Lindsey muttered.

Meg pointed to the stairs.

It looked as though Lindsey was about to argue; apparently she thought better of it. Her shoulders slumped forward and she moved slowly toward the stairs.

"I was just helping," she said under her breath.

"We'll talk about that later, young lady."

Lindsey's blue eyes met Steve's as she passed him. "I know I'm in trouble when she calls me *young lady.* She's mad. Be careful what you say. Don't ruin everything now."

"I'll try my best," Steve promised.

Meg waited until her daughter had reached the top of the stairs before she spoke. "I can't begin to tell you how sorry I am about that." Although her voice was calm, Steve wasn't fooled. Meg was angry, just as Lindsey had said.

"I'll have Lindsey apologize after I've had a chance to cool down," Meg was saying. "I don't dare speak to her now." She paced the carpet. "I want you to know I absolve you from everything that was said."

Steve rubbed his jaw. "Absolve me from what, precisely?"

"I want it understood, here and now, that I don't expect you to marry me."

"But I like the idea."

"I don't," she flared. "Not when my daughter practically ordered you to propose. Now," she said with a deep breath, "I think it might be best if you left."

Steve tried to protest, but Meg ushered him to the door and he could see that this wasn't the time to reason with her.

"I've never been so mortified in my life," Meg told Laura. She counted the change and put it in the cash register. The store was due to open in ten minutes and she felt far from ready to deal with customers.

"But he said he wanted to marry you, didn't he?"

"It was a pity proposal. Good grief, what else could he say?"

Laura restocked the front display with the latest best-sellers. "Steve doesn't look like the kind of guy who'd propose if he didn't mean it."

"He didn't mean it."

"What makes you so sure?"

Meg wanted to find a hole, crawl inside and hide for the rest of her natural life. No one seemed to appreciate the extent of her humiliation. Steve certainly hadn't. He'd tried to conceal it from her, but he'd viewed the incident with Lindsey as one big joke.

She hadn't intended to mention it to anyone. Laura knew because she'd sensed something was wrong with Meg, and in a moment of weakness, Meg had blurted out the entire episode.

"Have you talked to Lindsey about what she did?" Laura asked.

"In my current frame of mind," Meg told her, "I thought it better not to try. I'll talk to her when I can do so without screaming or weeping in frustration."

"What I don't understand," Laura said, hugging a book to her chest, "is what happened to bring about such a reversal in her attitude to Steve. The last time we talked, you were pulling out your hair because she refused to believe he wasn't a convicted felon."

"I don't know what's going on with her. I just don't get it."

"You've got to admit, this romance between you and Steve has taken some unexpected twists and turns," Laura said. "First, you didn't even *want* to meet him, then once you did you agreed not to see each other again. It would've ended there if not for the flowers."

"Which didn't even come from Steve. He was just glad to be done with me."

"That's not the way I remember it."

"I doubt I'll ever see him again," Meg said, slamming the cash drawer shut.

"Now you're being ridiculous," Laura said.

"I wouldn't blame him. No man in his right mind would want to get tangled up with Lindsey and me."

"I'm sure that's not true."

Laura sounded so definite about that. Meg desperately wanted to believe her, but she knew better. When she closed the shop at six that evening, she still hadn't heard from Steve, which convinced Meg that he was relieved to be free of her.

Lindsey was sitting in the living room reading when Meg got home from work. "Hi," she said, taking a huge bite out of a big red Delicious apple.

Meg set aside her purse and slipped off her shoes. The tiles in the entryway felt cool against her aching feet.

"You're not mad at me anymore, are you?" Lindsey asked. She got off the sofa and moved into the kitchen, where Meg was pouring herself a glass of iced tea.

"You embarrassed me."

"Steve wasn't embarrassed," Lindsey said. "I don't understand why you're so upset."

"How would you feel if I called up Dale Kotz and told him you wanted to go to the ninth-grade dance with him? He'd probably agree, because he likes you, but you'd never know if Dale would've asked you himself."

"Oh." Lindsey didn't say anything for several minutes.

"But it's more than that, Lindsey. I was mortified to the very marrow of my bones. I felt like you pressured Steve into proposing."

Lindsey sat in one of the kitchen chairs. "Would you believe me if I told you I was sorry?"

"Yes, but it doesn't change what happened."

"You are still angry, aren't you?"

"No," Meg said, opening the refrigerator and taking out

lettuce for a salad. "I'm not angry anymore, just incredibly embarrassed and hurt."

"I didn't mean to hurt you, Mom," Lindsey said in a low voice. "I was only trying to help."

"I know, honey, but you didn't. You made everything much, much worse."

Lindsey hung her head. "I feel just awful."

Meg didn't feel much better herself. She sat down at the table, next to her daughter, and patted Lindsey's hand.

Lindsey managed a weak smile, then fell into her mother's arms and hid her face against Meg's shoulder. "Men are so dumb sometimes," she murmured. "Brenda says love is like a game of connect the dots. Only with men, you have to make the dots and then draw the lines. They don't get it."

Meg stroked her daughter's hair.

"Do you love him, Mom?"

Meg smiled for the first time that day. "Yeah, I think I do. I certainly didn't plan on falling in love with him, that's for sure. It just sort of…happened."

"I don't think he expected to fall in love with you, either."

The doorbell chimed, and horrified that she might be caught crying, Lindsey broke away from her mother and hurriedly brushed the tears from her face.

"I'll get it," Meg said. She padded barefoot into the hallway and opened the door.

Steve stood on the other side, holding a dozen long-stemmed roses. He grinned. "Hello," he said, handing her the flowers. "I thought we'd try this marriage-proposal thing again, only this time we'll do it my way—not Lindsey's."

Nine

"Marriage proposal?" Meg repeated, staring down at the roses in her arms. "Really, Steve, there's no need to do this." Her throat was closing up on her; she could barely speak and she couldn't meet his eyes.

"I know exactly what I'm doing," Steve said.

"Is it Brenda?" Lindsey called from the kitchen.

"No, it's Steve."

"Steve!" Lindsey cried excitedly. "This is great. Maybe I didn't ruin everything after all."

"Hello, Meg," Steve said softly.

"Hi." She still couldn't look him in the eye.

"I'd like to talk to you."

"I...I was hoping we could do that," Meg told him. "They're lovely, thank you."

She handed Lindsey the flowers. "Would you take care

of these for me?" she asked her daughter. "Steve and I are going to talk and we'd appreciate some privacy. Okay?"

"Sure, Mom."

Lindsey disappeared into the kitchen and Meg sat down on the sofa. Steve sat beside her and took her hand. She wished he wasn't so close. The man had a way of muddling her most organized thoughts.

"Before you say anything, I have a couple of things I'd like to talk to you about," she began. She freed her hand from his and clasped her knees. "I've been doing a lot of thinking and...and I've come to a few conclusions."

"About what?"

"Us," she said. Dragging in a deep breath, she continued. "Laura reminded me this afternoon that our relationship has taken some unexpected twists and turns. Neither one of us wanted to meet the other—we were thrown into an impossible situation.

"We wouldn't have seen each other again if it wasn't for the flowers your sister sent me. From the moment we met, we've had two other people dictating our lives."

"To some extent that's true," Steve agreed, "but we wouldn't have allowed any of this to happen if we hadn't been attracted to each other from the beginning."

"Maybe," she admitted slowly.

"What do you mean, maybe?" Steve asked.

"I think we both need some time apart to decide what we really want."

"No way!" he said. "I've had thirty-eight years to look for what I want and I've found it. I'd like to make you and Lindsey a permanent part of my life."

"Ah, yes. Lindsey," Meg said. "As you might have noticed, she's fifteen going on thirty. I have a feeling this is what the rest of the teen years are going to be like."

"So you could use a gentle hand to help you steer her in the right direction." Steve leapt to his feet and jerked his fingers through his hair. "Listen, if you're trying to suggest you'd rather not marry me, just say so."

Meg straightened, keeping her back stiff. For a moment she couldn't speak. "That's what I'm saying," she finally managed.

Steve froze, and it was clear to Meg that he was in shock. "I see," he said after a long pause. "Then what do you want from me?"

Meg closed her eyes. "Maybe it'd be best if we—"

"Don't say it, Meg," he warned in low tones, "because we'll both know it's a lie."

"Maybe it'd be best if we—" she felt she had to say the words "—didn't see each other for a while."

Steve's smile was filled with sarcasm. "Let me tell you something, Meg Remington, because someone obviously needs to. Your husband walked out on you and your daughter. It happens. It wasn't the first time a man deserted his family for another woman and it won't be the last. But you've spent the past ten years building a wall around you and Lindsey.

"No one else was allowed in until Lindsey took matters into her own hands. Now that I'm here, you don't know what to do. You started to care for me and now you're scared to death."

"Steve..."

"Your safe, secure world is being threatened by another man. Do you think I don't know you love me?" he demanded. "You're crazy about me. I feel the same way about you, and to be fair, you've done a damned good job of shaking up my world, too.

"If you want it to end here and now, okay, but at least be honest about it. You're pushing me away because you're afraid of knocking down those walls of yours. You're afraid to trust another man with your heart."

"You seem to have me all figured out," she said, trying—without much success—to sound sarcastic. To sound as if her emotions were unaffected by his words.

"You want me to leave without giving you this diamond burning a hole in my pocket, then fine. But don't think it's over, because it isn't. I don't give up that easily." He stalked out of the room and paused at her front door. "Don't get a false sense of security. I'll be back and next time I'm bringing reinforcements." The door closed with a bang.

"Mom," Lindsey asked, slipping into the room and sitting down next to Meg. "What happened?"

Meg struggled not to weep. "I...got cold feet."

"But you told me you were in love with Steve."

"I am," she whispered.

"Then why'd you send him away?"

Meg released her breath. "Because I'm an idiot."

"Then stop him," Lindsey said urgently.

"I can't.... It's too late."

"No, it isn't," Lindsey argued and rushed out the front door. A part of Meg wanted to stop her daughter. Meg's pride had taken enough of a beating in the past few days. But her heart, her treacherous heart, knew that the battle had already been lost. She was in love with Steve Conlan.

A minute later Lindsey burst into the house, breathing hard. Panting, she said between giant gulps of air, "Steve says...if you want to talk to him...you're going to have to come outside...yourself."

Meg clasped her hands together. "Where is he?"

"Sitting in his truck. Hurry, Mom! I don't think...he'll wait much longer."

With her heart pounding, Meg walked onto the porch and leaned against the column. Steve's truck was parked at the curb.

He turned his head when he saw her. His eyes were cold. Unfriendly. Unwelcoming.

Meg bit her lip and met his gaze squarely. It took every

ounce of resolve she had to move off the porch and take a few steps toward him. She paused halfway across the freshly mowed lawn.

Steve rolled down the window. "What?" he demanded.

She blinked, her heart racing.

"Lindsey said you had something you wanted to tell me," he muttered.

Meg should've known better than to let Lindsey do her talking for her. She opened her mouth, but her throat was clogged with tears. She tried to swallow, refusing to cry in front of him.

"Say it!"

"I...don't know if I can."

"Either you say it or I'm leaving." He turned away from her and started the engine.

"Mom, we're going to lose him," Lindsey cried from the porch. "Don't let him go...."

"I...love you," she whispered.

Steve switched off the engine. "Did you say something?"

"I love you, Steve Conlan. I'm scared out of my wits. You're right—I have built a wall around us. I don't want to lose you. It's just that I'm...afraid." Her voice caught on the last word.

His eyes held hers and after a moment, he smiled. "That wasn't so difficult, now, was it?"

"Yes, it was," she countered. "It was incredibly hard."

He didn't seem to realize she was standing on her front lawn with half the neighborhood looking on as she told him how much she loved him.

"You're going to marry me, Meg Remington."

She sniffled. "Probably."

He got out of his truck, slammed the door and with three long strides eliminated the distance between them. "Will you or will you not marry me?"

"I will," she said, laughing and crying at the same time, then she ran to meet him halfway.

"That's what I thought." Steve hauled her into his arms and buried her in his embrace. He grabbed her about the waist and whirled her around, then half carried her back into the house.

Once inside, he kicked the door shut and and they leaned against it, kissing frantically.

Lindsey cleared her throat behind them. "I hate to interrupt, but I have a few important questions."

Steve hid his face in Meg's neck and mumbled something she couldn't hear, which was no doubt for the best.

"Okay, kiddo, what do you want to know?" Steve asked when he'd regrouped.

"We're getting married?" Lindsey asked. Meg liked the way she'd included herself.

"Yup," Steve assured her. "We're going to be a family."

Lindsey let out a holler that could be heard three blocks away.

"Where will we live? Your house or ours?"

Steve looked at Meg. "Do you care?"

She shook her head.

"We'll live wherever you want," Steve told the girl. "I imagine staying close to your friends is important, so we'll take that into consideration."

"Great." Lindsey beamed him a smile. "What about adding to the family? Mom's willing, I think."

Once more Steve looked at Meg, and laughing, she nodded. "Oh, yes," she murmured, "there'll be several additions to this family."

Steve's eyes grew intense, and Meg knew he was thinking the same thing she was. She wanted his babies as much as she wanted this man. She loved him, desired him, anticipating all they could discover together, all they could learn from each other.

"One last thing," Lindsey said.

It was hard to pull her eyes away from Steve, but she wanted to include Lindsey in these important decisions. "Yes, honey?"

"It's just that I'd rather you didn't go shopping for your wedding dress alone. You're really good at lots of things, but frankly, Mom, you don't have any fashion sense."

As it turned out, Lindsey, Brenda and Steve's sister, Nancy, were all involved in the process of choosing the all-important wedding dress. Steve, naturally, wasn't allowed within a hundred feet of Meg and her dress until the day of the ceremony.

The wedding took place three months later, with family and friends gathered around. Lindsey proudly served as her mother's maid of honor.

Steve endured all the formality because he knew it mattered to Meg and to Lindsey. Nancy and his mother seemed to enjoy making plans for the wedding, too. All that was required of him was to show up and say "I do," which suited Steve just fine.

In his view, this fuss over weddings was for women. Men considered it a necessary evil. Or so he believed until his wedding day. When he saw Meg walk down the aisle, the emotion that throbbed in his chest came as a complete and utter surprise.

He'd known he loved her—he must, to put up with all the craziness that had befallen their courtship. But he hadn't realized how deep that love went. Not until he saw Meg so solemn and so beautiful. His bride. She stole his breath as he gazed at her.

The reception was a blur. Every time he looked at Meg he found it difficult to believe that this beautiful, vibrant woman was his wife. His thoughts were a jumbled, confused mess as he greeted those he needed to greet and thanked those he needed to thank.

It seemed half a lifetime before he was alone with his wife. He'd booked the honeymoon suite at a hotel close to

Sea-Tac airport. The following morning they were flying to Hawaii for two weeks. Meg had never seen the islands. Steve suspected he didn't need a tropical playground to discover paradise. He would find that in her arms.

"My husband." Meg said the word shyly as Steve fumbled with the key card to unlock their suite. "I like the way it sounds."

"So do I, but not quite as much as I like the sound of wife." With the door open, he swept Meg into his arms and carried her into the room.

He hadn't taken two steps before they started to kiss.

Meg tasted of wedding cake and champagne, of passion and love. She wound her arms around his neck and enticed him to kiss her again. Steve didn't need much of an invitation.

At the unbridled desire he read in her eyes, Steve moaned and carried her to the bed. After he'd set her feet on the floor, he kissed her again, slowly, with all the pent-up desire inside him.

He reached behind her for the zipper of her dress. "I haven't made any secret of how much I want to make love to you."

"That's true," she whispered, kissing his jaw. "Thank you for agreeing to wait. It meant a lot to me to start our marriage this way."

He slipped the sleeve down her arm and kissed the ivory perfection of one shoulder. Then he kissed the other, his lips blazing a trail up the side of her neck to the hollow of her throat.

"You make my knees go weak," she told him in a low voice.

"Mine are, too."

Together they collapsed on the bed. Steve kissed her and loosened his tie. With their lips joined, Meg's fingers worked at his shirt, undressing him.

Soon they were lost in each other, loving each other, immersed in a world of their own. A world from which they didn't emerge until the summer sun had been replaced by a glittering moon and a sky full of stars.

Back at the reception, Lindsey sat with Steve's sister, Nancy, and licked the icing off their fingertips. "Do you suppose they'll ever figure it out?"

Nancy sipped champagne from a crystal flute. "I doubt either of them is thinking about much right now—except each other."

"We made some real mistakes, though."

"We?" Nancy said, eyeing Lindsey.

"Okay, me. I'll admit I nearly ruined everything by pushing the marriage issue. How was I to know my mother would take it so personally? Jeez, she just about had a heart attack, and all because I suggested Steve marry her."

"It worked out, though," Nancy said, looking pleased

with herself. "And I made a few blunders of my own. Getting my friend to go to the shop and say she was Meg wasn't the smartest thing I've ever done. Steve was bound to find out sooner or later that it wasn't Meg."

"But we had to do something," Lindsey insisted. "They were both being so stubborn. One of them had to give in. Besides, your ploy worked."

"Better than the flowers I sent."

Lindsey sampled another bite of wedding cake. "You know what was the hardest part?"

"I know what it was for me. I had one heck of a time keeping a straight face when your mother came to the house dressed in a Tina Turner wig and five-inch heels. Oh, Lindsey, if you could've seen her."

"Steve was pretty funny himself, with his leather jacket and that bad-boy smirk."

"Neither one of them's any good at acting," Nancy said, still grinning.

"Not like us."

"Not like us," Nancy agreed.

* * * * *

Father's Day

For Lois and Bill Hoskins,
living proof that love is
better the second time around.

One

"I can't believe I'm doing this," Robin Masterson muttered as she crawled into the makeshift tent, which was pitched over the clothesline in the backyard of her new home.

"Come on, Mom," ten-year-old Jeff urged, shifting to make room for her. "It's nice and warm in here."

Down on all fours, a flashlight in one hand, Robin squeezed her way inside. Jeff had constructed the flimsy tent using clothespegs to hold up the blankets and rocks to secure the base. The space was tight, but she managed to maneuver into her sleeping bag.

"Isn't this great?" Jeff asked. He stuck his head out of the front opening and gazed at the dark sky and the spattering of stars that winked back at them. On second thought, Robin decided they were laughing at her, those stars. And with good reason. There probably wasn't another thirty-year-old woman in the entire state of California who would've agreed to this craziness.

It was the first night in their new house and Robin was exhausted. They'd started moving out of the apartment before five that morning and she'd just finished unpacking the last box. The beds were assembled, but Jeff wouldn't hear of doing anything as mundane as sleeping on a real mattress. After waiting years to camp out in his own backyard, her son wasn't about to delay the adventure by even one night.

Robin couldn't let him sleep outside alone and, since he hadn't met any neighbors yet, there was only one option left. Surely there'd be a Mother of the Year award in this for her.

"You want to hear a joke?" Jeff asked, rolling on to his back and nudging her.

"Sure." She swallowed a yawn, hoping she could stay awake long enough to laugh at the appropriate time. She needn't have worried.

For the next half hour, Robin was entertained with a series of riddles, nonsense rhymes and off-key renditions of Jeff's favourite songs from summer camp.

"Knock knock," she said when it appeared her son had run through his repertoire.

"Who's there?"

"Wanda."

"Wanda who?"

"Wanda who thinks up these silly jokes?"

Jeff laughed as though she'd come up with the funniest line ever devised. Her son's enthusiasm couldn't help but rub off on Robin and some of her weariness eased. Camping was fun—sort of. But it'd been years since she'd slept on the ground and, frankly, she couldn't remember it being quite this hard.

"Do you think we'll be warm enough?" she teased. Jeff had used every blanket they owned, first to construct the tent and then to pad it. To be on the safe side, two or three more were piled on top of their sleeping bags on the off-chance an arctic frost descended upon them. It was spring, but a San Francisco spring could be chilly.

"Sure," he answered, missing the kidding note in her voice. "But if you get cold, you can have one of mine."

"I'm fine," she assured him.

"You hungry?"

Now that she thought about it, she was. "Sure. Whatcha got?"

Jeff disappeared into his sleeping bag and returned a moment later with a limp package of licorice, a small plastic bag full of squashed marshmallows and a flattened box of raisins. Robin declined the snack.

"When are we going to buy me my dog?" Jeff asked, chewing loudly on the raisins.

Robin listened to the sound and said nothing.

"Mom…the dog?" he repeated after a few minutes.

Robin had been dreading that question most of the day. She'd managed to forestall Jeff for the past month by telling him they'd discuss getting a dog after they were settled in their house.

"I thought we'd start looking for ads in the paper first thing tomorrow," Jeff said, still munching.

"I'm not sure when we'll start the search for the right dog." She was a coward, Robin freely admitted it, but she hated to disappoint Jeff. He had his heart set on a dog. How like his father he was, in his love for animals.

"I want a big one, you know. None of those fancy little poodles or anything."

"A golden retriever would be nice, don't you think?"

"Or a German shepherd," Jeff said.

"Your father loved dogs," she whispered, although she'd told Jeff that countless times. Lenny had been gone for so many years, she had trouble remembering what their life together had been like. They'd been crazy in love with each other and married shortly after their high-school graduation. A year later, Robin became pregnant. Jeff had been barely six months old when Lenny was killed in a freak car accident on his way home from work. In the span of mere moments, Robin's comfortable world had been sent into a tailspin, and ten years later it was still whirling.

With her family's help, she'd gone back to school and obtained her degree. She was now a certified public accountant working for a large San Francisco insurance firm. Over the years she'd dated a number of men, but none she'd seriously consider marrying. Her life was far more complicated now than it had been as a young bride. The thought of falling in love again terrified her.

"What kind of dog did Dad have when he was a kid?" Jeff asked.

"I don't think Rover was any particular breed," Robin answered, then paused to recall exactly what Lenny's childhood dog had looked like. "I think he was mostly… Labrador."

"Was he black?"

"And brown."

"Did Dad have any other animals?"

Robin smiled at her warm memories of her late husband. She enjoyed the way Jeff loved hearing stories about his father—no matter how many times he'd already heard them. "He collected three more pets the first year we were married. It seemed he was always bringing home a stray cat or lost dog. We couldn't keep them, of course, because we weren't allowed pets in the apartment complex. We went to great lengths to hide them for a few days until we could locate their owners or find them a good home. For our first wedding anniversary, he bought me a goldfish. Your father really loved animals."

Jeff beamed and planted his chin on his folded arms.

"We dreamed of buying a small farm someday and raising chickens and goats and maybe a cow or two. Your father wanted to buy you a pony, too." Hard as she tried, she couldn't quite hide the pain in her voice. Even after all these years, the memory of Lenny's sudden death still hurt. Looking at her son, so eager for a dog of his own, Robin missed her husband more than ever.

"You and Dad were going to buy a farm?" Jeff cried, his voice ebullient. "You never told me that before." He paused. "A pony for me? Really? Do you think we'll ever be able to afford one? Look how long it took to save for the house."

Robin smiled. "I think we'll have to give up on the idea of you and me owning a farm, at least in the near future."

When they were first married, Robin and Lenny had talked for hours about their dreams. They'd charted their lives, confident that nothing would ever separate them. Their love had been too strong. It was true that she'd never told Jeff about buying a farm, nor had she told him how they'd planned to name it Paradise. Paradise, because that was what the farm would be to them. In retrospect, not telling Jeff was a way of protecting him. He'd lost so much—not only the guidance and love of his father but all the things they could have had as a family. She'd never mentioned the pony before, or the fact that Lenny had always longed for a horse....

Jeff yawned loudly and Robin marvelled at his endurance. He'd carried in as many boxes as the movers had, racing up and down the stairs with an energy Robin envied. He'd unpacked the upstairs bathroom, as well as his own bedroom and had helped her organize the kitchen.

"I can hardly wait to get my dog," Jeff said, his voice fading. Within minutes he was sound asleep.

"A dog," Robin said softly as her eyes closed. She didn't know how she was going to break the bad news to Jeff. They couldn't get a dog—at least not right away. She was unwilling to leave a large dog locked indoors all day while she went off to work and Jeff was in school. Tying one up in the backyard was equally unfair, and she couldn't afford to build a fence. Not this year, anyway. Then there was the cost of feeding a dog and paying the vet's bills. With this new home, Robin's budget was already stretched to the limit.

Robin awoke feeling chilled and warm at the same time. In the gray dawn, she glanced at her watch. Six-thirty. At some point during the night, the old sleeping bag that dated back to her high-school days had come unzipped and the cool morning air had chilled her arms and legs. Yet her back was warm and cozy. Jeff had probably snuggled up to her during the night. She sighed, determined to sleep for another half hour or so. With that idea in mind, she reached for a blanket to wrap around her shoulders and met with some resistance. She tugged and pulled, to no avail. It was then that she felt something wet and warm close to her neck. Her eyes shot open. Very slowly, she turned her head until she came eyeball to eyeball with a big black dog.

Robin gasped loudly and struggled into a sitting position, which was difficult with the sleeping bag and several blankets wrapped around her legs, imprisoning her.

"Where did you come from?" she demanded, edging away from the dog. The Labrador had eased himself between her and Jeff and made himself right at home. His head rested on his paws and he looked perfectly content, if a bit disgruntled about having his nap interrupted. He didn't seem at all interested in vacating the premises.

Jeff rolled over and opened his eyes. Immediately he bolted upright. "Mom," he cried excitedly. "You got me a dog!"

"No—he isn't ours. I don't know who he belongs to."

"Me!" Jeff's voice was triumphant. "He belongs to me." His thin arms hugged the animal's neck. "You really got me a dog! It was supposed to be a surprise, wasn't it?"

"Jeff," she said firmly. "I don't know where this animal came from, but he isn't ours."

"He isn't?" His voice sagged in disappointment. "But who owns him, then? And how did he get inside the tent with us?"

"Heavens, I don't know." Robin rubbed the sleep from

her eyes while she attempted to put her garbled thoughts in order. "He looks too well fed and groomed to be a stray. He must belong to someone in the neighborhood. Maybe he—"

"Blackie!" As if in response, she was interrupted by a crisp male voice. "Blackie. Here, boy."

The Labrador lifted his head, but stayed where he was. Robin didn't blame him. Jeff was stroking his back with one hand and rubbing his ears with the other, all the while crooning to him softly.

With some effort, Robin managed to divest herself of the sleeping bag. She reached for her tennis shoes and crawled out of the tent. No sooner was she on her feet than she turned to find a lanky man standing a few yards from her, just on the other side of the three-foot hedge that separated the two properties. Obviously he was her neighbor. Robin smiled, but the friendly gesture was not returned. In fact, the man looked downright *un*friendly.

Her neighbor was also an imposing man, at least six feet tall. Since Robin was only five-three, he towered head and shoulders above her. Instinctively, she stiffened her back, meeting his dark eyes. "Good morning," she said coolly.

He barely glanced in her direction, and when he did, he dismissed her with little more than a nod. After a night on the ground, with her son and a dog for bedmates, Robin realized she wasn't looking her best, but she resented the way his eyes flicked disinterestedly over her.

Robin usually gave people the benefit of the doubt, but toward this man, she felt an immediate antipathy. His face was completely emotionless, which lent him an intimidating air. He was clearly aware of that and used it to his advantage.

"Good morning," she said again, clasping her hands tightly. She drew herself to her full height and raised her chin. "I believe your dog is in the tent with my son."

Her news appeared to surprise him; his expression softened. Robin was struck by the change. When his face relaxed, he was actually a very attractive man. For the most part, Robin hardly noticed how good-looking a man was or wasn't, but this time…she noticed. Perhaps because of the contrast with his forbidding demeanor of a moment before.

"Blackie knows better than to leave the yard. Here, boy!" He shouted for the Labrador again, this time including a sharp whistle loud enough to pierce Robin's eardrums. The dog emerged from the tent and approached the hedge, slowly wagging his tail.

"Is that your dog?" Jeff asked, dashing out behind Blackie. "He's great. How long have you had him?"

"I'll make sure he doesn't bother you again," the man said, ignoring Jeff's question. Robin supposed his words were meant to be an apology. "He's well trained—

he's never left my yard before. I'll make sure it doesn't happen again."

"Blackie wasn't any bother," Jeff hurried to explain, racing forward. "He crawled into the tent with us and made himself at home, which was all right with us, wasn't it, Mom?"

"Sure," Robin answered, flipping her shoulder-length auburn hair away from her face. She'd had it tied back when she'd gone to bed, but it had pulled free during the night. Robin could well imagine how it looked now. Most mornings it tended to resemble foam on a newly poured mug of beer.

"We're friends, aren't we, Blackie?" Jeff knelt, and without hesitation the dog came to him, eagerly licking his face.

The man's eyes revealed astonishment, however fleeting, and his dark brows drew together over his high-bridged nose. "Blackie," he snapped. "Come."

The Labrador squeezed between two overgrown laurel bushes and returned to his master, who didn't look any too pleased at his dog's affection for Jeff.

"My son has a way with animals," Robin said.

"Do you live here?" Jeff asked next. He seemed completely unaware of their new neighbor's unfriendliness.

"Next door."

"Oh, good." Jeff grinned widely and placed his right

hand on his chest. "I'm Jeff Masterson and this is my mom, Robin. We moved in yesterday."

"I'm Cole Camden. Welcome to the neighborhood."

Although his words were cordial, his tone wasn't. Robin felt about as welcome as a punk-rock band at a retirees' picnic.

"I'm getting a dog myself," Jeff went on affably. "That's why we moved out of the apartment building—I couldn't have a pet there except for my goldfish."

Cole nodded without comment.

Oh, great, Robin thought. After years of scrimping and saving to buy a house, they were going to be stuck with an ill-tempered next-door neighbor. His house was older than the others on the block. Much bigger, too. Robin guessed that his home, a sprawling three-story structure, had been built in the early thirties. She knew that at one time this neighborhood had been filled with large opulent homes like Cole Camden's. Gradually, over the years, the older places had been torn down and a series of two-story houses and trendy ramblers built in their place. Her neighbor's house was the last vestige of an era long past.

"Have you got any kids?" Jeff could hardly keep the eagerness out of his voice. In the apartment complex there'd always been plenty of playmates, and he was eager to make new friends, especially before he started classes in an unfamiliar school on Monday morning.

Cole's face hardened and Robin could have sworn the

question had angered him. An uncomfortable moment passed before he answered. "No, I don't have any kids." His voice held a rough undertone, and for a split second Robin was sure she saw a flash of pain in his eyes.

"Would it be okay if I played with Blackie sometimes? Just until I get my own dog?"

"No." Cole's response was sharp, but, when Jeff flinched at his vehemence, Cole appeared to regret his harsh tone. "I don't mean to be rude, but it'd probably be best if you stayed in your own yard."

"That's all right," Jeff said. "You can send Blackie over here to visit anytime you want. I like dogs."

"I can see that." A hint of a smile lifted the corners of his mouth. Then his cool gaze moved from Jeff to Robin, his face again expressionless, but she sensed that he'd made up his mind about them, categorized them and come to his own conclusions.

If Cole Camden thought he could intimidate her, Robin had news for him. He'd broadcast his message loud and clear. He didn't want to be bothered by her or her son, and in exchange he'd stay out of her way. That was fine with her. Terrific, in fact. She didn't have time for humoring grouches.

Without another word, Cole turned and strode toward his house with Blackie at his heels.

"Goodbye, Mr. Camden," Jeff called, raising his hand.

Robin wasn't surprised when their neighbor didn't give them the courtesy of a reply.

In an effort to distract Jeff from Cole Camden's unfriendliness, she said brightly, "Hey, I'm starving. How about you?"

Jeff didn't answer right away. "Do you think he'll let me play with Blackie?"

Robin sighed, considering the dilemma that faced her. She didn't want Cole to hurt Jeff's feelings, but it wasn't likely their neighbor would appreciate her son's affinity with his Labrador. By the same token, a neighbor's dog, even one that belonged to a grouch, would ease her guilt over not being able to provide Jeff with the dog she'd promised him.

"What do you think, Mom?" Jeff prompted. "He'll probably let me play with Blackie sometimes, don't you think?"

"I don't know, honey," she whispered. "I just don't know."

Later the same day, after buying groceries to stock their bare kitchen shelves and picking up other necessities, Robin counted the change at the bottom of her purse. She needed to be sure she had money for the subway on Monday morning. Luckily she had enough spare change for BART—Bay Area Rapid Transit—to last the week, but it was packed lunches for her and Jeff until her next payday, which was in two weeks.

Her finances would've been in better shape if she'd waited another year to move out of the apartment. But interest rates were at a two-year low and she'd decided soon after the first of the year that if they were ever going to move out of the apartment this was the time.

"Mom!" Jeff crashed through the back door, breathless. "We're in trouble."

"Oh?" Robin glanced up from the salad she was mixing. A completely disgusted look on his face, her son flung himself into a chair and propped his elbows on the table. Then he let out a forceful sigh.

"What's wrong, Jeff?"

"I'm afraid we made a bad mistake."

"How's that?"

"There's nothing but girls in this neighborhood." He made it sound as though they'd unexpectedly landed in enemy territory. "I rode my bike up and down the street and all I saw were *girls*." He wrinkled his nose.

"Don't worry, you'll be meeting lots of boys in school on Monday."

"You aren't taking this seriously!" Jeff cried. "I don't think you understand what this means. There are seven houses on this block. Six of them have kids and only one has a boy, and that's me. I'm surrounded by women!"

"How'd you find all this out?"

"I asked, of course." He sighed again. "What are you going to do about it, Mom?"

"Me?" Robin asked. "Are you suggesting we move back to the apartment?"

Jeff considered this for only a moment. "I'd think we should if it wasn't for two things. We can't have a dog there. And I found a fort."

"A fort?"

"Yes," he said solemnly. "It's hidden way back in Mr. Camden's yard and covered by a bunch of brush. It's real neat there. I don't think he knows about it, because the word on the street is he doesn't like kids. Someone must've built it and I'm going to find out who. If there's a club going, I want in. I've got the right—I live closer to Mr. Camden than anyone else does."

"Agreed." Robin munched on a slice of green pepper and handed one to Jeff. "So you think it'd be all right if we stayed?"

"I guess so," Jeff conceded, "at least until I find out more about the fort."

Robin was about to say something else when the door-bell chimed.

Jeff's blue eyes met hers. "I bet it's one of those pesky girls," he said in disgust.

"Do you want me to get rid of her?"

Jeff nodded emphatically.

Robin was smiling when she answered the front door.

Jeff was right; it was a girl, one who seemed to be a couple of years younger than her son. She hadn't come alone, though. Standing with the youngster was an adult.

"Hi," the woman said cheerfully, flashing Robin a warm smile. "I know you've hardly had a chance to get settled, but I wanted to introduce myself. I'm Heather Lawrence and this is my daughter, Kelly. We live next door, and we'd like to welcome you to the neighborhood."

Robin introduced herself as she opened the door and invited them in. Heather was cute and perky. Her hair was cut in a short bob that bounced when she spoke. Robin knew right away that she was going to like these neighbors. Heather's warm reception was a pleasant change from the way Cole Camden had greeted her.

"Would you like some coffee?" Robin asked.

"If you're sure I'm not interrupting anything."

"I'm sure." Robin led her into the kitchen, where Jeff sat waiting. He cast her a look that suggested she should be shot for treason, then muttered something about forgetting that mothers were really *girls* in disguise. Then he headed out the front door.

Robin reached for two matching ceramic mugs and poured coffee for herself and her new friend. She offered Kelly a glass of juice, then slid into a chair across the table from the girl and her mother. "I'm sorry about Jeff." She felt obliged to apologize. "He's at the age where he thinks girls are a plague to society."

"Don't worry about it," Heather said, smiling. "Kelly isn't keen on boys herself."

"They're creeps. I'd rather ride my bicycle than play with a boy," the girl announced. "But Mom wanted me to come over with her so she didn't look like a busybody. Right, Mom?"

Heather blushed and threw her daughter a murderous glance.

Robin laughed. "I thought it would take several weeks to get to know my neighbors and I've met two in one day."

"Someone else has already been over?"

"Cole Camden introduced himself this morning," she explained, keeping her eyes averted to hide the resentment she felt toward her unfriendly neighbor. Even now, hours later, she couldn't help thinking about the way he'd reacted to her and Jeff.

"Cole Camden introduced himself?" Heather repeated, sounding shocked. She frowned, staring into space as though digesting the fact.

"To be honest, I think he would've preferred to avoid me, but his dog wanted to make friends with Jeff."

Heather's mouth opened and closed twice. "Blackie did?"

"Is there something strange about that?"

"Frankly, yes. To say Cole keeps to himself is an understatement. I don't think he's said more than a handful of words to me in the entire two years since Kelly and

I moved here. I don't know why he stays in the neighborhood." She paused to respond to her daughter, who was asking permission to go home. "Thank Robin for the juice, honey. Anyway," she went on, turning back to Robin when her daughter had skipped out the door, "he's all alone in that huge house and it's ridiculous, really. Can you imagine what his heating bills must be? Although, personally, I don't think money is much of a problem for him. But I've never heard any details."

It didn't surprise Robin to learn Cole lived alone. She'd barely met the man, but guessed that life held little joy for him. It was as though love, warmth and friendship had all been found lacking and had therefore been systematically dismissed.

"Apparently, he was married once, but he was divorced long before I came here."

Robin had dealt with unfriendly men before, but something about Cole struck her hard and deep, and she wasn't sure what it was or why he evoked such a strong feeling within her.

"He and his dog are inseparable," Heather added.

Robin nodded, hardly listening. He'd intimidated her at first, but when she'd pulled herself together and faced him squarely he'd loosened up a bit and, later, even seemed amused. But then Jeff had asked him about children, and Robin had seen the pain in his eyes.

As if by magic, her son's face appeared around the

door. When he saw that Kelly was gone, he walked into the room, hands in his back pockets.

"Do you have a dog?" he asked Heather.

"Unfortunately, no. Kelly's allergic."

Jeff nodded as though to say that was exactly the kind of thing he expected from a girl. "We're getting a German shepherd soon, aren't we, Mom?"

"Soon," Robin responded, feeling wretched. After Heather left, she was going to tell Jeff the truth. She fully intended to let him have his dog, but he'd have to wait a while. She'd been practicing what to say. She'd even come up with a compromise. They could get a cat. Cats didn't seem to mind being left on their own, and they didn't need to be walked. Although she wasn't happy about keeping a litter box in the house, Robin was willing to put up with that inconvenience. Then, when she could afford to have a fence built, they'd get a dog. She planned to be positive and direct with Jeff. He'd understand. At least she hoped he would.

Heather stayed only a few more minutes. The visit had been a fruitful one. Robin had learned that Heather was divorced, worked mornings in an office and provided af-ter-school day care in an effort to spend more time with Kelly. This information was good news to Robin, and the two women agreed that Jeff would go to the Lawrence house before and after school, instead of the community center several blocks away. The arrangement suited them both; even Jeff shrugged in agreement.

Robin would've liked to ask her new friend more about Cole, but his name didn't come up again, and she didn't want to seem too curious about him.

After Heather left, Robin braced herself for the talk with Jeff about getting a dog. Unfortunately, it didn't go well. It seemed that after waiting nearly ten years, a few more months was completely unacceptable.

"You promised!" he shouted. "You said I could have a dog when we moved into the house!"

"You can, sweetheart, but not right away."

Unusual for Jeff, tears gathered in his eyes, and he struggled to hold them back. Soon Robin felt moisture filling her own eyes. She hated disappointing Jeff more than anything. His heart was set on getting a dog right away, and he considered the offer of a cat a poor substitute.

He left the house soon afterward. In an effort to soothe his hurt feelings, Robin cooked her son's favorite meal—macaroni and cheese with sliced sausage and lots of ketchup.

She didn't see him on the pavement or the street when she went to check half an hour later. She stood on the porch, wondering where he'd gone. His bike was inside the garage, and he'd already aired his views about playing with any of the girls in the neighborhood.

It would be just like him to storm into his room in a fit of indignation and promptly fall asleep. Robin hurried upstairs to his bedroom, which was across the hall from her own.

His bed was made and his clothes hung neatly in the closet. Robin decided that in another day or two, everything would be back to normal.

It wasn't until she turned to leave that she saw the note on his desk. Picking it up, Robin read the first line and felt a swirling sense of panic.

Dear Mom,
You broke your promise. You said I could have a dog and now you say I have to wait. If I can't have a dog, then I don't want to live with you anymore. This is goodbye forever.

Love, Jeff

Two

For a moment, Robin was too stunned to react. Her heart was pounding so hard it echoed in her ears like thunder, so loud it seemed to knock her off balance.

Rushing down the stairs, she stood on the porch, cupped her hands over her mouth and screamed frantically. "Jeff! Jeffy!"

Cole Camden was standing on his front porch, too. He released a shrill whistle and stood waiting expectantly. When nothing happened, he called, "Blackie!"

"Jeff!" Robin tried again.

"Blackie!"

Robin called for Jeff once more, but her voice cracked as the panic engulfed her. She paused, placed her hand over her mouth and closed her eyes, trying to regain her composure.

"Blackie!" Cole yelled. He looked furious about his dog's disappearance.

It took Robin only a moment to put two and two together. "Cole," she cried, running across the lawn toward him. "I think Jeff and Blackie might have run away together."

Cole looked at her as if she was deranged, and Robin couldn't blame him. "Jeff left me a note. He wants a dog so badly and we can't get one right now because...well, because we can't, and I had to tell him, and he was terribly disappointed and he decided to run away."

Cole's mouth thinned. "The whole idea is ridiculous. Even if Jeff did run away, Blackie would never go with him."

"Do you honestly think I'd make this up?" she shrieked. "The last time I saw Jeff was around four-thirty, and I'd bet cold cash that's about the same time Blackie disappeared."

Cole's gaze narrowed. "Then where are they?"

"If I knew that, do you think I'd be standing around here arguing with you?"

"Listen, lady, I don't know your son, but I know my dog and—"

"My name's not lady," Robin flared, clenching her hands at her sides. He was looking at her as though she were a madwoman on the loose—which she was where her son was concerned. "I'm sorry to have troubled you. When I find Jeff, I'll make sure your dog gets home."

Cole's eyes shot sparks in her direction, but she ignored them. Turning abruptly, she ran back to her own house. Halfway there, she stopped dead and whirled around to face Cole again. "The fort."

"What fort?" Cole demanded.

"The one that's in the back of your yard. It's covered with brush…. Jeff found it earlier today. He wouldn't know anywhere else to go and that would be the perfect hiding place."

"No one's been there in years," Cole said, discounting her suggestion.

"The least we can do is look."

Cole's nod was reluctant. He led the way to his backyard, which was much larger than hers. There was a small grove of oak trees at the rear of the property and beyond that a high fence. Apparently the fort was situated between the trees and the fence. A few minutes later, in the most remote corner of the yard, nestled between two trees, Robin saw the small wooden structure. It blended into the terrain, and if she hadn't been looking for the hideaway, she would never have seen it.

It was obvious when they neared the space that someone had taken up residence. Cole lowered himself down to all fours, peered inside, then looked back at Robin with a nod. He breathed in sharply, apparently irritated by this turn of events, and crawled through the narrow entrance.

Not about to be left standing by herself, Robin got down on her knees and followed him in.

Just as she'd suspected, Jeff and Blackie were huddled together in a corner. Jeff was fast asleep and Blackie was curled up by his side, guarding him. When Cole and Robin entered, the Labrador lifted his head and wagged his tail in greeting.

The fort wasn't much bigger than the tent Jeff had constructed the night before, and Robin was forced to pull her knees close and loop her arms around them. Cole's larger body seemed to fill every available bit of space.

Jeff must have sensed that his newfound home had been invaded because his eyes fluttered open and he gazed at Robin, then turned his head to stare at Cole.

"Hi, Mom," he said sheepishly. "I bet I'm in trouble, aren't I?"

Robin was so grateful to find him that all she could do was nod. If she'd tried to speak, her voice would've been shaking with emotion, which would only have embarrassed them both.

"So, Jeff," Cole said sternly. "You were going to run away from home. I see you brought everything you needed." He pushed the frying pan and atlas into the middle of their cramped quarters. "What I want to know is how you convinced Blackie to join you."

"He came on his own," Jeff murmured, but his eyes avoided Cole's. "I wouldn't have taken him on purpose—he's your dog."

"I'm glad you didn't…coerce him."

"All you took was a frying pan and an atlas!" Robin cried, staring at the cast-iron skillet and the atlas with its dog-eared pages.

Cole and Jeff both ignored her outburst.

"I take it you don't like living here?" Cole asked.

Jeff stiffened, then shook his head vigorously. "Mom told me that when we moved I could have a dog and now I can't. And…and she dragged me into a neighborhood filled with girls. That might've been okay if I had a dog, but then she broke her promise. A promise is a promise and it's sacred. A guy would never do that."

"So you can't have a dog until later?"

"All because of a stupid fence."

Cole nodded. "Fences are important, you know. And you know what else? Your mom was worried about you."

Jeff looked at Robin, who was blinking furiously to keep the tears from dripping down her face. The upheaval and stress of the move had drained her emotionally and she was an unmitigated mess. Normally, she was a calm, controlled person, but this whole drama with Jeff was her undoing. That and the fact she'd hardly slept the night before in his makeshift tent.

"Mom," Jeff said, studying her anxiously, "are you all right?"

She covered her face with both hands. "I slept with a dog and you ran away and all you took was a frying pan and an atlas." That made no sense whatsoever, but she couldn't help it, and once the tears started they wouldn't stop.

"I'm sorry, Mom," Jeff said softly. "I didn't mean to make you cry."

"I know," she whimpered. "I want you to have a dog, I really do, but we can't keep one locked up in the house all day and we don't have a fence and…and the way you just looked at me, I swear it was Lenny all over again."

"Who's Lenny?" Cole cocked his head toward Jeff, speaking in a whisper.

"Lenny was my dad. He died when I was real little. I don't even remember him."

Cole shared a knowing look with her son. "It might be a good idea if we got your mother back inside the house."

"You think I'm getting hysterical, don't you?" Robin burst out. "I want you both to know I'm in perfect control. A woman can cry every now and then if she wants. Venting your emotions is healthy—all the books say so."

"Right, Mom." Jeff gently patted her shoulder, then crawled out of the fort. He waited for Robin, who emerged after him, and offered her a hand. Cole and Blackie followed.

Jeff took Robin's arm, holding her elbow as he led her to the back door of their house, as if he suspected she couldn't find her way without his guidance.

Once inside, Robin grabbed a tissue and loudly blew her nose. Her composure was shaky, but when she turned to Cole, she intended to be as reasonable as a judge. As polite as a preacher.

"Have you got any aspirin?" Cole asked Jeff.

Jeff nodded, and dashed up the stairs to the bathroom, returning in thirty seconds flat with the bottle. Cole filled a glass with water and delivered both to Robin. How he knew she had a fierce headache she could only guess.

"Why don't you lie down for a few minutes? I'm sure you'll feel better."

"I feel just fine, thank you," she snapped, more angry with herself for overreacting than with him for taking charge.

"Do you have family close by?" Again Cole directed the question to Jeff, which served to further infuriate Robin. Jeff was ten years old! She, on the other hand, was an adult. If this man had questions they should be directed to her, not her son.

"Not anymore," Jeff answered in an anxious whisper. "Grandma and Grandpa moved to Arizona last year, and my uncle lives in LA."

"I don't need to lie down," Robin said forcefully. "I'm perfectly fine."

"Mom," Jeff countered, his voice troubled, "you don't look so good."

"You were talking about frying pans and sleeping with dogs in the same breath," Cole elaborated, his eyebrows raised.

"I think Mr. Camden's right," Jeff said. "You need rest—lots of rest."

Her own son had turned traitor on her. Robin was shocked. Jeff took her hand and led her into the family room, which was off the kitchen. He patted the quilted pillow on the sofa, wordlessly suggesting she place her head there. When she resisted, he pulled the afghan from the chair and draped it around her, tucking the ends behind her shoulders.

Robin couldn't believe she was allowing herself to be led around like a…like a puppy. As if reading her thoughts, Blackie wandered over to her side and lowered his bulk onto the carpet beside the sofa.

"That's a neat fort you've got there," Jeff told Cole once he'd finished tucking in the blanket. Robin watched him hurry back to the kitchen, grab a plate, then load it with macaroni and cheese and hand it to Cole, apparently wanting to share his favorite meal with their neighbor.

Cole set the plate on the counter. "Thanks anyway, Jeff, but I've got to get back to the house. In the future, if you're thinking about running away—don't."

"Yeah, I guess you're right," Jeff said with a mildly guilty look. "My mom turned into a basket case."

Cole smiled—at least, it was as close to a smile as Robin had seen. "You're both going to be fine. She intends to get you that dog, you know. Just hang on. It'll be sooner than you think."

Jeff walked to the sliding glass door with Cole. "Mr. Camden, can I ask you something important?"

"Sure."

"Is anyone using the fort?"

"Not that I know of."

Jeff's expression was hopeful. "It didn't look like anyone had been inside for a long time."

"Six years," Cole murmured absently.

"That long? How come?" Jeff asked. "It's a *great* fort. If it's all right with you I'd like to go over there sometimes. I promise not to walk in any flowerbeds or anything, and I won't leave a mess. I'll take real good care of everything."

Cole hesitated for a moment. He looked at Jeff, and Robin held her breath. Then he shook his head. "Maybe sometime in the future, but not now."

Jeff's deep blue eyes brightened; apparently the refusal didn't trouble him. "Okay. When I can use the fort, would it be all right if I took Blackie with me? He followed me today, you know. I didn't have to do anything to get him to tag along." Jeff paused and lowered his eyes. "Well, hardly anything."

"I thought as much. As your mom said, you have a way with animals."

"My dad did, too. If he hadn't died he would've gotten me a pony and everything."

There was such pride in Jeff's voice that Robin bit her bottom lip to keep from crying all over again. Jeff and Lenny were so much alike. What she'd told her son earlier was true. More and more, Jeff was starting to take on his father's looks and personality.

Cole gazed down at Jeff, and an emotion flashed in his eyes, so transient Robin couldn't recognize it. He laid his hand on Jeff's shoulder. "Since your mother explained there's going to be a delay in getting you a dog, it'd be okay with me if you borrowed Blackie every now and then. You have to stay in your own yard, though. I don't want him running in the neighborhood unless he's on a leash."

"Do you mean it? Thanks, Mr. Camden! I'll do everything you ask."

Robin had the feeling Jeff would've agreed to just about any terms as long as he could see Blackie. It wasn't a dog of his own, but it was as close as he was going to get for the next few months.

Once Cole had left, Jeff joined her on the sofa, his hands folded on his lap. "I'm sorry, Mom," he muttered, his chin buried in his chest. "I promise I'll never run away again."

"I should hope not," she said. Wrapping her arms around him, she hugged him close, kissing his cheek.

"Gee whiz," Jeff grumbled, rubbing his face. "I'd never have apologized if I'd known you were going to kiss me."

A week passed. Jeff liked his new school and, as Robin had predicted, found his class contained an equal number of boys and girls. With his outgoing personality, he quickly collected new friends.

On Sunday afternoon, Robin was in the family room reading the paper when Jeff ambled in and sat down across from her. He took the baseball cap from his head and studied it for a moment.

"Something bothering you?" she asked, lowering the paper to get a better view of her son.

He shrugged. "Did you know Mr. Camden used to be married?"

"That's what I heard," Robin said absently. But other than Heather's remarks the previous week, she hadn't heard anything else. In fact, she'd spoken to her neighbor only when she'd gone to pick up Jeff every afternoon. The child-care arrangement with Heather was working beautifully, but there'd been little opportunity to chat.

As for Cole, Robin hadn't seen him at all. Since he'd been so kind and helpful in the situation with Jeff, Robin had revised her opinion of him. He liked his privacy and that was fine by her; she had no intention of interrupting his serene existence. The memory of their first meeting still rankled, but she was willing to overlook that shaky beginning.

"Mr. Camden had a son who died."

Robin's heart constricted. It made sense: the pain she'd seen when Jeff had asked him about children, the word on the street that Cole didn't like kids, the abandoned fort. "I… How did you find that out?"

"Jimmy Wallach. He lives two streets over and has an older brother who used to play with Bobby Camden. Jimmy told me about him."

"I didn't know," Robin murmured, saddened by the information. She couldn't imagine her life without Jeff—the mere thought of losing him was enough to tear her apart.

"Mrs. Wallach heard Jimmy talking about Bobby Camden, and she said Mr. Camden got divorced and it was real bad, and then a year later Bobby died. She said Mr. Camden's never been the same since."

Robin ached for Cole, and she regretted all the uncharitable thoughts she'd had that first morning.

"I feel sad," Jeff whispered, frowning. His face was as intent as she'd ever seen it.

"I do, too," Robin returned softly.

"Mrs. Wallach seemed real surprised when I told her Mr. Camden said I could play in Bobby's fort someday. Ever since his son died, he hasn't let any kids in the yard or anything. She said he hardly talks to anyone in the neighborhood anymore."

Heather Lawrence had said basically the same thing, but hadn't explained the reason for it. Probably because she didn't know.

"Are you still going to barbecue hamburgers for dinner tonight?"

Robin nodded, surprised by the abrupt way Jeff had changed the subject. "If you want." Next to macaroni and cheese, grilled burgers were Jeff's all-time favorite food.

"Can I invite Mr. Camden over to eat with us?"

Robin hated to refuse her son, but she wasn't sure a dinner invitation was a good idea. She didn't know Cole very well, but she'd already learned he wasn't one to socialize with the neighbors. In addition, Jeff might blurt out questions about Cole's dead son that would be terribly painful for him.

"Mom," Jeff pleaded, "I bet no one ever invites him to dinner and he's all alone."

"Sweetheart, I don't know if that would be the right thing to do."

"But we *owe* him, Mom," Jeff implored. "He let me throw sticks for Blackie twice this week."

"I don't think Mr. Camden's home," Robin said, picking up the newspaper while she weighed the pros and cons of Jeff's suggestion. Since last Sunday, Robin hadn't spoken to Cole once, and she wasn't eager to initiate a conversation. He might read something into it.

"I'll go and see if he's home." Before she could react, Jeff was out the front door, letting the screen door slam in his wake.

He returned a couple of minutes later breathless and excited. "Mr. Camden's home and he said he appreciates the invitation, but he has other plans for tonight."

"That's too bad," Robin said, hoping she sounded sincere.

"I told him we were having strawberry shortcake for dessert and he said that's his favorite."

Robin didn't want to admit it, but she was relieved Cole wouldn't be showing up for dinner. The man made her feel nervous and uncertain. She didn't know why that should be, only that it was a new and unfamiliar sensation.

"Thanks, Mom."

Robin jerked her head up from the paper. "Thanks for what?" She hadn't read a word in five minutes. Her thoughts had been on her neighbor.

Jeff rolled his eyes. "For letting me take a piece of strawberry shortcake over to Mr. Camden."

"I said you could do that?"

"Just now." He walked over to her and playfully tested her forehead with the back of his hand. "You don't feel hot, but then, with brain fever you never know."

Robin swatted playfully at her son's backside.

Laughing, Jeff raced outdoors, where his bicycle was waiting. A half hour later, he was back in the house. "Mom! Mom!" he cried, racing into the kitchen. "Did you know Mr. Camden owns a black Porsche?"

"I can't say I did." She was more interested in peeling potatoes for the salad than discussing fancy cars. She didn't know enough about sports cars to get excited about them.

Jeff jerked open the bottom drawer and rooted through the rag bag until he found what he was looking for. He pulled out a large square that had once been part of his flannel pyjamas, then started back outside. "He has another car, too, an SUV."

"Just where are you going, young man?" Robin demanded.

"Mr. Camden's waxing his car and I'm gonna help him."

"Did he ask for your help?"

"No," Jeff said impatiently.

"He may not want you to."

"Mom!" Jeff rolled his eyes as if to suggest she was overdoing this mothering thing. "Can I go now?"

"Ah…I suppose," she agreed, but her heart was in her throat. She moved into the living room and watched as Jeff strolled across the lawn to the driveway next door, where Cole was busy rubbing liquid wax on the gleaming surface of his Porsche. Without a word, Jeff started polishing the dried wax with his rag. Cole straightened and stopped smearing on the wax, obviously surprised to see Jeff. Robin bit her lip, not knowing how her neighbor would react to Jeff's willingness to help. Apparently he said something, because Jeff nodded, then walked over and sat cross-legged on the lawn. They didn't seem to be carrying on a conversation and Robin wondered what Cole had said to her son.

Robin returned to the kitchen, grateful that Cole's rejection had been gentle. At least he hadn't sent Jeff away. She peeled another potato, then walked back to the living room and glanced out the window again. This time she saw Jeff standing beside Cole, who was, it seemed, demonstrating the correct way to polish a car. He made wide circular motions with his arms, after which he stepped aside to let Jeff tackle the Porsche again. Cole smiled, then patted him on the head before walking around to the other side of the car.

Once the salad was ready, Robin ventured outside.

Jeff waved enthusiastically when he caught sight of her on the porch. "Isn't she a beaut?" he yelled.

It looked like an ordinary car to Robin, but she nodded enthusiastically. "Wonderful," she answered. "Afternoon, Cole."

"Robin." He returned her greeting absently.

He wore a sleeveless gray sweatshirt and she was surprised by how muscular and tanned his arms were. From a recent conversation with Heather Lawrence, Robin had learned Cole was a prominent attorney. And he seemed to fit the lawyer image to a T. Not anymore. The lawyer was gone and the *man* was there, bold as could be. Her awareness of him as an attractive virile male was shockingly intense.

The problem, she decided, lay in the fact that she hadn't expected Cole to look so…fit. The sight of all that lean muscle came as a pleasant surprise. Cole's aggressive, unfriendly expression had been softened as he bantered with Jeff.

Blackie ambled to her side and Robin leaned over to scratch the dog's ears while she continued to study his master. Cole's hair was dark and grew away from his brow, but a single lock flopped stubbornly over his forehead and he had to toss it back from his face every once in a while. It was funny how she'd never noticed that about him until now.

Jeff must've made some humorous remark because Cole threw back his head and chuckled loudly. It was the first time she'd ever heard him laugh. She suspected he didn't often give in to the impulse. A smile crowded Robin's face as Jeff started laughing, too.

In that moment the oddest thing happened. Robin felt something catch in her heart. The tug was almost physical, and she experienced a completely unfamiliar feeling of vulnerability….

"Do you need me to roll out the barbecue for you?" Jeff shouted when he saw that she was still on the porch. He'd turned his baseball cap around so the bill faced backward. While he spoke, his arm continued to work feverishly as he buffed the passenger door with his rag.

"Not...yet."

"Good, 'cause Mr. Camden needs me to finish up this side for him. We're on a tight schedule here, and I don't have time. Cole's got a dinner date at five-thirty."

"I see." Standing on the porch, dressed in her old faded jeans, with a mustard-spotted terrycloth hand towel tucked in the waistband, Robin felt as appealing as Ma Kettle. "Any time you're finished is fine."

So Cole Camden's got a date, Robin mused. *Of course he's got a date,* she told herself. Why should she care? And if watching Jeff and Cole together was going to affect her like this, it would be best to go back inside the house now.

Over dinner, all Jeff could talk about was Cole Camden. Every other sentence was Cole this and Cole that, until Robin was ready to slam her fist on the table and demand Jeff never mention their neighbor's name again.

"And the best part is, he *paid* me for helping him wax his car," Jeff continued, then stuffed the hamburger into his mouth, chewing rapidly in his enthusiasm.

"That was generous of him."

Jeff nodded happily. "Be sure and save some shortcake

for him. He said not to bring it over 'cause he didn't know exactly when he'd get home. He'll stop by, he said."

"I will." But Robin doubted her neighbor would. Jeff seemed to be under the impression that Cole would show up at any time; Robin knew better. If Cole had a dinner date, he wasn't going to rush back just to taste her dessert, although she did make an excellent shortcake.

As she suspected, Cole didn't come over. Jeff grumbled about it the next morning. He was convinced Cole would've dropped by if Robin hadn't insisted Jeff go to bed at his regular time.

"I'll make shortcake again soon," Robin promised, hurrying to pack their lunches. "And when I do, you can take a piece over to him."

"All right," Jeff muttered.

That evening, when Robin returned home from work, she found Jeff playing with Blackie in Cole's backyard.

"Jeff," she cried, alarmed that Cole might discover her son on his property. He'd made it clear Jeff wasn't to go into his yard. "What are you doing at Mr. Camden's? And why aren't you at Heather's?" She walked over to the hedge and placed her hands on her hips in frustration.

"Blackie's chain got all tangled up," Jeff said, looking sheepish. "He needed my help. I told Heather it would be okay with you and…" His voice trailed off.

"He's untangled now," Robin pointed out.

"I know, but since I was here it seemed like a good time for the two of us to—"

"Play," Robin completed for him.

"Yeah," her son said, nodding eagerly. Jeff was well aware he'd done something wrong, but had difficulty admitting it.

"Mr. Camden doesn't want you in his yard, and we both know it." Standing next to the laurel hedge, Robin watched with dismay as Cole opened his back door and stepped outside. Blackie barked in greeting, and his tail swung with enough force to knock Jeff off balance.

When Cole saw Jeff in his yard, he frowned and cast an accusing glare in Robin's direction.

"Jeff said Blackie's chain was tangled," she rushed to explain.

"How'd you get over here?" Cole asked her son, and although he didn't raise his voice it was clear he was displeased. "The gate's locked and the hedge is too high for him to jump over."

Jeff stared down at the lawn. "I came through the gap in the hedge—the same one Blackie uses. I crawled through it."

"Was his chain really tangled?"

"No, sir," Jeff said in a voice so low Robin had to strain to hear him. "At least not much… I just thought, you know, that maybe he'd like company."

"I see."

"He was all alone and so was I." Jeff lifted his eyes defiantly to his mother's, as if to suggest the fault was entirely hers. "I go to Mrs. Lawrence's after school, but it's all girls there."

"Don't you remember what I said about coming into my yard?" Cole asked him.

Jeff's nod was sluggish. "Yeah. You said maybe I could sometime, but not now. I thought…I hoped that since you let me help you wax your car, you wouldn't mind."

"I mind," Cole said flatly.

"He won't do it again," Robin promised. "Will you, Jeff?"

"No," he murmured. "I'm sorry, Mr. Camden."

For a whole week Jeff kept his word. The following Monday, however, when Robin came home from the BART station, Heather told her Jeff had mysteriously disappeared about a half hour earlier. She assumed he'd gone home; he'd said something about expecting a call.

Unfortunately, Robin knew exactly where to look for him, and it wasn't at home. Even more unfortunate was the fact that Cole's car pulled into the driveway just as she was opening her door. Throwing aside her briefcase and purse, she rushed through the house, jerked open the sliding glass door at the back and raced across her yard.

Her son was nowhere to be seen, but she immediately realized he'd been with Blackie. The dog wasn't in evidence, either, and she could see Jeff's favorite baseball cap on the lawn.

"Jeff," she called, afraid to raise her voice. She sounded as though she was suffering from a bad case of laryngitis.

Neither boy nor dog appeared.

She tried again, taking the risk of shouting for Jeff in a normal tone, praying it wouldn't attract Cole's attention. No response. Since Jeff and Blackie didn't seem to be within earshot, she guessed they were in the fort. There was no help for it; she'd have to go after him herself. Her only hope was that she could hurry over to the fort, get Jeff and return to her own yard, all without being detected by Cole.

Finding the hole in the laurel proved difficult enough. The space was little more than a narrow gap between two thick plants, and for a distressing moment, Robin doubted she was slim enough to squeeze through. Finally, she lowered herself to the ground, hunched her shoulders and managed to push her way between the shrubs. Her head had just emerged when she noticed a pair of polished men's shoes on the other side. Slowly, reluctantly, she glanced up to find Cole towering above her, eyes narrowed with suspicion.

"Oh, hi," she said, striving to sound as though it was perfectly normal for her to be crawling into his yard on her hands and knees. "I suppose you're wondering what I'm doing here...."

"The question did cross my mind."

Three

"It was the most embarrassing moment of my entire life," Robin repeated for the third time. She was sitting at the kitchen table, resisting the urge to hide her face in her hands and weep.

"You've already said that," Jeff grumbled.

"What possessed you to even *think* about going into Mr. Camden's yard again? Honestly, Jeff, you've been warned at least half a dozen times. What do I have to do? String barbed wire between our yards?"

Although he'd thoroughly disgraced himself, Jeff casually rotated the rim of his baseball cap between his fingers. "I said I was sorry."

A mere apology didn't begin to compensate for the humiliation Robin had suffered when Cole found her on all fours, crawling through his laurel hedge. If she lived to be an old woman, she'd never forget the look on his face.

"You put me on TV, computer and phone restriction already," her son reminded her.

That punishment could be another mistake to add to her growing list. At times like this, she wished Lenny were there to advise her. She needed him, and even after all these years, still missed him. Often, when there was no one else around, Robin found herself talking to Lenny. She wondered if she'd made the right decision, wondered what her husband would have done. Without television, computer or phone, the most attractive form of entertainment left open to her son was playing with Blackie, which was exactly what had gotten him into trouble in the first place.

"Blackie belongs to Mr. Camden," Robin felt obliged to tell him. Again.

"I know," Jeff said, "but he likes me. When I come home from school, he goes crazy. He's real glad to see me, Mom, and since there aren't very many boys in this neighborhood—" he paused as if she was to blame for that "—Blackie and I have an understanding. We're buds."

"That's all fine and dandy, but you seem to be forgetting that Blackie doesn't belong to you." Robin stood and opened the refrigerator, taking out a package of chicken breasts.

"I wish he was my dog," Jeff grumbled. In an apparent effort to make peace, he walked over to the cupboard, removed two plates and proceeded to set the table.

After dinner, while Robin was dealing with the dishes, the doorbell chimed. Jeff raced down the hallway to answer it, returning a moment later with Cole Camden at his side.

Her neighbor was the last person Robin had expected to see—and the last person she *wanted* to see.

"Mom," Jeff said, nodding toward Cole, "it's Mr. Camden."

"Hello, again," she managed, striving for a light tone, and realizing even as she spoke that she'd failed. "Would you like a cup of coffee?"

"No, thanks. I'd like to talk to both of you about—"

Not giving him the opportunity to continue, Robin nodded so hard she nearly dislocated her neck. "I really am sorry about what happened. I've had a good long talk with Jeff and, frankly, I understand why you're upset and I don't blame you. You've been very kind about this whole episode and I want you to know there won't be a repeat performance."

"From either of you?"

"Absolutely," she said, knowing her cheeks were as red as her nail polish. Did he have to remind her of the humiliating position he'd found her in earlier?

"Mom put me on TV, computer and phone restriction

for an entire week," Jeff explained earnestly. "I promise not to go into your fort again, Mr. Camden. And I promise not to go in my backyard after school, either, because Blackie sees me and gets all happy and excited—and I guess I get all happy and excited, too—and that's when I do stuff I'm not supposed to."

"I see." Cole smiled down at Jeff. Robin thought it was a rather unusual smile. It didn't come from his lips as much as his eyes. Once more she witnessed a flash of pain, and another emotion she could only describe as longing. Slowly his gaze drifted to Robin. When his dark eyes met hers, she suddenly found herself short of breath.

"Actually I didn't come here to talk to you about what happened this afternoon," Cole said. "I'm going to be out of town for the next couple of days, and since Jeff and Blackie seem to get along so well I thought Jeff might be willing to look after him. That way I won't have to put him in the kennel. Naturally I'm prepared to pay your son for his time. If he agrees, I'll let him play in the fort while I'm away, as well."

Jeff's eyes grew rounder than Robin had ever seen them. "You want me to watch Blackie?" he asked, his voice incredulous. "And you're going to *pay* me? Can Blackie spend the night here? Please?"

"I guess that answers your question," Robin said, smiling.

"Blackie can stay here if it's okay with your mom," Cole told Jeff. Then he turned to her. "Would that create a problem for you?"

Once more his eyes held hers, and once more she experienced that odd breathless sensation.

"I… No problem whatsoever."

Cole smiled then, and this time it was a smile so potent, so compelling, that it sailed straight through Robin's heart.

"Mom," Jeff hollered as he burst through the front door late Thursday afternoon. "Kelly and Blackie and I are going to the fort."

"Kelly? Surely this isn't the *girl* named Kelly, is it? Not the one who lives next door?" Robin couldn't resist teasing her son. Apparently Jeff was willing to have a "pesky" girl for a friend, after all.

Jeff shrugged as he opened the cookie jar and groped inside. He frowned, not finding any cookies and removed his hand, his fingertips covered with crumbs that he promptly licked off. "I decided Kelly isn't so bad."

"Have you got Blackie's leash?"

"We aren't going to need it. We're playing Sam Houston and Daniel Boone, and the Mexican army is attacking. I'm going to smuggle Blackie out and go for help. I can't use a leash for that."

"All right. Just don't go any farther than the Alamo and be back by dinnertime."

"But that's less than an hour!" Jeff protested.

Robin gave him one of her don't-argue-with-me looks.

"But I'm not hungry and—"

"Jeff," Robin said softly, widening her eyes just a bit, increasing the intensity of her look.

"You know, Mom," Jeff said with a cry of undisguised disgust, "you don't fight fair." He hurried out the front door with Blackie trotting faithfully behind.

Smiling to herself, Robin placed the meat loaf in the oven and carried her coffee into the backyard. The early evening air was filled with the scent of spring flowers. A gentle breeze wafted over the budding trees. How peaceful it seemed. How serene. All the years of pinching pennies to save for a house of their own seemed worth it now.

Her gaze wandered toward Cole Camden's yard. Jeff, Kelly and Blackie were inside the fort, and she could hear their raised voices every once in a while.

Cole had been on her mind a great deal during the past couple of days; she'd spent far too much time dwelling on her neighbor, thinking about his reputation in the neighborhood and the son he'd lost.

The tranquillity of the moment was shattered by the insistent ringing of the phone. Robin walked briskly to the kitchen, set her coffee on the counter and picked up the receiver.

"Hello."

"Robin, it's Angela. I'm not catching you at a bad time, am I?"

"No," Robin assured her. Angela worked in the same department as Robin, and over the years they'd become good friends. "What can I do for you?" she asked, as if she didn't already know.

"I'm calling to invite you to dinner—"

"On Saturday so I can meet your cousin Frank," Robin finished, rolling her eyes. Years before, Angela had taken on the task of finding Robin a husband. Never mind that Robin wasn't interested in meeting strangers! Angela couldn't seem to bear the thought of anyone spending her life alone and had appointed herself Robin's personal matchmaker.

"Frank's a really nice guy," Angela insisted. "I wouldn't steer you wrong, you know I wouldn't."

Robin restrained herself from reminding her friend of the disastrous date she'd arranged several weeks earlier.

"I've known Frank all my life," Angela said. "He's decent and nice."

Decent and *nice* were two words Robin had come to hate. Every man she'd ever met in this kind of arrangement was either decent or nice. Or both. Robin had come to think the two words were synonymous with dull, unattractive and emotionally manipulative. Generally these were recently divorced men who'd willingly placed themselves in the hands of family and friends to get them back into circulation.

"Didn't you tell me that Frank just got divorced?" Robin asked.

"Yes, about six months ago."

"Not interested."

"What do you mean you're not interested?" Angela demanded.

"I don't want to meet him. Angela, I know you mean well, and I apologize if I sound like a spoilsport, but I can't tell you the number of times I've had to nurse the fragile egos of recently divorced men. Most of the time they're emotional wrecks."

"But Frank's divorce was final months ago."

"If you still want me to meet him in a year, I'll be more than happy to have you arrange a dinner date."

Angela released a ragged sigh. "You're sure?"

"Positive."

There was a short disappointed silence. "Fine," Angela said in obvious frustration. "I'll see you in the morning."

"Right." Because she felt guilty, Robin added, "I'll bring the coffee."

"Okay."

Robin lingered in the kitchen, frowning. She hated it when her friends put her on the spot like this. It was difficult enough to say no, but knowing that Angela's intentions were genuine made it even worse. Just as she was struggling with another attack of guilt, the phone rang again. Angela! Her friend must have suspected that Robin's offer to buy the coffee was a sign that she was weakening.

Gathering her fortitude, Robin seized the receiver and said firmly, "I'm not interested in dating Frank. I don't want to be rude, but that's final!"

Her abrupt words were followed by a brief shocked silence, and then, "Robin, hello, this is Cole Camden."

"Cole," she gasped, closing her eyes. "Uh, I'm sorry, I thought you were someone else. A friend." She slumped against the wall and covered her face with one hand. "I have this friend who's always trying to arrange dates for me, and she doesn't take no for an answer," Robin quickly explained. "I suppose you have friends wanting to arrange dates for you, too."

"Actually, I don't."

Of course he didn't. No doubt there were women all over San Francisco who longed to go out with Cole. He didn't require a personal matchmaker. All someone like him had to do was look interested and women would flock to his side.

Her hand tightened around the receiver and a sick weightless feeling attacked the pit of her stomach. "I apologize. I didn't mean to shout in your ear."

"You didn't."

"I suppose you called to talk to Jeff," she said. "He's

with Blackie and Kelly—Kelly Lawrence, the little girl who lives on the other side of us."

"I see."

"He'll be back in a few minutes, if you'd like to call then. Or if you prefer, I could run and get him, but he said something about sneaking out and going for help and—"

"I beg your pardon? What's Jeff doing?"

"Oh, they're playing in the fort, pretending they're Houston and Daniel Boone. The fort is now the Alamo."

He chuckled. "I see. No, don't worry about chasing after him. I'd hate to see you waylaid by the Mexican army."

"I don't think I'd care for that myself."

"How's everything going?"

"Fine," she assured him.

She must have sounded rushed because he said, "You're sure this isn't a bad time? If you have company..."

"No, I'm here alone."

Another short silence, which was broken by Cole. "So everything's okay with Blackie? He isn't causing you any problems, is he?"

"Oh, no, everything's great. Jeff lavishes him with attention. The two of them are together practically every minute. Blackie even sleeps beside his bed."

"As you said, Jeff has a way with animals," Cole murmured.

His laugh, so tender and warm, was enough to jolt her. She had to pinch herself to remember that Cole was a prominent attorney, wealthy and respected. She was an accountant. A junior accountant at that.

The only thing they had in common was the fact that they lived next door to each other and her son was crazy about his dog.

The silence returned, only this time it had a relaxed, almost comfortable quality, as though neither wanted the conversation to end.

"Since Jeff isn't around," Cole said reluctantly, "I'll let you go."

"I'll tell him you phoned."

"It wasn't anything important," Cole said. "Just wanted to let you know when I'll be back—late Friday afternoon. Will you be home?"

"Of course."

"You never know, your friend might talk you into going out with Fred after all."

"It's Frank, and there isn't a snowball's chance in hell."

"Famous last words!"

"See you Friday," she said with a short laugh.

"Right. Goodbye, Robin."

"Goodbye, Cole."

Long after the call had ended, Robin stood with her hand on the receiver, a smile touching her eyes and her heart.

* * *

"Mom, I need my lunch money," Jeff yelled from the bottom of the stairs.

"I'll be down in a minute," she said. Mornings were hectic. In order to get to the Glen Park BART station on time, Robin had to leave the house half an hour before Jeff left for school.

"What did you have for breakfast?" she hollered as she put the finishing touches on her makeup.

"Frozen waffles," Jeff shouted back. "And don't worry, I didn't drown them in syrup and I rinsed off the plate before I put it in the dishwasher."

"Rinsed it off or let Blackie lick it for you?" she asked, as she hurried down the stairs. Her son was busy at the sink and didn't turn around to look at her.

"Blackie, honestly, is that maple syrup on your nose?"

At the sound of his name, the Labrador trotted over to her. Robin took a moment to stroke his thick fur before fumbling for her wallet to give Jeff his lunch money.

"Hey, Mom, you look nice."

"Don't act so surprised," she grumbled. "I'm leaving now."

"Okay," Jeff said without the slightest bit of concern. "You won't be late tonight, will you? Remember Mr. Camden's coming back."

"I remember, and no, I won't be late." She grabbed her

purse and her packed lunch, putting it in her briefcase, and headed for the front door.

Even before Robin arrived at the subway station, she knew the day would drag. Fridays always did.

She was right. At six, when the subway pulled into the station, Robin felt as though she'd been away forty hours instead of the usual nine. She found herself hurrying and didn't fully understand why. Cole was scheduled to return, but that didn't have anything to do with her, did it? His homecoming wasn't anything to feel nervous about, nor any reason to be pleased. He was her neighbor, and more Jeff's friend than hers.

The first thing Robin noticed when she arrived on Orchard Street was Cole's Porsche parked in the driveway of his house.

"Hi, Mom," Jeff called as he raced across the lawn between the two houses. "Mr. Camden's back!"

"So I see." She removed her keys from her purse and opened the front door.

Jeff followed her inside. "He said he'd square up with me later. I wanted to invite him to dinner, but I didn't think I should without asking you first."

"That was smart," she said, depositing her jacket in the closet on her way to the kitchen. She opened the refrigerator and took out the thawed hamburger and salad makings.

"How was your day?" she asked.

Jeff sat down at the table and propped his elbows on it. "All right, I guess. What are you making for dinner?"

"Taco salad."

"How about just tacos? I don't get why you want to ruin a perfectly good dinner by putting green stuff in it."

Robin paused. "I thought you liked my taco salad."

Jeff shrugged. "It's all right, but I'd rather have just tacos." Once that was made clear, he cupped his chin in his hands. "Can we rent a movie tonight?"

"I suppose," Robin returned absently as she added the meat to the onions browning in the skillet.

"But I get to choose this time," Jeff insisted. "Last week you picked a musical." He wrinkled his nose as if to suggest that being forced to watch men and women sing and dance was the most disgusting thing he'd ever had to endure.

"Perhaps we can find a compromise," she said.

Jeff nodded. "As long as it doesn't have a silly love story in it."

"Okay," Robin said, doing her best not to betray her amusement. Their difference in taste when it came to movies was legendary. Jeff's favorite was an older kids' film, *Scooby Doo,* that he watched over and over, which Robin found boring, to say the least. Unfortunately, her son was equally put off by the sight of men and women staring longingly into each other's eyes.

The meat was simmering in the skillet when Robin

glanced up and noted that her son was looking surprisingly thoughtful. "Is something troubling you?" she asked, and popped a thin tomato slice into her mouth.

"Have you ever noticed that Mr. Camden never mentions he had a son?"

Robin set the paring knife on the cutting board. "It's probably painful for him to talk about."

Jeff nodded, and, with the innocent wisdom of youth, he whispered, "That man needs someone."

The meal was finished, and Robin was standing in front of the sink rinsing off the dinner plates when the doorbell rang. Robin knew it had to be Cole.

"I'll get it," Jeff cried as he raced past her at breakneck speed. He threw open the door. "Hi, Mr. Camden!" he said eagerly.

By this time Robin had smoothed her peach-colored sweater over her hips and placed a friendly—but not too friendly—smile on her face. At the last second, she ran her fingers through her hair, striving for the casual I-didn't-go-to-any-trouble look, then wondered at her irrational behavior. Cole wasn't coming over to see *her*.

Robin could hear Jeff chatting away at ninety miles an hour, telling Cole they were renting a movie and how Robin insisted that every show he saw had to have the proper rating, which he claimed was totally ridiculous. He went on to explain that she considered choosing the film a mother's job and apparently a mere kid didn't have rights. When there was a pause in the conversation, she could envision Jeff rolling his eyes dramatically.

Taking a deep breath, she stepped into the entryway and smiled. "Hello, Cole."

"Robin."

Their eyes met instantly. Robin's first coherent thought was that a woman could get lost in eyes that dark and not even care. She swallowed and lowered her gaze.

"Would you like a cup of coffee?" she asked, having difficulty dragging the words out of her mouth.

"If it isn't too much trouble."

"It isn't." Or it wouldn't be if she could stop her heart from pounding so furiously.

"Where's Blackie?" Jeff asked, opening the screen door and glancing outside.

"I didn't bring him over. I thought you'd be tired of him by now."

"Tired of Blackie?" Jeff cried. "You've got to be kidding!"

"I guess I should've known better," Cole teased.

Robin returned to the kitchen and took mugs from the cupboard, using these few minutes to compose herself.

The screen door slammed, and a moment later Cole appeared in her kitchen. "Jeff went to my house to get Blackie."

She smiled and nodded. "Do you take cream or sugar?" she asked over her shoulder.

"Just black, thanks."

Robin normally drank hers the same way. But for some reason she couldn't begin to fathom, she added a generous teaspoonful of sugar to her own, stirring briskly as though she feared it wouldn't dissolve.

"I hope your trip went well," she said, carrying both mugs into the family room, where Cole had chosen to sit.

"Very well."

"Good." She sat a safe distance from him, across the room in a wooden rocker, and balanced her mug on her knee. "Everything around here went without a hitch, but I'm afraid Jeff may have spoiled Blackie a bit."

"From what he said, they did everything but attend school together."

"Having the dog has been wonderful for him. I appreciate your giving Jeff this opportunity. Not only does it satisfy his need for a dog, but it's taught him about responsibility."

The front door opened and the canine subject of their conversation shot into the room, followed by Jeff, who was grinning from ear to ear. "Mom, could Mr. Camden stay and watch the movie with us?"

"Ah..." Caught off guard, Robin didn't know what to say. After being away from home for several days, watch-

ing a movie with his neighbors probably held a low position on Cole's list of priorities.

To Robin's astonishment, Cole's eyes searched hers as
though seeking her approval.

"You'd be welcome...I mean, you can stay if you'd
like, unless...unless there's something else you'd rather
do," she stammered. "I mean, I'd...we'd like it if you did,
but..." She let whatever else she might have said fade
away. She was making a mess of this, and every time she
tried to smooth it over, she only stuck her foot further
down her throat.

"What movie did you rent?"

"We haven't yet," Jeff explained. "Mom and me had to
come to an understanding first. She likes mushy stuff and
gets all bent out of shape if there's an explosion or anything. You wouldn't believe the love story she made me
watch last Friday night." His voice dripped with renewed
disgust.

"How about if you and I go rent the movie while your
mother and Blackie make the popcorn?"

Jeff's blue eyes brightened immediately. "That'd be
great, wouldn't it, Mom?"

"Sure," she agreed, and was rewarded by Jeff's smile.

Jeff and Cole left a few minutes later. It was on the tip of
her tongue to give Cole instructions on the type of movie
appropriate for a ten-year-old boy, but she swallowed her
concerns, willing to trust his judgment. Standing on the

porch, she watched as they climbed inside Cole's expensive sports car. She pressed her hand to her throat, grateful when Cole leaned over the front seat and snapped Jeff's seat belt snugly in place. Suddenly Cole looked at her; she raised her hand in farewell, and he did the same. It was a simple gesture, yet Robin felt as if they'd communicated so much more.

"Come on, Blackie," Robin said, "let's go start the popcorn." The Lab trailed behind her as she returned to the kitchen. She placed a packet of popcorn in the microwave. It was while she was waiting for the kernels to start popping that the words slipped from her mouth.

"Well, Lenny, what do you think?" Talking to her dead husband came without conscious thought. It certainly wasn't that she expected him to answer. Whenever she spoke to him, the words came spontaneously from the deep well of love they'd once shared. She supposed she should feel foolish doing it, but so many times over the long years since his death she'd felt his presence. Robin assumed that the reason she talked to him came from her need to discuss things with the one other person who'd loved her son as much as she did. In the beginning she was sure she needed to visit a psychiatrist or arrange for grief counseling, but later she convinced herself that every widow went through this in one form or another.

"He's grown so much in the past year, hasn't he?" she asked, and smiled. "Meeting Cole has been good for Jeff.

He lost a child, you know, and I suppose having Jeff move in next door answers a need for him, too."

About ten minutes later, she'd transferred the popcorn to a bowl and set out drinks. Jeff and Cole came back with a movie that turned out to be an excellent compromise—a teen comedy that was surprisingly witty and entertaining.

Jeff sprawled on the carpet munching popcorn with Blackie by his side. Cole sat on the sofa and Robin chose the rocking chair. She removed her shoes and tucked her feet beneath her. She was enjoying the movie; in fact, several times she found herself laughing out loud.

Cole and Jeff laughed, too. The sounds were contrasting—one deep and masculine, the other young and pleasantly boyish—yet they harmonized, blending with perfect naturalness.

Soon Robin found herself watching Jeff and Cole more than the movie. The two…no, the three of them had grown comfortable together. Robin didn't try to read any significance into that. Doing so could prove emotionally dangerous, but the thought flew into her mind and refused to leave.

The credits were rolling when Cole pointed to Jeff, whose head was resting on his arms, his eyes closed.

"He's asleep," Cole said softly.

Robin smiled and nodded. She got up to bring the empty popcorn bowl into the kitchen. Cole stood, too, taking their glasses to the sink, then returned to the family room to remove the DVD.

"Do you want me to carry him upstairs for you?" he asked, glancing down at the slumbering Jeff.

"No," she whispered. "When he wakes up in the morning, he'll think you treated him like a little kid. Egos are fragile at ten."

"I suppose you're right."

The silence seemed to resound. Without Jeff, awake and chattering, as a buffer between them, Robin felt clumsy and self-conscious around Cole.

"It was nice of you to stay," she said, more to fill the silence than because she had anything important to communicate. "It meant a lot to Jeff."

Jeff had told her Cole had an active social life. Heather Lawrence had confirmed it by casually letting it drop that Cole was often away on weekends. Robin wasn't entirely sure what to think about it all. But if there was a woman in his life, that was his business, not hers.

"It meant a lot to me, too," he said, returning the DVD to its case.

The kitchen and family room, actually quite spacious, felt close and intimate with Cole standing only a few feet away.

Robin's fingers were shaking as she placed the bowls and soda glasses in the dishwasher. She tried to come up with some bright and witty comment, but her mind was blank.

"I should be going."

Was that reluctance she heard in his voice? Somehow Robin doubted it; probably wishful thinking on her part. Half of her wanted to push him out the door and the other half didn't want him to leave at all. But there really wasn't any reason for him to stay. "I'll walk you to the door."

"Blackie." Cole called for his dog. "It's time to go."

The Lab didn't look pleased. He took his own sweet time lumbering to his feet and stretching before trotting to Cole's side.

Robin was about to open the door when she realized she hadn't thanked Cole for getting the movie. She turned, and his dark eyes delved into hers. Whatever thoughts had been taking shape fled like leaves scattering in the wind. She tried to smile, however weakly, but it was difficult when he was looking at her so intently. His gaze slipped to her mouth, and in a nervous movement, she moistened her lips. Before she was fully aware of how it had happened, Cole's fingers were in her hair and he was urging her mouth to meet his.

His eyes held hers, as if he expected her to stop him, then they slowly closed and their lips touched. Robin's eyes drifted shut, but that was the only response she made.

He kissed her again, even more gently than the first time. Robin moaned softly, not in protest, but in wonder and surprise. It had been so long since a man had kissed her like this. So long that she'd forgotten the wealth of sensations a mere kiss could evoke. Her hands crept to his chest, and her fingers curled into the soft wool of his sweater. Hesitantly, timidly, her lips trembled beneath his. Cole sighed and took full possession of her mouth.

Robin sighed, too. The tears that welled in her eyes were a shock. She was at a loss to explain them. They slipped down her face, and it wasn't until then that she realized she was crying.

Cole must have felt her tears at the same moment, because he abruptly broke off the kiss and raised his head. His eyes searched hers as his thumb brushed the moisture from her cheek.

"Did I hurt you?" The question was whispered.

She shook her head vehemently.

"Then why…?"

"I don't know." She couldn't explain something she didn't understand herself. Rubbing her eyes, she attempted to wipe away the evidence. She forced a smile. "I'm nothing if not novel," she said with brittle cheerfulness. "I don't imagine many women break into tears when you kiss them."

Cole looked as confused as Robin felt.

"Don't worry about it. I'm fine." She wanted to reassure him, but was having too much trouble analyzing her own reactions.

"Let's sit down and talk about this."

"No," she said quietly. Adamantly. That was the last thing she wanted. "I'm sorry, Cole. I really am. This has never happened before and I don't understand it either."

"But…"

"The best thing we can do is chalk it up to a long work-week."

"It's not that simple."

"Probably, but I'd prefer to just forget it. Please?"

"Are you all right?"

"Emotionally or physically?" She tried to joke, but didn't succeed.

"Both."

He was so serious, so concerned, that it was all Robin could do not to dissolve into fresh tears. She'd made a world-class fool of herself with this man, not once but twice.

This man, who had suffered such a tremendous loss himself, was so gentle with her, and instead of helping, that only made matters worse. "I'm sorry, really I am," she said raggedly, "but perhaps you should go home now."

Four

"You know what I'm in the mood for?" Angela Lansky said as she sat on the edge of Robin's desk early Monday afternoon.

"I certainly hope you're going to say food," Robin teased. They had shared the same lunch hour and were celebrating a cost-of-living raise by eating out.

"A shrimp salad," Angela elaborated. "Heaped six inches high with big fresh shrimp."

"I was thinking Chinese food myself," Robin said, "but, now that you mention it, shrimp salad sounds good." She opened her bottom drawer and took out her purse.

Angela was short and enviably thin with thick brown hair that fell in natural waves over her shoulders. She used clips to hold the abundant curls away from her face and looked closer to twenty than the thirty-five Robin knew her to be.

"I know just the place," Angela was saying. "The Blue Crab. It's on the wharf and worth the trouble of getting there."

"I'm game," Robin said.

They stopped at the bank, then headed for the restaurant. They decided to catch the Market Street cable car to Fisherman's Wharf and joined the quickly growing line.

"So how's the kid doing?" Angela asked. She and her salesman husband didn't plan to have children themselves, but Angela enjoyed hearing about Jeff.

"He signed up for baseball through the park program and starts practice this week. I think it'll be good for him. He was lonely this weekend now that Blackie's back with Cole."

"But isn't Blackie over at your place as much as before?" Angela asked.

Robin shook her head. "Cole left early Saturday morning and took the dog with him. Jeff moped around for most of the weekend."

"Where'd your handsome neighbor go?"

"How am I supposed to know?" Robin asked with a soft laugh, hiding her disappointment at his disappearance. "Cole doesn't clear his schedule with me."

The way he'd left—without a word of farewell or explanation—still hurt. It was the kind of hurt that came from realizing what a complete fool she'd made of herself with this worldly, sophisticated man. He'd kissed her and she'd started crying. Good grief, he was probably doing backflips in order to avoid seeing her again.

"Do you think Cole was with a woman?"

"That's none of my business!"

"But I thought your neighbor said Cole spent his weekends with a woman."

Robin didn't remember mentioning that to Angela, but she obviously had, along with practically everything else. Robin had tried to convince herself that confiding in Angela about Cole was a clever way of thwarting her friend's matchmaking efforts. Unfortunately, the whole thing had backfired in her face. In the end, the last person she wanted to talk about was Cole, but of course Angela persisted in questioning her.

"Well?" Angela demanded. "Did he spend his weekend with a woman or not?"

"What he does with his time is his business, not mine," Robin reiterated. She pretended not to care. But she did. Too much. She'd promised herself she wasn't going to put any stock in the kiss or the powerful attraction she felt for Cole. Within the space of one evening, she'd wiped out every pledge she'd made to herself. She hadn't said anything to Jeff—how could she?—but she was just as disappointed as he was that Cole had left for the weekend.

"I was hoping something might develop between the

two of you," Angela murmured. "Since you're obviously not interested in meeting Frank, it would be great if you got something going with your neighbor."

Robin cast her a plaintive look that suggested otherwise. "Cole Camden lives in the fanciest house in the neighborhood. He's a partner in the law firm of Blackwell, Burns and Dailey, which we both know is one of the most prestigious in San Francisco. And he drives a car with a name I can barely pronounce. Now, what would someone like that see in me?"

"Lots of things," Angela said.

Robin snickered. "I hate to disillusion you, my friend, but the only thing Cole Camden and I have in common is the fact that my small yard borders his massive one."

"Maybe," Angela agreed, raising her eyebrows. "But I could tell you were intrigued by him the very first time you mentioned his name."

"That's ridiculous!"

"It isn't," Angela insisted. "I've watched you with other men over the past few years. A guy will show some interest, and at first everything looks peachy-keen. You'll go out with him a couple of times, maybe even more, but before anything serious can develop you've broken off the relationship without really giving it a chance."

Robin didn't have much of an argument, since that was true, but she made a token protest just the same. "I can't help it if I have high standards."

"High standards!" Angela choked back a laugh. "That's got to be the understatement of the century. You'd find fault with Prince Charming."

Robin rolled her eyes, but couldn't hold back a smile. Angela was right, although that certainly hadn't slowed her matchmaking efforts.

"From the time you started talking about your neighbor," Angela went on, "I noticed something different about you, and frankly I'm thrilled. In all the years we've known each other, this is the first time I can remember you giving a man this much attention. Until now, it's always been the other way around."

"I'm not interested in Cole," she mumbled. "Oh, honestly, Angela, I can't imagine where you come up with these ideas. I think you've been reading too many romance novels."

Angela waved her index finger under Robin's nose. "Listen, I'm on to you. You're not going to divert me with humor, or weasel your way out of admitting it. You can't fool me—you're attracted to this guy and it's scaring you to death. Right?"

The two women gazed solemnly at each other, both too stubborn to admit defeat. Under the force of her friend's unyielding determination, Robin was the one who finally gave in.

"All right!" she cried, causing the other people waiting

for the cable car to turn and stare. "All right," she repeated in a whisper. "I like Cole, but I don't understand it."

Angela's winged brows arched speculatively. "He's attractive and wealthy, crazy about your son, generous and kind, and you haven't figured it out yet?"

"He's also way out of my league."

"I wish you'd quit categorizing yourself. You make it sound as though you aren't good enough for him, and that's not true."

Robin just sighed.

The cable car appeared then, its bell clanging as it drew to a stop. Robin and Angela boarded and held on tight.

Jeff loved hearing about the history of the cable cars, and Robin loved telling him the story. Andrew Hallidie had designed them because of his deep love for horses. Day after day, Hallidie had watched them struggling up and down the treacherous hills of the city, dragging heavy burdens. Prompted by his concern for the animals, he'd invented the cable cars that are pulled by a continuously moving underground cable. To Jeff and to many others, Andrew Hallidie was a hero.

Robin and Angela were immediately caught up in the festive atmosphere of Fisherman's Wharf. The rows of fishing boats along the dock bobbed gently with the tide, and although Robin had never been to the Mediterranean the view reminded her of pictures she'd seen of French and Italian harbors.

The day was beautiful, the sky blue and cloudless, the ocean sparkling the way it did on a summer day. This spring had been exceptionally warm. It wasn't uncommon for Robin to wear a winter coat in the middle of July, especially in the mornings, when there was often a heavy fog accompanied by a cool mist from the Bay. But this spring, they'd experienced some lovely weather, including today's.

"Let's eat outside," Angela suggested, pointing at a free table on the patio.

"Sure," Robin agreed cheerfully. The Blue Crab was a popular restaurant and one of several that lined the wharf. More elegant dining took place inside, but the pavement was crowded with diners interested in a less formal meal.

Once they were seated, Robin and Angela were waited on quickly and ordered their shrimp salads.

"So," Angela said, spreading out her napkin while closely studying Robin. "Tell me more about your neighbor."

Robin froze. "I thought we were finished with this subject. In case you hadn't noticed, I'd prefer not to discuss Cole."

"I noticed, but unfortunately I was just getting started. It's unusual for you to be so keen on a man, and I know hardly anything about him. It's time, Robin Masterson, to tell all."

"There's nothing to tell. I already told you everything

I care to," Robin said crossly. She briefly wondered if Angela had guessed that Cole had kissed her. At the rate things were going, she'd probably end up admitting it before lunch was over. Robin wished she could think of some surefire way to change the subject.

Tall glasses of iced tea arrived and Robin was reaching for a packet of sugar when she heard a masculine chuckle that reminded her instantly of Cole. She paused, savoring the husky sound. Without really meaning to, she found herself scanning the tables, certain Cole was seated a short distance away.

"He's here," she whispered before she could guard her tongue.

"Who?"

"Cole. I just heard him laugh."

Pushing back her chair in order to get a fuller view of the inside dining area, Robin searched through a sea of faces, but didn't find her neighbor's.

"What's he look like?" Angela whispered.

Ten different ways to describe him shot through her mind. To say he had brown hair, neatly trimmed, coffee-colored eyes and was about six foot two seemed inadequate. To add that he was strikingly attractive further complicated the problem.

"Tell me what to look for," Angela insisted. "Come on, Robin, this is a golden opportunity. I want to check this guy out. I'm not letting a chance like this slip through my fingers. I'll bet he's gorgeous."

Reluctantly, Robin continued to scan the diners, but she didn't see anyone who remotely resembled Cole. Even if she did see him, she wasn't sure she'd point him out to Angela, although she hated to lie. Perhaps she wouldn't have to. Perhaps she'd imagined the whole thing. It would've been easy enough to do. Angela's questions had brought Cole to the forefront of her mind; they'd just been discussing him and it was only natural for her to—

Her heart pounded against her rib cage as Cole walked out of the restaurant foyer. He wasn't alone. A tall, slender woman with legs that seemed to go all the way up to her neck and a figure as shapely and athletic as a dancer's was walking beside him. She was blond and, in a word, gorgeous. Robin felt as appealing as milkweed in comparison. The woman's arm was delicately tucked in Cole's, and she was smiling up at him with eyes big and blue enough to turn heads.

Robin's stomach tightened into a hard knot.

"Robin," Angela said anxiously, leaning toward her, "what is it?"

Cole was strolling past them, and in an effort not to be seen, Robin stuck her head under the table pretending to search for her purse.

"Robin," Angela muttered, lowering her own head and

peeking under the linen tablecloth, "what's the matter with you?"

"Nothing." Other than the fact that she was going to be ill. Other than the fact that she'd never been more out-classed in her life. "I'm fine, really." A smile trembled on her pale lips.

"Then what are you doing with your head under the table?"

"I don't suppose you'd believe my napkin fell off my lap?"

"No."

A pair of shiny black shoes appeared. Slowly, Robin twisted her head and glanced upward, squinting at the flash of sunlight that nearly blinded her. It was their waiter. Heaving a giant sigh of relief, Robin straightened. The first thing she noticed was that Cole had left.

The huge shrimp salads were all but forgotten as Angela, eyes narrowed and elbows braced on the table, confronted her. "You saw him, didn't you?"

There was no point in pretending otherwise, so Robin nodded.

"He was with someone?"

"Not just someone! The most beautiful woman in the world was draped all over his arm."

"That doesn't mean anything," Angela said. "Don't you think you're jumping to conclusions? Honestly, she could've been anyone."

"Uh-huh." Any fight left in Robin had long since evaporated. There was nothing like seeing Cole with another woman to bring her firmly back to earth—which was right where she belonged.

"She could've been a client."

"She probably was," Robin concurred, reaching for her fork. She didn't know how she was going to manage one shrimp, let alone a whole plate of them. Heaving another huge sigh, she plowed her fork into the heap of plump pink darlings. It was then that she happened to glance across the street. Cole and Ms. Gorgeous were walking along the sidewalk, engrossed in their conversation. For some reason, known only to the fates, Cole looked across the street at that very moment. His gaze instantly narrowed on her. He stopped midstride as though shocked to have seen her.

Doing her best to pretend she hadn't seen *him,* Robin took another bite of her salad and chewed vigorously. When she glanced up again, Cole was gone.

"Mom, I need someone to practice with," Jeff pleaded. He stood forlornly in front of her, a baseball mitt in one hand, a ball in the other.

"I thought Jimmy was practicing with you."

"He had to go home and then Kelly threw me a few pitches, but she had to go home, too. Besides, she's a girl."

"And what am I?" Robin muttered.

"You're a mom," Jeff answered, clearly not understanding her question. "Don't you see? I've got a chance of making pitcher for our team if I can get someone to practice with me."

"All right," Robin agreed, grumbling a bit. She set aside her knitting and followed her son into the backyard. He handed her his old catcher's mitt, which barely fit her hand, and positioned her with her back to Cole's yard.

Robin hadn't been able to completely avoid her neighbor in the past week, but she'd succeeded in keeping her distance. For that matter, he didn't seem all that eager to run into her, either. Just as well, she supposed.

He stayed on his side of the hedge. She stayed on hers.

If he passed her on his way to work, he gave an absent wave. She returned the gesture.

If they happened to be outside at the same time, they exchanged smiles and a polite greeting, but nothing more. It seemed, although Robin couldn't be sure, that Cole spent less time outside than usual. So did she.

"Okay," Jeff called, running to the end of their yard. "Squat down."

"I beg your pardon?" Robin shouted indignantly. "I agreed to play catch with you. You didn't say anything about having to squat!"

"Mom," Jeff said impatiently, "think about it. If I'm going to be the pitcher, you've got to be the catcher, and catchers have to be low to the ground."

Complaining under her breath, Robin sank to her knees, worried the grass would stain her jeans.

Jeff tossed his arms into the air in frustration. "Not like that!" He said something else that Robin couldn't quite make out—something about why couldn't moms be guys.

Reluctantly, Robin assumed the posture he wanted, but she didn't know how long her knees would hold out. Jeff wound up his arm and let loose with a fastball. Robin closed her eyes, stuck out the mitt and was so shocked when she caught the ball that she toppled backward into the wet grass.

"You all right?" Jeff yelled, racing toward her.

"I'm fine, I'm fine," she shouted back, discounting his concern as she brushed the dampness from the seat of her jeans. She righted herself, assumed the position and waited for the second ball.

Jeff ran back to his mock pitcher's mound, gripped both hands behind his back and stepped forward. Robin closed her eyes again. Nothing happened. She opened her eyes cautiously, puzzled about the delay. Then she recalled the hand movements she'd seen pitchers make and flexed her fingers a few times.

Jeff straightened, placed his hand on his hip and stared at her. "What was that for?"

"It's a signal…I think. I've seen catchers do it on TV."

"Mom, leave that kind of stuff to the real ballplayers.

All I want you to do is catch my pitches and throw them back. It might help if you kept your eyes open, too."

"I'll try."

"Thank you."

Robin suspected she heard a tinge of sarcasm in her son's voice. She didn't know what he was getting so riled up about; she was doing her best. It was at times like these that she most longed for Lenny. When her parents had still lived in the area, her dad had stepped in whenever her son needed a father's guiding hand, but they'd moved to Arizona a couple of years ago. Lenny's family had been in Texas since before his death. Robin hadn't seen them since the funeral, although Lenny's mother faithfully sent Jeff birthday and Christmas gifts.

"You ready?" Jeff asked.

"Ready." Squinting, Robin stuck out the mitt, prepared to do her best to catch the stupid ball, since it seemed so important to her son. Once more he swung his arms behind him and stepped forward. Then he stood there, poised to throw, for what seemed an eternity. Her knees were beginning to ache.

"Are you going to throw the ball, or are you going to stare at me all night?" she asked after a long moment had passed.

"That does it!" Jeff tossed his mitt to the ground. "You just broke my concentration."

"Well, for crying out loud, what's there to concentrate

on?" Robin grimaced, rising awkwardly to her feet. Her legs had started to lose feeling.

"This isn't working," Jeff cried, stalking toward her. "Kelly's only in third grade and she does a better job than you do."

Robin decided to ignore that comment. She pressed her hand to the small of her back, hoping to ease the ache she'd begun to feel.

"Hello, Robin. Jeff."

Cole's voice came at her like a hangman's noose. She straightened abruptly and winced at the sharp pain shooting through her back.

"Hi, Mr. Camden!" Jeff shouted as though Cole was a conquering hero returned from the war. He dashed across the yard, past Robin and straight to the hedge. "Where have you been all week?"

"I've been busy." He might've been talking to Jeff, but his eyes were holding Robin's. She tried to look away— but she couldn't.

His eyes told her she was avoiding him.

Hers answered that he'd been avoiding *her*.

"I guess you *have* been busy," Jeff was saying. "I haven't seen you in days and days and days." Blackie squeezed through the hedge and Jeff fell to his knees, his arms circling the dog's neck.

"So how's the baseball going?" Cole asked.

Jeff sent his mother a disgusted look, then shrugged. "All right, I guess."

"What position are you playing?"

"Probably outfield. I had a chance to make pitcher, but I can't seem to get anyone who knows how to catch a ball to practice with me. Kelly tries, but she's a girl and I hate to say it, but my mother's worthless."

"I did my best," Robin protested.

"She catches with her eyes closed," Jeff said.

"How about if you toss a few balls at me?" Cole offered.

Jeff blinked as if he thought he'd misunderstood. "You want me to throw you a few pitches? You're sure?"

"Positive."

The look on her son's face defied description as Cole jumped over the hedge. Jeff's smile stretched from one side of his face to the other as he tore to the opposite end of the yard, unwilling to question Cole's generosity a second time.

For an awkward moment, Robin stayed where she was, not knowing what to say. She looked up at Cole, her emotions soaring—and tangling like kites in a brisk wind. She was deeply grateful for his offer, but also confused. Thrilled by his presence, but also frightened.

"Mom?" Jeff muttered. "In case you hadn't noticed, you're in the way."

"Are you going to make coffee and invite me in for a chat later?" Cole asked quietly.

Her heart sank. "I have some things that need to be done, and…and…"

"Mom?" Jeff shouted.

"I think it's time you and I talked," Cole said, staring straight into her eyes.

"Mom, are you moving or not?"

Robin looked frantically over her shoulder. "Oh…oh, sorry," she whispered, blushing. She hurried away, then stood on the patio watching as the ball flew across the yard.

After catching a dozen of Jeff's pitches, Cole got up and walked over to her son. They spoke for several minutes. Reluctantly, Robin decided it was time to go back in.

She busied herself wiping kitchen counters that were already perfectly clean and tried to stop thinking about the beautiful woman she'd seen with Cole on the Wharf.

Jeff stormed into the house. "Mom, would it be okay if Mr. Camden strings up an old tire from the apple tree?"

"I suppose. Why?"

"He said I can use it to practice pitching, and I wouldn't have to bother you or Kelly."

"I don't think I have an old tire."

"Don't worry, Mr. Camden has one." He ran outside again before she could comment.

Jeff was back in the yard with Cole a few minutes later,

far too soon to suit Robin. She forced a weak smile. That other woman was a perfect damsel to his knight in shining armor, she thought wryly. Robin, on the other hand, considered herself more of a court jester.

Her musings were abruptly halted when Cole walked into the kitchen, trailed by her son.

"Isn't it time for your bath, Jeff?" Cole asked pointedly.

It looked for a minute as though the boy was going to argue. For the first time in recent memory, Robin would've welcomed some resistance from him.

"I guess," he said. Bathing was about as popular as homework.

"I didn't make any coffee," Robin said in a small voice. She simply couldn't look at Cole and not see the beautiful blonde on his arm.

"That's fine. I'm more interested in talking, anyway," he said. He walked purposefully to the table and pulled out a chair, then gestured for her to sit down.

Robin didn't. Instead, she frowned at her watch. "My goodness, will you look at the time?"

"No." Cole headed toward her, and Robin backed slowly into the counter.

"We're going talk about that kiss," Cole warned her.

"Please don't," she whispered. "It meant nothing! We'd both had a hectic week. We were tired…. I wasn't myself."

Cole's eyes burned into hers. "Then why did you cry?"

"I...don't know. Believe me, if I knew I'd tell you, but I don't. Can't we just forget it ever happened?"

His shoulders rose in a sigh as he threaded his long fingers through his hair. "That's exactly what I've tried to do all week. Unfortunately it didn't work."

Five

"**I**'ve put it completely out of my mind," Robin said, resuming her string of untruths. "I wish you'd do the same."

"I can't. Trust me, I've tried," Cole told her softly. He smiled and his sensuous mouth widened as his eyes continued to hold hers. The messages were back. Less than subtle messages. *You can't fool me,* they said, and *I didn't want to admit it either.*

"I..."

The sense of expectancy was written across his face. For the life of her, Robin couldn't tear her eyes from him.

She didn't remember stepping into his arms, but suddenly she was there, encompassed by his warmth, feeling more sheltered and protected than she had since her husband's death. This comforting sensation spun itself around her as he wove his fingers into her hair, cradling her head. He hadn't kissed her yet, but Robin felt the promise of it in every part of her.

Deny it though she might, she knew in her heart how badly she wanted Cole to hold her, to kiss her. He must have read the longing in her eyes, because he lowered his mouth to hers, stopping a fraction of an inch from her parted lips. She could feel warm moist breath, could feel a desire so powerful that she wanted to drown in his kiss.

From a reservoir of strength she didn't know she possessed, Robin managed to shake her head. "No…please."

"Yes…please," he whispered just before his mouth settled firmly over hers.

His kiss was the same as it had been before, only more intense. More potent. Robin felt rocked to the very core of her being. Against her will, she felt herself surrendering to him. She felt herself forgetting to breathe. She felt herself weakening.

His mouth moved to her jaw, dropping small, soft kisses there. She sighed. She couldn't help it. Cole's touch was magic. Unable to stop herself, she turned her head, yearning for him to trace a row of kisses on the other side, as well. He complied.

Robin sighed again, her mind filled with dangerous, sensuous thoughts. It felt so good in his arms, so warm and safe…but she knew the feeling was deceptive. She'd seen him with another woman, one far more suited to him than she could ever be. For days she'd been tormented by the realization that the woman in the restaurant was probably the one he spent his weekends with.

"No, please don't." Once more she pleaded, but even to her own ears the words held little conviction.

In response, Cole brought a long slow series of featherlight kisses to her lips, effectively silencing any protest. Robin trembled, breathless.

"Why are you fighting me so hard?" he whispered. His hands framed her face, his thumbs stroking her cheeks. They were damp and she hadn't even known she was crying.

Suddenly she heard footsteps bounding down the stairs. At the thought of Jeff finding her in Cole's arms, she abruptly broke away and turned to stare out the darkened window, hoping for a moment to compose herself.

Jeff burst into the room. "Did you kiss her yet?" he demanded. Not waiting for an answer, Jeff ran toward Robin and grabbed her by the hand. "Well, Mom, what do you think?"

"About…what?"

"Mr. Camden kissing you. He did, didn't he?"

It was on the tip of her tongue to deny the whole thing, but she decided to brazen it out. "You want me to rate him? Like on a scale of one to ten?"

Jeff blinked, uncertain. His questioning glance flew to Cole.

"She was a ten," Cole said, grinning.

"A…high seven," Robin returned.

"A high seven!" Jeff cried, casting her a disparaging look. He shook his head and walked over to Cole. "She's out of practice," he said confidingly. "Doesn't know how to rate guys. Give her a little time and she'll come around."

"Jeff," Robin gasped, astounded to be having this kind of discussion with her son, let alone Cole, who was looking all too smug.

"She hardly goes out at all," Jeff added. "My mom's got this friend who arranges dates for her, and you wouldn't believe some of the guys she's been stuck with. One of them came to the door—"

"Jeff," Robin said sharply, "that's enough!"

"But one of us needs to tell him!"

"Mr. Camden was just leaving," Robin said, glaring at her neighbor, daring him to contradict her.

"I was? Oh, yeah. Your mom was about to walk me to the door, isn't that right, Robin?"

She gaped at Cole as he reached for her hand and gently led her in the direction of the front door. Meekly she submitted, but not before she saw Jeff give Cole a thumbs-up.

"Now," Cole said, standing in the entryway, his hands heavy on her shoulders. "I want to know what's wrong."

"Wrong? Nothing's wrong."

"It's because of Victoria, isn't it?"

"Victoria?" she asked, already knowing that had to be the woman with him the day she'd seen him at the restaurant.

"Yes. Victoria. I saw you practically hiding under your table, pretending you didn't notice me."

"I... Why should I care?" She hated the way her voice shook.

"Yes, why should you?"

She didn't answer him. Couldn't answer him. She told herself it didn't matter that he was with another woman. Then again, it mattered more than she dared admit.

"Tell me," he insisted.

Robin lowered her gaze. If only he'd stop holding her, stop touching her. Then she might be able to think clearly. "You looked right together. She was a perfect complement to you. She's tall and blond and—"

"Cold as an iceberg. Victoria's a business associate— we had lunch together. Nothing more. I find her as appealing as...as dirty laundry."

"Please, don't explain. It's none of my business who you have lunch with or who you date or where you go every weekend or who you're with. Really. I shouldn't have said anything. I don't know why I did. It was wrong of me—very wrong. I can't believe we're even talking about this."

Jeff poked his head out from the kitchen. "How are things going in here?"

"Good," Robin said. "I was just telling Cole how much we both appreciated his help with your pitching."

"I was having real problems until Cole came along," Jeff confirmed. "Girls are okay for some things, but serious baseball isn't one of them."

Robin opened the front door. "Thanks," she whispered, her eyes avoiding Cole's, "for everything."

"Everything?"

She blushed, remembering the kisses they'd shared. But before she could think of a witty reply, Cole brushed his lips across hers.

"Hey, Cole," Jeff said, hurrying to the front door. "I've got a baseball game Thursday night. Can you come?"

"I'd love to," Cole answered, his eyes holding Robin's. Then he turned abruptly and strode out the door.

"Jeff, we're going to be late for the game if we don't leave now."

"But Cole isn't home yet," Jeff protested. "He said he'd be here."

"There's probably a very good explanation," Robin said calmly, although she was as disappointed as Jeff. "He could be tied up in traffic, or delayed at the office, or any one of a thousand other things. He wouldn't purposely not come."

"Do you think he forgot?"

"I'm sure he didn't. Come on, sweetheart, let's get a

move on. You've got a game to pitch." The emphasis came on the last word. The first game of the season and Jeff had won the coveted position of first-string pitcher. Whether it was true or not, Jeff believed Cole's tutoring had given him an advantage over the competition. Jeff hadn't told him the news yet, keeping it a surprise for today.

"When you do see Cole, don't say anything, all right?" Jeff pleaded as they headed toward the car. "I want to be the one who tells him."

"My lips are sealed," she said, holding up her hand. For good measure, she pantomimed zipping her mouth closed. She slid into the car and started the engine, but glanced in the rearview mirror several times, hoping Cole would somehow miraculously appear.

He didn't.

The game was scheduled for the baseball diamond in Balboa Park, less than two miles from Robin's house. A set of bleachers had been arranged around the diamonds, and Robin climbed to the top. It gave her an excellent view of the field—and of the parking area.

Cole knew the game was at Balboa Park, but he didn't know which diamond and there were several. Depending on how late he was, he could waste valuable time looking for the proper field.

The second inning had just begun when Heather Lawrence joined Robin. Robin smiled at her.

"Hi," Heather said. "What's the score?"

"Nothing nothing. It's the top of the second inning."

"How's the neighborhood Randy Johnson doing?"

"Jeff's doing great. He managed to keep his cool when the first batter got a hit off his second pitch. I think I took it worse than Jeff did."

Heather grinned and nodded. "It's the same with me. Kelly played goalie for her soccer team last year, and every time the opposing team scored on her I took it like a bullet to the chest."

"Where's Kelly now?"

Heather motioned toward the other side of the field. The eight-year-old was leaning casually against a tall fir tree. "She didn't want Jeff to know she'd come to watch him. Her game was over a few minutes ago. They lost, but this is her first year and just about everyone else's, too. The game was more a comedy of errors than anything."

Robin laughed. It was thoughtful of Heather to stop by and see how Jeff's team was doing.

Heather laced her fingers over her knees. "Jeff's been talking quite a bit about Cole Camden." She made the statement sound more like a question and kept her gaze focused on the playing field.

"Oh?" Robin wasn't sure how to answer. "Cole was kind enough to give Jeff a few pointers about pitching techniques."

"Speaking of pitching techniques, you two certainly seem to be hitting it off."

Heather was beginning to sound a lot like Angela, who drilled her daily about her relationship with Cole, offering advice and unsolicited suggestions.

"I can't tell you how surprised I am at the changes I've seen in Cole since you two moved in. Kelly's been wanting to play in that fort from the moment she heard about it, but it's only since Jeff came here that she was even allowed in Cole's yard."

"He's been good for Jeff," Robin said, training her eyes on the game. Cole's relationship with her son forced Robin to examine his motives. He'd lost a son, and there was bound to be a gaping hole in his heart. At first he hadn't allowed Jeff in his yard or approved of Blackie and Jeff's becoming friends. But without anything ever being said, all that had fallen to the wayside. Jeff played in Cole's yard almost every day, and with their neighbor's blessing. Jeff now had free access to the fort and often brought other neighborhood kids along. Apparently Cole had given permission. Did he consider Jeff a sort of substitute son? Robin shook off the thought.

"Jeff talks about Cole constantly," Heather said. "In fact, he told me this morning that Cole was coming to see him pitch. What happened? Did he get hung up at the office?"

"I don't know. He must've been delayed, but—"

"There he is! Over there." Heather broke in excitedly. "You know, in the two years we've lived on Orchard

Street, I can only recall talking to Cole a few times. He was always so standoffish. Except when we were both doing yard work, I never saw him, and if we did happen to meet we said hello and that was about it. The other day we bumped into each other at the grocery store and he actually smiled at me. I was stunned. I swear that's the first time I've seen that man smile. I honestly think you and Jeff are responsible for the change in him."

"And I think you're crediting me with more than my due," Robin said, craning her head to look for Cole.

"No, I'm not," Heather argued. "You can't see the difference in him because you're new to the neighborhood, but everyone who's known him for any length of time will tell you he's like a different person."

Jeff was sitting on the bench while his team was up at bat. Suddenly he leapt to his feet and waved energetically, as though he was flagging down a rescue vehicle. His face broke into a wide, eager smile. His coach must have said something to him because Jeff nodded and took off running toward the parking area.

Robin's gaze followed her son. Cole had indeed arrived. The tension eased out of her in a single breath. She hadn't realized how edgy she'd been. In her heart she knew Cole would never purposely disappoint Jeff, but her son's anxiety had been as acute as her own.

"Listen," Heather said, standing, "I'll talk to you later."

"Thanks for stopping by."

"Glad to." Heather climbed down the bleachers. She paused when she got to the ground and wiggled her eyebrows expressively, then laughed merrily at Robin's frown.

Heather must have passed Cole on her way out, but Robin lost sight of them as Jeff raced on to the pitcher's mound for the bottom of the second inning. Even from this distance Robin could see that his eyes were full of happy excitement. He discreetly shot her a look and Robin made a V-for-victory sign, smiling broadly.

Cole vaulted up the bleachers and sat down beside her. "Sorry I'm late. I was trapped in a meeting, and by the time I could get out to phone you I knew you'd already left for the field. I would've called your cell," he added, "but I didn't have the number."

"Jeff and I figured it had to be something like that."

"So he's pitching!" Cole's voice rang with pride.

"He claims it's all thanks to you."

"I'll let him believe that," Cole said, grinning, "but he's a natural athlete. All I did was teach him a little discipline and give him a means of practicing on his own."

"Well, according to Jeff you taught him everything he knows."

He shook his head. "I'm glad I didn't miss the whole game."

"There'll be others," she said, but she was grateful he'd come when he had. From the time they'd left the house,

Robin had been tense and guarded. Cole could stand *her* up for any date, but disappointing Jeff was more than she could bear. Rarely had she felt this emotionally unsettled. And all because Cole had been late for a Balboa Park Baseball League game. It frightened her to realize how much Jeff was beginning to depend on him. And not just Jeff, either....

"This is important to Jeff," Cole said as if reading her mind, "and I couldn't disappoint him. If it had been anyone else it wouldn't have been as important. But Jeff matters—" his eyes locked with hers "—and so do you."

Robin felt giddy with relief. For the first time since Lenny's tragic death, she understood how carefully, how completely, she'd anesthetized her life, refusing to let in anyone or anything that might cause her or Jeff more pain. For years she'd been drifting in a haze of denial and grief, refusing to acknowledge or deal with either. What Angela had said was true. Robin had dated infrequently and haphazardly, and kept any suitors at a safe distance.

For some reason, she hadn't been able to do that with Cole. Robin couldn't understand what was different or why; all she knew was that she was in serious danger of falling for this man, and falling hard. It terrified her....

"Have you and Jeff had dinner?" Cole asked.

Robin turned to face him, but it was a long moment before she grasped that he'd asked her a question. He repeated it and she shook her head. "Jeff was too excited to eat."

"Good. There's an excellent Chinese restaurant close by. The three of us can celebrate after the game."

"That'd be nice," she whispered, thinking she should make some excuse to avoid this, and accepting almost immediately that she didn't want to avoid it at all.

"Can I have some more pork-fried rice?" Jeff asked.

Cole passed him the dish and Robin watched as her son heaped his plate high with a third helping.

"You won," she said wistfully.

"Mom, I wish you'd stop saying that. It's the fourth time you've said it. I *know* we won," Jeff muttered, glancing at Cole as if to beg forgiveness for his mother, who was obviously suffering from an overdose of maternal pride.

"But Jeff, you were fantastic," she couldn't resist telling him.

"The whole team was fantastic." Jeff reached for what was left of the egg rolls and added a dollop of plum sauce to his plate.

"I had no idea you were such a good hitter," Robin said, still impressed with her son's athletic ability. "I knew you could pitch—but two home runs! Oh, Jeff, I'm so proud of you—and everyone else." It was difficult to remember that Jeff was only one member of a team, and that his success was part of a larger effort.

"I wanted to make sure I played well, especially 'cause you were there, Cole." Jeff stretched his arm across the table again, this time reaching for the nearly empty platter of almond chicken.

As for herself, Robin couldn't down another bite. Cole had said the food at the Golden Wok was good, and he hadn't exaggerated. It was probably the best Chinese meal she'd ever tasted. Jeff apparently thought so, too. The boy couldn't seem to stop eating.

It was while they were laughing over their fortune cookies that Robin heard bits and pieces of the conversation from the booth behind them.

"I bet they're celebrating something special," an elderly gentleman remarked.

"I think their little boy must have done well at the baseball game," his wife said.

Their little boy, Robin mused. The older couple dining directly behind them thought Cole and Jeff were father and son.

Robin's eyes flew to Cole, but if he had heard the comment he didn't give any sign.

"His mother and father are certainly proud of him."

"It's such a delight to see these young people so happy. A family should spend time together."

A family. The three of them looked like a family.

Once more Robin turned to Cole, but once more he seemed not to hear the comments. Or if he had, he ignored them.

But Cole must have sensed her scrutiny because his gaze found hers just then. Their eyes lingered without a hint of the awkwardness Robin had felt so often before.

Jeff chatted constantly on the ride home with Robin. Since she and Cole had both brought their cars, they drove home separately. They exchanged good-nights in the driveway and entered their own houses.

Jeff had some homework to finish and Robin ran a load of clothes through the washing machine. An hour later, after a little television and quick baths, they were both ready for bed. Robin tucked the blankets around Jeff's shoulders, although he protested that he was much too old for her to do that. But he didn't complain too loudly or too long.

"Night, Jeff."

"Night, Mom. Don't let the bedbugs bite."

"Don't go all sentimental on me, okay?" she teased as she turned off his light. He seemed to fall asleep the instant she left the room. She went downstairs to secure the house for the night, then headed up to her own bedroom. Once upstairs, she paused in her son's doorway and smiled gently. They'd both had quite a day.

At about ten o'clock, she was sitting up in bed reading

a mystery when the phone rang. She answered quickly, always anxious about late calls. "Hello."

"You're still awake." It was Cole, and his voice affected her like a surge of electricity.

"I…was reading," she said.

"It suddenly occurred to me that we never had the chance to finish our conversation the other night."

"What conversation?" Robin asked.

"The one at the front door…that Jeff interrupted. Remind me to give that boy lessons in timing, by the way."

"I don't even remember what we were talking about." She settled back against the pillows, savoring the sound of his voice, enjoying the small intimacy of lying in bed, listening to him. Her eyes drifted shut.

"As I recall, you'd just said something about how it isn't any of your business who I lunch with or spend my weekends with. I assume you think I'm with a woman."

Robin's eyes shot open. "I can assure you, I don't think anything of the sort."

"I guess I should explain about the weekends."

"No. I mean, Cole, it really isn't my business. It doesn't matter. Really."

"I have some property north of here, about forty acres," he said gently, despite her protests. "The land once belonged to my grandfather, and he willed it to me when he passed away a couple of years back. This house was part of the estate, as well. My father was born and raised here. I've been spending a lot of my free time remodeling the old farmhouse. Sometime in the future I might move out there."

"I see." She didn't want to think about Cole leaving the neighborhood, ever.

"The place still needs a lot of work, and I've enjoyed doing it on my own. It's coming along well."

She nodded and a second later realized he couldn't see her action. "It sounds lovely."

"Are there any other questions you'd like to ask me?" His voice was low and teasing.

"Of course not," she denied immediately.

"Then would you be willing to admit you enjoy it when I kiss you? A high seven? Really? I think Jeff's right—we need more practice."

"Uh…" Robin didn't know how to answer that.

"I'm willing," he said, and she could almost hear him smile.

Robin lifted the hair from her forehead with one hand. "I can't believe we're having this discussion."

"Would it help if I told you how much I enjoy kissing you?"

"Please…don't," she whispered. She didn't want him to tell her that. Every time he kissed her, it confused her more. Despite the sheltered feeling she experienced in his arms, something deep and fundamental inside her was afraid of loving again. No, terrified. She was terrified of falling in love with Cole. Terrified of what the future might hold.

"The first time shook me more than I care to admit," he said. "Remember that Friday night we rented the movie?"

"I remember."

"I tried to stay away from you afterward. For an entire week I avoided you."

Robin didn't answer. She couldn't. Lying back against the pillows, she stared at the ceiling as a sense of warmth enveloped her. A feeling of comfort...of happiness.

There was a short silence, and in an effort to bring their discussion back to a less intimate—less risky—level, she said, "Thank you for dinner. Jeff had the time of his life." She had, too, but she couldn't find the courage to acknowledge it.

"You're welcome."

"Are you going away this weekend to work on the property?"

She had no right to ask him that, and was shocked at how easily the question emerged.

"I don't think so." After another brief pause, he murmured, "When's the last time you went on a picnic and flew a kite?"

"I don't recall."

"Would you consider going with me on Saturday afternoon? You and Jeff. The three of us together."

"Yes…Jeff would love it."

"How about you? Would you love it?"

"Yes," she whispered.

There didn't seem to be anything more to say, and Robin ended the conversation. "I'll tell Jeff in the morning. He'll be thrilled. Thank you."

"I'll talk to you tomorrow, then."

"Yes. Tomorrow."

"Good night, Robin."

She smiled softly. He said her name the way she'd always dreamed a man would, softly, with a mixture of excitement and need. "Good night, Cole."

For a long time after they'd hung up Robin lay staring at her bedroom walls. When she did flick off her light, she fell asleep as quickly as Jeff seemed to have. She woke about midnight, surprised to find the sheets all twisted as if she'd tossed and turned frantically. The bedspread had slipped onto the floor, and the top sheet was wound around her legs, trapping her.

Sitting up, she untangled her legs and brushed the curls from her face, wondering what had caused her restlessness. She didn't usually wake abruptly like this.

She slid off the bed, found her slippers and went downstairs for a glass of milk.

It was while she was sitting at the table that it came to her. Her hand stilled. Her heartbeat accelerated. The couple in the Chinese restaurant. Robin had overheard them and she was certain Cole had, too.

Their little boy. A family.

Cole had lost a son. From the little Robin had learned, Cole's son had been about the same age Jeff was now when he'd died. First divorce, and then death.

Suddenly it all made sense. A painful kind of sense. A panicky kind of sense. The common ground between them wasn't their backyards, but the fact that they were both victims.

Cole was trying to replace the family that had been so cruelly taken from him.

Robin was just as guilty. She'd been so caught up in the tide of emotion and attraction that she'd refused to recognize what was staring her in the face. She'd ignored her own suspicions and fears, shoving them aside.

She and Cole were both hurting, needy people.

But once the hurt was assuaged, once the need had been satisfied, Cole would discover what Robin had known from the beginning. They were completely different people with little, if anything, in common.

Six

"What do you mean you want to meet my cousin?" Angela demanded, glancing up from her desk, a shocked look on her face.

"You've been after me for weeks to go out with Fred."

"Frank. Yes, I have, but that was B.C."

"B.C.?"

"Before Cole. What happened with you two?"

"Nothing!"

"And pigs have wings," Angela said with more than a trace of sarcasm. She stood up and walked around to the front of her desk, leaning against one corner while she folded her arms and stared unblinkingly at Robin.

Robin knew it would do little good to try to disguise her feelings. She'd had a restless night and was convinced it showed. No doubt her eyes were glazed; they ached. Her bones ached. But mostly her heart ached. Arranging a date with Angela's cousin was a sure indication of her distress.

"The last thing I heard, Cole was supposed to attend Jeff's baseball game with you."

"He did." Robin walked to her own desk and reached for the cup of coffee she'd brought upstairs with her. Peeling off the plastic lid, she cautiously took a sip.

"And?"

"Jeff pitched and he played a fabulous game," Robin said, hoping her friend wouldn't question her further.

Angela continued to stare at Robin. Good grief, Robin thought, the woman had eyes that could cut through solid rock.

"What?" Robin snapped when she couldn't stand her friend's scrutiny any longer. She took another sip of her coffee and nearly scalded her lips. If the rest of her day followed the pattern set that morning, she might as well go home now. The temptation to climb back into bed and hide her head under the pillow was growing stronger every minute.

"Tell me what happened with Cole," Angela said again.

"Nothing. I already told you he was at Jeff's baseball game. What more do you want?"

"The least you can do is tell me what went on last night," Angela said slowly, carefully enunciating each word as though speaking to someone who was hard of hearing.

"Before or after Jeff's game?" Robin pulled out her chair and sat down.

"Both."

Robin gave up. Gesturing weakly with her hands, she shrugged, took a deep breath and poured out the whole story in one huge rush. "Cole was held up at the office in a meeting, so we didn't meet at the house the way we'd planned. Naturally Jeff was disappointed, but we decided that whatever was keeping Cole wasn't his fault, and we left for Balboa Park without him. Cole arrived at the bottom of the second inning, just as Jeff was ready to pitch. Jeff only allowed three hits the entire game, and scored two home runs himself. Afterward Cole took us all out for Chinese food at a fabulous restaurant I've never heard of but one you and I will have to try sometime. Our next raise, okay? Later Cole phoned and asked to take Jeff and me on a picnic Saturday. I think we're going to Golden Gate Park because he also talked about flying kites." She paused, dragged in a fresh gulp of air and gave Angela a look that said "make something out of that if you can!"

"I see," Angela said after a lengthy pause.

"Good."

Robin wasn't up to explaining things, so if Angela really *didn't* understand, that was just too bad. She only knew that she was dangerously close to letting her emotions take charge of her life. She was becoming increasingly attracted to a man who could well be trying to replace the son he'd lost. Robin needed to find a way to keep from following her heart, which was moving at breakneck speed straight into Cole's arms.

"Will you introduce me to Frank or not?" she asked a second time, strengthening her voice and her conviction.

Angela was still watching her with those diamond-cutting eyes. "I'm not sure yet."

"You're not sure!" Robin echoed, dismayed. "For weeks you've been spouting his virtues. According to you, this cousin is as close to a god as a human being can get. He works hard, buys municipal bonds, goes to church regularly and flosses his teeth."

"I said all that?"

"Just about," Robin muttered. "I made up the part about flossing his teeth. Yet when I ask to meet this paragon of limitless virtue, you say you're not sure you want to introduce me. I would've thought you'd be pleased."

"I am pleased," Angela said, frowning, "but I'm also concerned."

"It's not your job to be concerned. All you have to do is call Fred and let him know I'm available Saturday evening for drinks or dinner or a movie or whatever. I'll let him decide what he's most comfortable with."

"It's Frank, and I thought you said you were going on a picnic with Cole on Saturday."

Robin turned on her computer, prepared to check several columns of figures. If she looked busy and suitably nonchalant, it might prompt Angela to agree. "Jeff and I will be with Cole earlier in the day. I'll simply make sure we're back before late afternoon, so there's no reason to worry."

Robin's forehead puckered. "I *am* worried. I can't help being worried. Honestly, Robin, I've never seen you like this. You're so…so determined."

"I've always been determined," Robin countered, glancing up from the computer.

"Oh, I agree one hundred percent," Angela said with a heavy sigh, "but not when it comes to anything that has to do with men. My thirteen-year-old niece has more savvy with the opposite sex than you do!"

"Mom, look how high my kite is," Jeff hollered as his box kite soared toward the heavens.

"It's touching the sky!" Robin shouted, and laughed with her son as he tugged and twisted the string. Despite all her misgivings about her relationship with Cole, she was thoroughly enjoying the afternoon. At first, she'd been positive the day would turn into a disaster. She was sure Cole would take one look at her and know she was going out with another man that evening. She was equally sure she'd blurt it out if he didn't immediately guess.

Cole had been as excited as Jeff about the picnic and kite-flying expedition. The two of them had been fussing with the kites for hours—buying, building and now flying them. For her part, Robin was content to soak up the sunshine.

The weather couldn't have been more cooperative. The sky was a brilliant blue and the wind was perfect. Sailboats scudding on the choppy green waters added dashes of bright color.

In contrast to all the beauty surrounding her, Robin's heart was troubled. Watching Cole, so patient and gentle with her son, filled her with contradictory emotions. Part of her wanted to thank him. Thank him for the smile that lit up Jeff's face. Thank him for throwing open the shades and easing her toward the light. And part of her wanted to shut her eyes and run for cover.

"Mom, look!" Jeff cried as the kite whipped and kicked in the wind. Blackie raced at his side as the sleek red-and-blue kite sliced through the sky, then dipped sharply and crashed toward the ground at heart-stopping speed, only to be caught at the last second and lifted higher and higher.

"I'm looking, I'm looking!" Robin shouted back. She'd never seen Jeff happier. Pride and joy shone from his face, and Robin was moved almost to tears.

Cole stood behind Jeff, watching the kite. One hand rested on the boy's shoulder, the other shaded his eyes as he gazed up at the sky. They laughed, and once more Robin was struck by the mingling of their voices. One mature and measured, the other young and excited. Both happy.

A few minutes later, Cole jogged over to Robin's blanket and sat down beside her. He did nothing more than smile at her, but she felt an actual jolt.

Cole stretched out and leaned back on his elbows, grinning at the sun. "I can't remember the last time I laughed so much."

"You two seem to be enjoying this," Robin said.

If Cole noticed anything awry, he didn't comment. She'd managed not to tell him about the date with Angela's cousin; she certainly didn't want him to think she was trying to make him jealous. That wasn't the evening's purpose at all. Actually she wasn't sure *what* she hoped to accomplish by dating Fred...Frank. She mentally shouted the name five times. Why did she keep calling him Fred? She didn't know that any more than she knew why she was going out with him. On the morning she'd talked Angela into making the arrangements for her, it had seemed a matter of life and death. Now she only felt confused and regretful.

"Jeff says you've got a date this evening."

So much for her worry that she might blurt it out herself, Robin thought. She glanced at Cole. He might've been referring to the weather for all the emotion revealed in his voice.

"A cousin of a good friend. She's been after me for months to meet Frank—we're having dinner."

"Could this be the Frank you weren't going out with and that was final?"

Robin stared at him blankly.

"You answered the phone with that when I called to inquire about Blackie. Remember?"

"Oh, yes…" Suddenly she felt an intense need to justify her actions. "It's just that Angela's been talking about him for so long and it seemed like the right thing to do. He's apparently very nice and Angela's been telling me he's a lot of fun and I didn't think it would hurt to meet him…." Once she got started, Robin couldn't seem to stop explaining.

"Robin," Cole said, his eyes tender. "You don't owe me any explanations."

She instantly grew silent. He was right, she knew that, yet she couldn't help feeling guilty. She was making a terrible mess of this.

"I'm not the jealous type," Cole informed her matter-of-factly.

"I'm not trying to make you jealous," she returned stiffly.

"Good," Cole said and shrugged. His gaze moved from

her to Jeff, who was jogging across the grass. Blackie was beside him, barking excitedly.

He hadn't asked, but she felt obliged to explain who'd be looking after her son while she was out. "Jeff's going to the movies with Heather and Kelly Lawrence while I'm out."

Cole didn't say anything. All he did was smile. It was the same smile he'd flashed at her earlier. The same devastating, wickedly charming smile.

He seemed to be telling her she could dine with a thousand different men and it wouldn't disturb him in the least. As he'd said, he wasn't the jealous type. Great. This was exactly the way she'd wanted him to respond, wasn't it? She could date a thousand different men, because Cole didn't care about her. He cared about her son.

"Let me know when you want to leave," he said with infuriating self-assurance. "I wouldn't want you to be late."

On that cue, Robin checked her watch and was surprised to note that it was well past four. They'd been having so much fun, the day had simply slipped away. When she looked up, she found Cole studying her expectantly. "It's... I'm not meeting Frank until later," she said, answering his unspoken question evasively while she gathered up the remains of their picnic.

An hour later, they decided to leave Golden Gate Park. Jeff and Cole loaded up the kites, as well as the picnic cooler, in the back of Cole's car. It took them another hour to get back to Glen Park because of the traffic, which made Robin's schedule even tighter. But that was hardly Cole's fault—it wasn't as if he'd *arranged* for an accident on the freeway.

Cole and Jeff chatted easily for most of the ride home. When they finally arrived at the house, both Robin and Jeff helped Cole unload the car. Blackie's barking only added to the confusion.

"I suppose I'd better get inside," Robin said, her eyes briefly meeting Cole's. She felt awkward all of a sudden, wishing Jeff was standing there as a barrier, instead of busily carrying things onto Cole's porch.

"We had a great time," she added self-consciously. She couldn't really blame her nervousness on Cole; he'd been the perfect companion all day. "Thank you for the picnic."

Jeff joined them, his eyes narrowing as he looked at Cole. "Are you gonna let her do it?"

"Do what?" Robin asked.

"Go out with that other man," Jeff said righteously, inviting Cole to leap into the argument. "I can't believe you're letting her get away with this."

"Jeff. This isn't something we should be discussing with Mr. Camden."

"All right," he murmured with a sigh. "But I think you're making a mistake." He cast a speculative glance in Cole's direction. "Both of you," he mumbled under his breath and headed for the house.

"Thanks for the wonderful afternoon, Cole," Robin said again.

"No problem," he responded, hands in his pockets, his stance relaxed. "Have a good time with Frank."

"Thanks, I will," she said, squinting at him suspiciously just before she turned toward the house. Darn it, she actually felt guilty! There wasn't a single solitary reason she should feel guilty for agreeing to this dinner date with Angela's cousin, yet she did. Cole must've known it, too, otherwise he wouldn't have made that remark about having a good time. Oh, he knew all right.

As Robin was running the bath, Jeff raced up the stairs. "Mom, I need money for the movie." He thrust her purse into her hands. "How much are you giving me for goodies?"

"Goodies?"

"You know, popcorn, pop, a couple of candy bars. I'm starving."

"Jeff, you haven't stopped eating all day. What about the two hot dogs I just fixed you?"

"I ate them, but that was fifteen minutes ago. I'm hungry again."

Robin handed him fifteen dollars, prepared for an argument. That amount should be enough to pay his way into the movie and supply him with popcorn and a soda. Anything beyond that he could do without.

Jeff took the money from her and slowly shook his head. "That's it, kid," she said in a firm voice.

"Did I complain?" Bright blue eyes gazed innocently back at her.

"You didn't have to. I could see it in your face."

Jeff was ready to leave a few minutes later, just as Robin was getting dressed. He stood outside her bedroom door and shouted that Kelly and her mom were there to pick him up.

"Have fun. I won't be any later than ten-thirty," she assured him.

"Can't I wait for you over at Cole's after the movie?"

"Absolutely not!" Robin's heart skidded to a dead stop at the suggestion. The last person she wanted to face at the end of this evening was Cole Camden. "You didn't ask him, did you?"

"No…but I'm not all that excited about going to Kelly's. I'm there every day, you know."

"Sweetie, I'm sorry. I promise I won't be late."

"You're sure I can't go over to Cole's?"

"Jeffrey Leonard Masterson, don't you *dare* bother Cole. Do you understand me?"

He blinked. She rarely used that tone with him, but she didn't have the time or energy to argue about this.

"I guess," he said with an exaggerated sigh. "But could you make it home by ten?"

"Why ten?"

"Because I don't want to do anything stupid like fall asleep in front of Kelly," he whispered heatedly.

"I'll be back as soon as I can," Robin said.

Glancing at her clock radio, she gasped at the time. She was running late. From the moment she'd made the arrangements to meet Frank, she hadn't given the reality of this evening much thought. Just forcing herself to go through with it had depleted her of energy.

Robin had always hated situations like this. Always. She was going to a strange restaurant, meeting a strange man, and for what? She didn't know.

Tucking her feet into her pumps, Robin hurried to the bathroom to spray on a little perfume. Not much, just enough to give herself some confidence. She rushed down the stairs and reached for her purse.

Her hand was on the doorknob when the phone rang. For a moment, Robin intended to ignore it. It was probably for Jeff. But what if the call was from her parents? Or Frank—calling to cancel? Ridiculous though it was, each ring sounded more urgent than the last. She'd have to answer or she'd spend all evening wondering who it was. Muttering under her breath, she dashed into the kitchen.

"Hello," she said impatiently.

At first there was no response. "Robin, it's Cole." He

sounded nothing like himself. "I lied." With that the line was abruptly disconnected.

Robin held the receiver away from her ear and stared at it for several seconds. He'd lied? About what? Good heavens, why had he even phoned? To tell her he'd lied.

There wasn't time to phone him back and ask what he'd meant.

"Would you care for something to drink?" Frank Eberle asked, glancing over the wine list.

"Nothing, thanks," Robin said. Frank had turned out to be a congenial sort, which was a pleasant surprise. He was quite attractive, with light blue eyes and a thick head of distinguished-looking salt-and-pepper hair. Angela had once mentioned he was "a little bit" shy, which had panicked Robin since she was a whole lot shy, at least around men. The way she'd figured it, they'd stare at each other most of the night, with no idea what to say. However, they did have Angela in common. Whereas with Cole, all she shared was—

Her thoughts came to an abrupt halt. She refused to think about her neighbor or his last-minute phone call. She balked at the idea of dining with one man while wistfully longing for another—which was exactly what she was doing.

Robin studied the menu, pretending to decide between the prime-rib special and the fresh halibut. But the entire time she stared at the menu, she was racking her brain for a topic of conversation.

Frank saved her the trouble. "For once," he said, "Angela didn't exaggerate. You're a delightful surprise."

"I am?" It was amusing to hear him echo her own reaction.

Frank nodded, his smile reserved. "When Angie phoned earlier in the week, I wasn't sure what to expect. She keeps wanting me to date her friends. And to hear her talk, she's close friends with dozens of gorgeous women all interested in meeting me."

Robin grinned. "She should run a dating service. I can't tell you the number of times she's matched me up with someone, or tried to, anyway."

"But you're a comfortable person to be around. I could sense that right away."

"Thank you. I...wasn't sure what to expect, either. Angela's raved about you for weeks, wanting to get the two of us together." Robin glanced from the menu to her companion, then back again. She felt the same misgivings every time she agreed to one of these arranged dates.

"I've been divorced six months now," Frank volunteered, "but after fourteen years of married life, I don't think I'll ever get accustomed to dating again."

Robin found herself agreeing. "I know what you mean. It all seems so awkward, doesn't it? When Lenny and I were dating, I was in high school, and there was so little to worry about. We knew what we wanted and knew what we had to do to get there."

Frank sent her a smile. "Now that we're older and—" he paused "—I hesitate to use the word *wiser*...."

"More sophisticated?"

"Right, more sophisticated," Frank repeated. His hand closed around the water glass. "Life seems so complicated now. I've been out of the swing of things for so long...."

The waitress came for their order then, and from that point on the evening went smoothly. The feeling of kinship she felt with Frank astonished Robin. He was obviously at ease with her, too. Before she knew it, Robin found herself telling him about Cole.

"He sounds like the kind of guy most women would leap off a bridge to meet."

Robin nodded. "He's wonderful to Jeff, too."

"Then what's the problem?"

"His wife and son."

Frank's mouth sagged open. "He's married?"

"Was," she rushed to explain. "From what I understand, his wife left him and sometime later his son died."

"That's tough," Frank said, picking up his coffee. "But that was years ago, wasn't it?"

"I...don't know. Cole's never told me these things himself. In fact, he's never mentioned either his wife or his son."

"He's *never* mentioned them?"

"Never," she confirmed. "I heard it from a neighbor."

"That's what's bothering you, isn't it?"

The question was sobering. Subconsciously, from the moment Robin had learned of Cole's loss, she'd been waiting for him to tell her. Waiting for him to trust her enough.

Frank and Robin lingered over coffee, chatting about politics and the economy and a number of other stimulating topics. But the question about Cole refused to fade from her mind.

They parted outside the restaurant and Frank kissed her cheek, but they were both well aware they wouldn't be seeing each other again. Their time together had been a brief respite. It had helped Frank deal with his loneliness and helped Robin understand what was troubling her about Cole.

The first thing Robin noticed when she pulled into her driveway was that Cole's house was dark. Dark and silent. Lonely. So much of her life had been like that—before she'd met him.

She needed to talk to him. She wanted to ask about his phone call. She wanted to ask about his wife and the son he'd lost. But the timing was all wrong.

For a long moment Robin sat alone in her car, feeling both sad and disappointed.

Heather greeted her with a smile and a finger pressed

to her lips. "Both kids were exhausted. They fell asleep in the living room almost as soon as we got back."

After Jeff's busy day, she could hardly believe he'd lasted through the movie. "I hope he wasn't cranky."

"Not in the least," Heather assured her.

Robin yawned, completely exhausted. She wanted nothing more than to escape to her room and sleep until noon the following day.

"Would you like a cup of coffee before you go?" Heather asked.

"No, thanks." Robin had been blessed with good neighbors. Heather on her right and Cole on her left….

Together Robin and Heather woke Jeff, who grumbled about his mother being late. He was too drowsy to realize it was only nine-thirty or that she'd returned ahead of schedule.

After telling Heather a little about her evening, Robin guided her son across the yard and into the house. She walked upstairs with him and answered the slurred questions he struggled to ask between wide, mouth-stretching yawns.

Tugging back his quilt, Robin urged him into his bed. Jeff kicked off his shoes and reached for the quilt. It wasn't the first time he'd slept in his clothes and it probably wouldn't be the last.

Smiling to herself, Robin moved quietly down the stairs.

On impulse, she paused in the kitchen and picked up the phone. When Cole answered on the first ring, she swallowed a gasp of surprise.

"Hello," he said a second time.

"What did you lie about?" she asked softly.

"Where are you?"

"Home."

"I'll be right there." Without a further word, he hung up.

A minute later, Cole was standing at her front door, hands in his back pockets. He stared at her as if it had been months since they'd seen each other.

"You win," he said, edging his way in.

"Win what? The door prize?" she asked, controlling her amusement with difficulty.

Not bothering to answer her, Cole stalked to the kitchen, where he sank down in one of the pine chairs. "Did you have a good time?"

She sat down across from him. "I really did. Frank's a very pleasant, very caring man. We met at the Higher Ground—that's a cute little restaurant close to the BART station and—"

"I know where it is."

"About your phone call earlier. You said—"

"What's he like?"

"Who? Frank?"

Cole gave her a look that suggested she have her intelligence tested.

"Like I said, he's very pleasant. Divorced and lonely."

"What's he do for a living?"

"He works for the city, I think. We didn't get around to talking about our careers." No doubt Cole would be shocked if he knew she'd spent the greater part of the evening discussing her relationship with *him!*

"What did you talk about, then?"

"Cole, honestly, I don't think we should discuss my evening with Frank. Would you like some coffee? I'll make decaf."

"Are you going to see him again?"

Robin ignored the question. Instead she left the table and began to make coffee. She was concentrating so carefully on her task that she didn't notice Cole was directly behind her. She turned—and found herself gazing into the darkest, most confused and frustrated pair of eyes she'd ever seen.

"Oh," she said, startled. "I didn't realize you were so close."

His hands gripped her shoulders. "Why did you go out with him?"

Surely that wasn't distress she heard in Cole's voice? Not after all that casual indifference this afternoon. She frowned, bewildered by the pain she saw in his eyes.

And she finally understood. Contrary to everything he'd claimed, Cole was jealous. Really and truly jealous.

"Did he kiss you?" he asked with an urgency, an intensity, she'd never heard in his voice before.

Robin stared, frozen by the stark need she read in him.

Cole's finger rested on her mouth. "Did Frank kiss you?" he repeated.

She shook her head and the motion brushed his finger across her bottom lip.

"He wanted to, though, didn't he?" Cole asked with a brooding frown.

"He didn't kiss me." She was finally able to say the words. She couldn't kiss Frank or anyone else. The only man she wanted to kiss and be kissed by was the man looking down at her now. The man whose lips were descending on hers....

Seven

"So, did you like this guy you had dinner with last night?" Jeff asked, keeping his eyes on his bowl of cold cereal.

"He was nice," Robin answered, pouring herself a cup of coffee and joining him at the table. They'd slept late and were spending a lazy Sunday morning enjoying their breakfast before going to the eleven o'clock service at church.

Jeff hesitated, his spoon poised in front of him. "Is he nicer than Cole?"

"Cole's...nicer," Robin admitted reluctantly. *Nice* and *nicer* weren't terms she would've used to describe the differences between Frank and Cole, but in her son's ten-year-old mind they made perfect sense.

A smile quivered at the edges of Jeff's mouth. "I saw you two smooching last night," he said, grinning broadly.

"When?" Robin demanded—a ridiculous question. It could only have happened when Cole had come over to talk to her. He'd confessed how jealous he'd been of Frank and how he'd struggled with the emotion and felt like a fool. Robin had been convinced she was the one who'd behaved like an idiot. Before either of them could prevent it, they were in each other's arms, seeking and granting reassurance.

"You thought I was asleep, but I heard Cole talking and I wanted to ask him what he was gonna do about you and this other guy, so I came downstairs and saw you two with your faces stuck together."

The boy certainly had a way with words.

"You didn't look like you minded, either. Cole and me talked about girls once, and he said they aren't much when they're ten, but they get a whole lot more interesting later on. He said girls are like green apples. At first they're all sour and make your lips pucker, but a little while later they're real good."

"I see," Robin muttered, not at all sure she liked being compared to an apple.

"But when I got downstairs I didn't say anything," Jeff said, "because, well, you know."

Robin nodded and sipped her coffee in an effort to hide her discomfort.

Jeff picked up his cereal bowl and drank the remainder of the milk in loud gulps. He wiped the back of his hand across his lips. "I suppose this means you're going to have a baby now."

Robin was too horrified to speak. The swallow of coffee got stuck in her throat and she started choking. Trying to help her breathe, Jeff pounded her back with his fist, which only added to her misery.

By the time she caught her breath, tears were streaking down her face.

"You all right, Mom?" Jeff asked, his eyes wide with concern. He rushed into the bathroom and returned with a wad of tissue.

"Thanks," she whispered, wiping her face. It took her a moment or two to regain her composure. This was a talk she'd planned on having with him soon—but not quite yet. "Jeff, listen…kissing doesn't make babies."

"It doesn't? But I thought… I hoped… You mean you won't be having a baby?"

"I… Not from kissing," she whispered, taking in deep breaths to stabilize her pulse.

"I suppose the next thing you're gonna tell me is we'll have to save up for a baby the way we did for the house and now the fence before we get me a dog."

This conversation was getting too complicated. "No, we wouldn't have to save for a baby."

"Then what's the holdup?" her son demanded. "I like

the idea of being a big brother. I didn't think much about it until we moved here. Then when we were having dinner at the Chinese restaurant I heard this grandma and grandpa in the booth next to us talking, and they were saying neat things about us being a family. That's when I started thinking about babies and stuff."

"Jeff," Robin said, rubbing her hands together as she collected her thoughts. "There's more to it than that. Before there's a baby, there should be a husband."

"Well, of course," Jeff returned, looking at her as if she'd insulted his intelligence. "You'd have to marry Cole first, but that'd be all right with me. You like him, don't you? You must like him or you wouldn't be kissing him that way."

Robin sighed. Of course she *liked* Cole, but it wasn't that simple. Unfortunately she wasn't sure she could explain it in terms a ten-year-old could understand. "I—"

"I can't remember ever seeing you kiss a guy like that. You looked real serious. And when I was sneaking back up the stairs, I heard him ask you to have dinner alone with him tonight and that seemed like a real good sign."

The next time Cole kissed her, Robin thought wryly, they'd have to scurry into a closet. The things that child came up with...

"You *are* going to dinner with him, aren't you?"

"Yes, but—"

"Then what's the problem? I'll ask him to marry you if you want."

"Jeff!" she cried, leaping to her feet. "Absolutely not! That's between Cole and me, and neither of us would appreciate any assistance from you. Is that clearly understood?"

"All right," he sighed, but he didn't look too pleased. He reached for a piece of toast, shredding it into thirds. "But you're going to marry him, aren't you?"

"I don't know."

"Why not? Cole's the best thing that's ever happened to us."

Her son was staring at her intently, his baseball cap twisted around to the back of his head. Now that she had his full attention, Robin couldn't find the words to explain. "It's more complicated than you realize, sweetie." She made a show of glancing at the clock. "Anyway, it's time to change and get ready for church."

Jeff nodded and rushed up the stairs. Robin followed at a much slower pace, grateful to put an end to this difficult and embarrassing subject.

The minute they were home from the service, Jeff grabbed his baseball mitt. "Jimmy Wallach and I are going to the school yard to practice hitting balls. Okay?"

"Okay," Robin said absently. "How long will you be gone?"

"An hour."

"I'm going grocery shopping, so if I'm not home when you get back you know what to do?"

"Of course," he muttered.

"You're Robin Masterson, aren't you?" a tall middle-aged woman asked as she maneuvered her grocery cart alongside Robin's.

"Yes," Robin said. The other woman's eyes were warm and her smile friendly.

"I thought you must be—I've seen you from a distance. I'm Joyce Wallach. Jimmy and Jeff have become good friends. In fact, they're at the school yard now."

"Of course," Robin said, pleased to make the other woman's acquaintance. They'd talked on the phone several times, and she'd met Joyce's husband once, when Jimmy had spent the night. The boys had wanted to play on the same baseball team and were disappointed when they'd been assigned to different teams. It had been Jimmy who'd told Jeff about the death of Cole's son.

"I've been meaning to invite you to the house for coffee," Joyce went on to say, "but I started working part-time and I can't seem to get myself organized."

"I know what you mean." Working full-time, keeping up with Jeff and her home was about all Robin could manage herself. She didn't know how other mothers were able to accomplish so much.

"There's a place to sit down here," Joyce said, and her

eyes brightened at the idea. "Do you have time to chat now?"

Robin nodded. "Sure. I've been wanting to meet you, too." The Wallachs lived two streets over, and Robin fully approved of Jimmy as a friend for Jeff. He and Kelly had become friends, too, but her ten-year-old son wasn't as eager to admit being buddies with a girl. Kelly was still a green apple in Jeff's eye, but the time would come when he'd appreciate having her next door.

"I understand Jeff's quite the baseball player," Joyce said at the self-service counter.

Robin smiled. She poured herself a plastic cup of iced tea and paid for it. "Jeff really loves baseball. He was disappointed he couldn't play with Jimmy."

"They separate the teams according to the kid's year of birth. Jimmy's birthday is in January so he's with another group." She frowned. "That doesn't really make much sense, does it?" She chuckled, and Robin couldn't help responding to the soft infectious sound of Joyce's laughter. She found herself laughing, too.

They pulled out chairs at one of the small tables in the supermarket's deli section.

"I feel like throwing my arms around you," Joyce said with a grin. "I saw Cole Camden at Balboa Park the other day and I couldn't believe my eyes. It was like seeing him ten years ago, the way he used to be." She glanced at Robin. "Jeff was with him."

"Cole came to his first game."

"Ah." She nodded slowly, as if that explained it. "I don't know if anyone's told you, but there's been a marked difference in Cole lately. I can't tell you how happy I am to see it. Cole's gone through so much heartache."

"Cole's been wonderful for Jeff," Robin said, then swallowed hard. She felt a renewed stab of fear that Cole was more interested in the idea of having a son than he was in a relationship with her.

"I have the feeling you've *both* been wonderful for him," Joyce added.

Robin's smile was losing its conviction. She lowered her eyes and studied the lemon slice floating in her tea.

"My husband and I knew Cole quite well before the divorce," Joyce went on to say. "Larry, that's my husband, and Cole played golf every Saturday afternoon. Then Jennifer decided she wanted out of the marriage, left him and took Bobby. Cole really tried to save that marriage, but the relationship had been in trouble for a long time. Cole doted on his son, though—he would've done anything to spare Bobby the trauma of a divorce. Jennifer, however—" Joyce halted abruptly, apparently realizing how much she'd said. "I didn't mean to launch into all of this—it's ancient history. I just wanted you to know how pleased I am to meet you."

Since Cole had told her shockingly little of his past, Robin had to bite her tongue not to plead with Joyce to continue. Instead, she bowed her head and said, "I'm pleased to meet you, too."

Then she looked up with a smile as Joyce said, "Jimmy's finally got the friend he's always wanted. There are so few boys his age around here. I swear my son was ready to set off fireworks the day Jeff registered at the school and he learned you lived only two blocks away."

"Jeff claimed he couldn't live in a house that's surrounded by girls." Robin shook her head with a mock grimace. "If he hadn't met Jimmy, I might've had a mutiny on my hands."

Joyce's face relaxed into another warm smile. She was energetic and animated, gesturing freely with her hands as she spoke. Robin felt as if she'd known and liked Jimmy's mother for years.

"There hasn't been much turnover in this neighborhood. We're a close-knit group, as I'm sure you've discovered. Heather Lawrence is a real sweetie. I wish I had more time to get to know her. And Cole, well… I realize that huge house has been in his family forever, but I half expected him to move out after Jennifer and Bobby were killed."

The silence that followed was punctuated by Robin's soft, involuntary gasp. "What did you just say?"

"That I couldn't understand why Cole's still living in the house on Orchard Street. Is that what you mean?"

"No, after that—about Jennifer and Bobby." It was difficult for Robin to speak. Each word felt as if it had been scraped from the roof of her mouth.

"I assumed you knew they'd both been killed," Joyce said, her eyes full of concern. "I mean, I thought for sure that Cole had told you."

"I knew about Bobby. Jimmy said something to Jeff, who told me, but I didn't have any idea that Jennifer had died, too. Heather Lawrence told me about the divorce, but she didn't say anything about Cole's wife dying…."

"I don't think Heather knows. She moved into the neighborhood long after the divorce, and Cole's pretty close-mouthed about it."

"When did all this happen?"

"Five or six years ago now. It was terribly tragic," Joyce said. "Just thinking about it makes my heart ache all over again. I don't mean to be telling tales, but if there's any blame to be placed I'm afraid it would fall on Jennifer. She wasn't the kind of woman who's easy to know or like. I shouldn't speak ill of the dead, and I don't mean to be catty, but Jen did Cole a favor when she left him. Naturally, he didn't see it that way—he was in love with his wife and crazy about his son. Frankly, I think Cole turned a blind eye to his wife's faults because of Bobby."

"What happened?" Perhaps having a neighbor fill in the details of Cole's life was the wrong thing to do; Robin no longer knew. Cole had never said a word to her about Jennifer or Bobby, and she didn't know if he ever would.

"Jen was never satisfied with Cole's position as a city attorney," Joyce explained. "We'd have coffee together every now and then, and all she'd do was complain how Cole was wasting his talents and that he could be making big money and wasn't. She had grander plans for him. But Cole loved his job and felt an obligation to follow through with his commitments. Jennifer never understood that. She didn't even try to sympathize with Cole's point of view. She constantly wanted more, better, newer things. She didn't work herself, so it was all up to Cole." Joyce shrugged sadly.

"Jen was never happy, never satisfied," she went on. "She hated the house and the neighborhood, but figured out that all the whining and manipulating in the world wasn't going to do one bit of good. Cole intended to finish out his responsibilities to the city, so she played her ace. She left him, taking Bobby with her."

"But didn't Cole try to gain custody of Bobby?"

"Of course. He knew, and so did everyone else, that Jennifer was using their son as a pawn. She was never the motherly type, if you know what I mean. If you want the truth, she was an alcoholic. There were several times I dropped Bobby off at the house and suspected Jen had been drinking heavily. I was willing to testify on Cole's behalf, and I told him so. He was grateful, but then the accident happened and it was too late."

"The accident?" A heaviness settled in her chest. Each

breath pained her and brought with it the memories she longed to forget, memories of another accident—the one that had taken her husband.

"It was Jennifer's fault—the accident, I mean. She'd been drinking and should never have been behind the wheel. The day before, Cole had been to see his attorneys, pleading with them to move quickly because he was afraid Jennifer was becoming more and more irresponsible. But it wasn't until after she'd moved out that Cole realized how sick she'd become, how dependent she was on alcohol to make it through the day."

"Oh, no," Robin whispered. "Cole must've felt so guilty."

"It was terrible," Joyce returned, her voice quavering. "I didn't know if Cole would survive that first year. He hid inside the house and severed relationships with everyone in the neighborhood. He was consumed by his grief. Later he seemed to come out of it a little, but he's never been the same.

"The irony of all this is that eventually Jen would've gotten exactly what she wanted if she'd been more patient. A couple of years ago, Cole accepted a partnership in one of the most important law firms in the city. He's made a real name for himself, but money and position don't seem to mean much to him—they never have. I wouldn't be surprised if he walked away from the whole thing someday."

"I think you're right. Cole told me not long ago that he

has some property north of here that he inherited from his grandfather. He's restoring the house, and he said something about moving there. It's where he spends most of his weekends."

"I wondered if that was it," Joyce said, nodding. "There were rumors floating around the neighborhood that he spent his weekends with a woman. Anyone who knew Cole would realize what a crock that is. Cole isn't the type to have a secret affair."

Robin felt ashamed, remembering how she'd been tempted to believe the rumor herself.

"For a long time," Joyce murmured, "I wondered if Cole was ever going to recover from Jennifer's and Bobby's deaths, but now I believe he has. I can't help thinking you and Jeff had a lot to do with that."

"I…think he would gradually have come out of his shell."

"Perhaps, but the changes in him lately have been the most encouraging things so far. I don't know how you feel about Cole or if there's anything between you, but you couldn't find a better man."

"I…I'm falling in love with him," Robin whispered, voicing her feelings for the first time. The words hung there, and it was too late to take them back.

"I think that's absolutely wonderful, I really do!" Joyce said enthusiastically.

"I don't." Now that the shock had worn off, Robin was

forced to confront her anger. Cole had told her none of this. Not a single word. That hurt. Hurt more than she would've expected. But the ache she felt was nothing compared to the grief Cole must face each morning, the pain that weighed down his life.

"Oh, dear," Joyce said. "I've really done it now, haven't I? I knew I should've kept my mouth shut. You're upset and it's my fault."

"Nonsense," Robin whispered, making an effort to bring a smile to her dry lips and not succeeding. "I'm grateful we met, and more than grateful you told me about Jennifer, and about Cole's son." The knowledge produced a dull ache in Robin's heart. She felt grief for Cole and a less worthy emotion, too—a sense of being slighted by his lack of trust in her.

She was so distressed on the short drive home that she missed the turn and had to take a side street and double back to Orchard Street.

As she neared the house, she saw that Cole was outside watering his lawn. He waved, but she pretended not to see him and pulled into her driveway. Desperate for some time alone before facing Cole, Robin did her best to ignore him as she climbed out of the car. She needed a few more minutes to gather her thoughts and control her emotions.

She was almost safe, almost at the house, when Cole stopped her.

"Robin," he called, jogging toward her. "Hold on a minute, would you?"

She managed to compose herself, squaring her shoulders and drawing on her dignity.

His wonderful eyes were smiling as he hurried over. Obviously he hadn't noticed there was anything wrong. "Did Jeff happen to say anything about seeing us kiss last night?" he asked.

Her mouth was still so dry she had to swallow a couple of times before she could utter a single syllable. "Yes, but don't worry, I think I've got him squared away."

"Drat!" he teased, snapping his fingers. "I suppose this means I don't have to go through with the shotgun wedding?"

She nodded, keeping her eyes lowered, fearing he'd be able to read all the emotion churning inside her.

"You have nothing to fear but fear itself," she said, forcing a lightness into her tone.

"Robin?" He made her name a question and a caress. "Is something wrong?"

She shook her head, shifting the bag of groceries from one arm to the other. "Of course not," she said with the same feigned cheerfulness.

Cole took the bag from her arms. Robin knew she should have resisted, but she couldn't; she felt drained of strength. She headed for the house, knowing Cole would follow her inside.

"What's wrong?" he asked a second time, setting the groceries on the kitchen counter.

It was difficult to speak and even more difficult, more exhausting, to find the words that would explain what she'd learned.

"Nothing. It's just that I've got a lot to do if we're going out for dinner tonight."

"Wear something fancy. I'm taking you to a four-star restaurant."

"Something fancy?" Mentally she reviewed the contents of her closet, which was rather lacking in anything fancy.

"I'm not about to be outclassed by Frank," Cole said with a laugh. "I'm going to wine and dine you and turn your head with sweet nothings."

He didn't need to do any of those things to turn her head. She was already dangerously close to being in love with him, so close that she'd blurted it out to a woman she'd known for a total of twelve minutes.

Abruptly switching her attention to the bag of groceries, Robin set several packages on the counter. When Cole's hands clasped her shoulders, her eyes drifted shut. "It isn't necessary," she whispered.

Cole turned her around to face him. "What isn't?"

"The dinner, the wine, the...sweet nothings."

Their eyes held. As if choreographed, they moved into each other's arms. With a groan that came from deep in his throat, Cole kissed her. His hands tangled in the auburn thickness of her hair. His lips settled on hers with fierce protectiveness.

Robin curled her arms tightly around his neck as her own world started to dip and spin and whirl. She was standing on tiptoe, her heart in her throat, when she heard the front door open.

Moaning, she dragged her mouth from Cole's and broke away just as her son strolled into the kitchen.

Jeff stopped, his brow furrowed, when he saw the two of them in what surely looked like suspicious circumstances.

"Hi, Mom. Hi, Cole." He went casually to the refrigerator and yanked open the door. "Anything decent to drink around this place?"

"Water?" Robin suggested.

Jeff rolled his eyes. "Funny, Mom."

"There are a few more sacks of groceries in the car. Would you get them for me?" He threw her a disgruntled look, until Robin added, "You'll find a six-pack of soda in there."

"Okay." He raced out of the house and returned a minute later, carrying one sack and sorting through its contents as he walked into the kitchen.

"I'll help you," Cole said, placing his hand on Jeff's shoulder. He glanced at Robin and his eyes told her they'd continue their discussion at a more opportune moment.

Robin started emptying the sacks, hardly paying attention as Jeff and Cole brought in the last couple of bags. Cole told her he'd pick her up at six, then left.

"Can I play with Blackie for a while?" Jeff asked her, a can of cold soda clenched in his hand.

"Sure," Robin answered, grateful to have a few minutes alone.

Robin cleared the counters and made Jeff a sandwich for his lunch. He must've become involved in his game with Cole's dog because he didn't rush in announcing he was hungry.

She went outside to stand on her small front porch and smiled as she watched Jeff and Blackie. Her son really had a way with animals—like his father. Every time Robin saw him play with Cole's Labrador, she marveled at how attuned they were to each other.

She smiled when she realized Cole was outside, too; he'd just finished watering his lawn.

"Jeff, I made a sandwich for you," she called.

"In a minute. Hey, Mom, watch," he yelled as he tossed a ball across the lawn. Blackie chased after it, skidding to a stop as he caught the bright red ball.

"Come on, Blackie," Jeff urged. "Throw me the ball."

"He can't do that," Robin said in astonishment.

"Sure, he can. Watch."

And just as Jeff had claimed, Blackie leapt into the air, tossed his head and sent the ball shooting into the street.

"I'll get it," Jeff hollered.

It was Cole's reaction that Robin noticed first. A horrified look came over his face and he threw down the hose. He was shouting even as he ran.

Like her son, Robin had been so caught up in Blackie's antics that she hadn't seen the car barreling down the street, directly in Jeff's path.

Eight

"Jeff!" Robin screamed, fear and panic choking her. Her hands flew to her mouth in relief as Cole grabbed Jeff around the waist and swept him out of the path of the speeding car. Together they fell backward onto the wet grass. Robin ran over to them.

"Jeff, how many times have I told you to look before you run into the street? How many times?" Her voice was high and hysterical. "You deserve the spanking of your life for that stunt!"

"I saw the car," Jeff protested loudly. "I did! I was going to wait for it. Honest." He struggled to his feet, looking insulted at what he obviously considered an overreaction.

"Get into the house," Robin demanded, pointing furiously. She was trembling so badly she could barely speak.

Jeff brushed the grass from his jeans and raised his head to a dignified angle, then walked toward the house. Not understanding, Blackie followed him, the ball in his mouth, wanting to resume their play.

"I can't, boy," Jeff mumbled just loudly enough for her to hear. "My mother had some kind of anxiety attack that I'm gonna get punished for."

Cole's recovery was slower than Jeff's. He sat up and rubbed a hand across his eyes. His face was ashen, his expression stark with terror.

"Everything's all right. Jeff isn't hurt," Robin assured him. She slipped to her knees in front of him.

Cole nodded without looking at her. His eyes went blank and he shook his head, as if to clear his mind.

"Cole," Robin said softly, "are you okay?"

"I... I don't know." He gave her a faint smile, but his eyes remained glazed and distant. He placed one hand over his heart and shook his head again. "For a minute there I thought Jeff hadn't seen that car and...I don't know... If that boy had been hurt..."

"Thank you for acting so quickly," Robin whispered, gratitude filling her heart. She ran her hands down the sides of his face, needing to touch him, seeking a way to comfort him, although her heart ached at his words. So many times over the past few weeks, she'd suspected— and feared—that Cole's feelings had more to do with replacing the family he'd lost than love for her and Jeff.

With a shudder, Cole locked his arms around her waist and pulled her close, burying his face in the curve of her neck as he dragged deep gulps of air into his lungs.

"Come inside and I'll get us some coffee," Robin suggested.

Cole murmured agreement, but he didn't seem in any hurry to release her. Nor she him. Her hands were in his hair and she rested her cheek against his, savoring these moments of closeness now that the panic was gone.

"I lost my son," Cole whispered and the words seemed to be wrenched from the deepest part of his soul. His voice held an agony only those who had suffered such a loss could understand. "In a car accident six years ago."

Robin kissed the crown of his head. "I know."

Cole broke away from her, slowly raising his eyes to meet hers. Mingled with profound grief was confusion. "Who told you?"

"Joyce Wallach."

Cole closed his eyes. "I could use that coffee."

They both stood, and when Cole wrapped his arm around her waist Robin couldn't be sure if it was to lend support or to offer it.

Inside the house, Jeff was sitting at the bottom of the stairs, his knees under his chin. Ever loyal, Blackie lay beside him.

Jeff looked up when Robin opened the front door. "I saw the car," he repeated. "You're getting upset over nothing. I hope you realize that. Hey, what's wrong with Cole?" he asked abruptly. He glanced from Robin to their neighbor and then back to his mother. "He looks like he's seen a ghost."

In some way, Robin supposed, he had.

"You all right, sport?" Cole asked. "I didn't hurt you when we fell, did I?"

"Nah." He bit his lip, eyes lowered.

Cole frowned. "You don't sound all that certain. Are you sure you're okay?"

Jeff nodded reluctantly. "I will be once I find out what my mother plans to do to me. I really was gonna stop at the curb. Honest."

The kid would make an excellent attorney, Robin thought wryly.

"I think I might've overreacted," Cole said. He held open his arms and Jeff flew into them without a second's hesitation. Briefly Cole closed his eyes, as though in silent thanksgiving for Jeff's safety.

"I didn't mean to scare you," Jeff murmured. "I would've stopped."

"I know."

"I promise to be more careful."

"I certainly hope so," Robin said.

Cole released Jeff and sighed deeply, then looked at Robin. "You said something about coffee?"

She smiled and nodded. "I'll get it in a minute. Jeff, you

can go outside, but from now on if you're playing ball with Blackie, do it in the backyard. Understand?"

"Sure, Mom," her son said eagerly. "But—" he paused "—you mean that's it? You aren't going to ground me or anything? I mean, of course you're not because I did everything I was supposed to—well, almost everything. Thanks, Mom." He tossed the red ball in the air and caught it deftly with one hand. "Come on, Blackie, we just got a pardon from the governor."

Robin followed the pair into the kitchen and watched as Jeff opened the sliding glass door and raced into the backyard with Blackie in hot pursuit. Reassured, she poured two mugs of coffee while Cole pulled out one of the kitchen chairs. She carried the mugs to the table, then sat down across from him.

Cole reached for her hand, lacing her fingers with his own. He focused his concentration on their linked hands. "Bobby was my son. He died when he was ten."

"Jeff's age," Robin said as a chill surrounded her heart.

"Bobby was so full of life and laughter I couldn't be around him and not smile."

Talking about Bobby was clearly difficult for Cole, and Robin longed to do or say something that would help. But she could think of nothing to ease the agony etched so deeply on his face.

"He was the kind of boy every father dreams of having.

Inquisitive, sensitive, full of mischief. Gifted with a vivid imagination."

"A lot like Jeff," she said, and her hands tightened around the mug.

Cole nodded. "Bobby used to tell me I shouldn't worry about Jennifer—she was my ex-wife—because *he,* my ten-year-old son, was taking care of her."

Robin held her breath as she watched the fierce pain in his eyes. "You don't need to tell me this." Not if it was going to rip open wounds that weren't properly healed.

"I should've told you before this," he said, frowning slightly. "It's just that even now, after all this time, it's difficult to talk about my son. For a good many years, I felt as though part of me had died with Bobby. The very best part of me. I don't believe that anymore."

"Jeff reminds you a lot of Bobby, doesn't he?" Robin doubted Cole fully grasped that he was transferring his love from one boy to the other.

A smile tugged at the corners of his mouth. "Bobby had a huskier build and was taller than Jeff. His sport was basketball, but he was more of a spectator than a participant. His real love was computers. Had he lived, I think Bobby would have gone into that field. Jen never understood that. She wanted him to be more athletic, and he tried to please her." Cole's gaze dropped to his hands. "Jennifer and I were divorced before the accident. She died with him. If there's anything to be grateful for in their deaths, it's the knowledge that they both went instantly. I couldn't have stood knowing they'd suffered." He paused long enough to take a sip of the coffee, and grimaced once. "You added sugar?"

"I thought you might need it."

He chuckled. "I have so much to thank you for."

"Me?"

"Do you remember the afternoon Jeff ran away?"

She wasn't likely to forget it. With Jeff around, Robin always figured she didn't need exercise to keep her heart in shape. Her son managed to do it with his antics.

"I left on a business trip to Seattle soon afterward," he reminded her.

She nodded. That was when Jeff had looked after Blackie for him.

"Late one afternoon, when the meeting was over and dinner wasn't scheduled for another couple of hours, I went for a stroll," Cole said. "It was still light and I found myself on the waterfront. The sky was a vivid blue and the waters green and clear. It's funny I'd remember that, but it's all so distinct in my memory. I stood alone on the pier and watched as a ferry headed for one of the islands, cutting a path through the waves. Something brought Bobby to my mind, although he's never far from my thoughts, even now. The most amazing thing happened that afternoon. It's difficult to find the words to explain." He hesitated, as though searching for a way to make Robin understand. Then apparently he gave up the effort and shook his head.

"Tell me about it," Robin said in a quiet voice.

"Well, standing there at the end of the pier...I don't know. For the first time since I lost my son, I felt his presence more than I did his absence. It was as if he was there at my side, pointing out the Olympic Mountains and asking questions. Bobby was always full of questions. My heart felt lighter than it had in years—as though the burden of pain and grief had been lifted from my shoulders. For no reason whatsoever, I started to smile. I think I've been smiling ever since. And laughing. And feeling.

"When I got back to the hotel, I had the sudden urge to hear your voice. I didn't have any excuse to call you, so I phoned on the pretense of talking to Jeff and checking up on Blackie. But it was your voice I wanted to hear."

Robin smiled through the unexpected rush of tears, wondering if Cole realized what he was saying. It might've been her voice he *thought* he wanted to hear, but it was Jeff he'd called.

"I discovered a new freedom on that Seattle pier. It was as if, in that moment, I was released from the past. I can't say exactly what changed. Meeting you and Jeff played a big role in it, I recognize that much, but it was more than that. It was as if something deep inside me was willing to admit that it was finally time to let go."

"I'm glad for you," Robin whispered.

"The problem is, I never allowed myself to grieve properly or deal with the anger I felt toward Jennifer. She was driving at the time and the accident was her fault. Yet deep in my heart I know she'd never purposely have done anything to hurt Bobby. She loved him as much as I did. He was her son, too.

"It wasn't until I met you that I knew I had to forgive her. I was never the kind of husband she needed and I'm afraid I was a disappointment to her. Only in the last few years of our marriage was I willing to accept that she suffered from a serious emotional and mental illness. Her addiction to alcohol was as much a disease as cancer. I didn't understand her illness, and because of that we all suffered."

"You're being too hard on yourself," Robin said, but she doubted Cole even heard her.

"After the accident, the anger and the grief were a constant gnawing pain. I refused to acknowledge or deal with either emotion. Over the years, instead of healing, I let the agony of my loss grow more intense. I closed myself off from friends and colleagues and threw myself into work, spending far more time in the office than I did at home. Blackie was virtually my only companion. And then a few years ago I started working on my place in the country. But the pleasure that gave me came from hard physical work, the kind that leaves you too tired to think." His features softened and he smiled at her. "I'd forgotten what it was like to fly a kite or laze in the sunshine."

"That's why you suggested the picnic with Jeff and me?"

He grinned and his dark eyes seemed almost boyish. "The last time I was in Golden Gate Park was with Bobby, shortly before the accident. Deciding to have a picnic there was a giant step for me. I half expected to feel pangs of grief, if not a full-blown assault. Instead I experienced joy—and appreciation for the renewal I felt. Laughter is a gift I'd forgotten. You and Jeff helped me see that, as well."

Everything Cole was saying confirmed her worst fears.

"Mom!" Jeff roared into the kitchen with Blackie at his heels. "Is there anything to eat? Are you guys still going out to dinner? I don't suppose you'd bring me, would you?"

Cole chuckled, then leapt to his feet to playfully muss Jeff's hair. "Not this time, sport. Tonight's for your mother and me."

Two hours later, as Robin stood in front of the bathroom mirror, she had her reservations about this dinner date. She was falling in love with a man who hadn't fully dealt with the pain of losing his wife and his son. Perhaps she recognized it in Cole because she saw the same thing in herself. She loved Lenny and always would. He'd died

years ago, and she still found herself talking to him, refusing to involve herself in another relationship. A part of her
continued to grieve and she suspected it always would.

Examining herself in the mirror, Robin surveyed her
calf-length skirt of soft blue velvet and white silk blouse
with a pearl necklace.

She was fussing with her hair, pinning one side back
with combs and studying the effect, when Jeff wandered
in. He leaned casually against the doorway, a bag of
potato chips in his hand.

"Hey, you look nice."

"Don't sound so surprised." She decided she'd spent
enough time on her hair and fastened her pearl earrings.
Jeff was disappointed about not joining them, but he'd
been a good sport—especially after Cole promised him
lunch at a fish-and-chip place on the Wharf the following
Saturday.

"You're wearing your pearls," Jeff mumbled, his mouth
full.

"Yes," Robin said, turning to face him. "Do they look
all right?"

Jeff's halfhearted shrug didn't do a lot to boost
Robin's confidence. "I suppose. I don't know about stuff like
that. Mrs. Lawrence could probably tell you." He popped
another potato chip in his mouth and crunched loudly.
"My dad gave you those earrings, didn't he? And the
necklace?"

"For our first wedding anniversary."

Jeff nodded. "I thought so." His look grew reflective. "When I grow up and get married, will I do mushy stuff like that?"

"Probably," Robin said, not bothering to disguise her amusement. "And lots of other things, too. Like taking your wife out to dinner and telling her how beautiful she is and how much you love her."

"Yuck!" Jeff wrinkled his nose. "You really know how to ruin a guy's appetite." With that he turned to march down the stairs, taking his potato chips with him.

Robin stood at the top of the staircase. "Cole will be here any minute, so you can go over to Kelly's now," she called down.

"Okay. I put my plate in the dishwasher. Is there anything you want me to tell Kelly's mom?"

"Just that I won't be too late."

"You're sure I can't come with you?" Jeff tried one more time.

Robin didn't give him an answer, knowing he didn't really expect one. After a moment, Jeff grumbled, more for show than anything, then went out the front door to their neighbor's.

Robin returned to the bathroom and smiled into the mirror, picturing Jeff several years into the future and seeing Lenny's handsome face smiling back at her. She was warmed by the image, certain that her son would grow into as fine a young man as his father had been.

"You don't mind that I'm wearing the pearls for Cole, do you?" she asked her dead husband, although she knew he wouldn't have objected. She ran the tips of her fingers over the earrings, feeling reassured.

The doorbell chimed just as Robin was dabbing perfume on her wrists. She drew in a calming breath, glanced quickly at her reflection one last time, then walked down the stairs to answer the door.

Cole was dressed in a black pin-striped suit and looked so handsome that her breath caught. He smiled as she let him in, but for the life of her she couldn't think of a thing to say.

His eyes held hers as he reached for her hands. Slowly he lowered his gaze, taking in the way she'd styled her hair, the pearl necklace and the outfit she'd chosen with such care.

"You are so beautiful," he said.

"I was just thinking the same about you," she confessed.

His mouth tilted in a grin. "If I kiss you, will it ruin your lipstick?"

"Probably."

"I'm going to kiss you, anyway," he said in a husky murmur. Tenderly he fit his mouth to hers, slipping his fingers through her hair. The kiss was gentle and thorough and slow. A single kiss, and she was like clay ready to be molded. The realization struck her hard—when Cole touched her, Robin felt alive all the way to the soles of her feet. *Alive.* Healthy. A red-blooded woman. He released her, and she was shocked to find she was trembling. From the inside out.

"I've mussed your hair," he apologized. His hands slid under the soft cloud of hair to her nape.

"And you've got lipstick on your mouth," she said with a quaver, reaching up to wipe it away. "There. It'll only take me a moment to fix my hair," she said, picking up her purse and moving to the hallway mirror.

He stood behind her, hands on her shoulders as she brushed her hair, then carefully tucked the loose curls back into place with the tortoiseshell combs.

"Are you ready?" he asked when she'd finished.

Robin nodded, unable to speak.

Cole led her outside to his car and held the passenger door. He dropped a quick kiss on her unsuspecting lips, then hurried around the car, his movements lighthearted, and got into the driver's seat.

"You didn't tell me where we're having dinner."

"I told Heather Lawrence in case she needs to get hold of you, but otherwise it's a surprise."

Robin wasn't sure what to think. A number of San Francisco's restaurants were internationally famous, but her knowledge of fancy dining places was limited. She assumed this one was somewhere in the heart of the city, until he exited from the freeway heading south along Highway 101 toward the ocean.

"Cole?" she asked hesitantly.

"Don't worry," he said, casting her a swift glance that didn't conceal the mischievous twinkle in his eyes. "I promise you dinner will be worth the drive."

The restaurant sat high on a cliff, with a stunning view of the surf battering the jagged rocks below.

Cole parked the Porsche, then came around to help her out, taking the opportunity to steal another kiss. It was with obvious reluctance that he let her go. His arm around her waist, he directed her toward the doors leading into the elegant restaurant. The maître d' escorted them to a table that overlooked the water and with a flourish presented them with elaborate menus.

Robin scanned the entrées, impressed with the interesting variations on basic themes. She was less impressed with the prices—a single dinner cost as much as an entire week's worth of lunches. For her *and* Jeff.

"When you said fancy you weren't joking, were you?" she whispered, biting her lip.

Cole lowered his menu and sent her a vibrant smile. "Tonight is special," he said simply.

"You're telling me. If I wasn't having dinner with you, I'd probably have eaten a toasted cheese sandwich and a bowl of tomato soup with Jeff."

Their waiter appeared and they ordered wine—a bottle of sauvignon blanc. Then they each chose the restaurant's specialty—a scallop and shrimp sauté—which proved as succulent and spicy as the menu had promised.

They talked through dinner and afterward, over steaming cups of Irish coffee. It astonished Robin that they had so much to say to each other, although they hadn't touched on the issue closest to her heart. But she hesitated to broach the subject of Cole's relationship with Jeff. She didn't want to risk the delightful camaraderie they were sharing tonight. Their conversation could have gone on for hours and in fact did. They talked about books they'd read, recent movies they'd seen, music they liked. It came as a pleasant surprise to discover that their tastes were similar.

All evening they laughed, they argued, they talked, as if they'd been friends most of their lives. Cole grinned so often, it was hard for Robin to remember that at one time she'd actually wondered if the man ever smiled.

Robin told Cole about her job and how much she enjoyed accounting. She voiced her fears about not being the kind of mother she wanted to be for Jeff. "There are so many things I want to share with him that I don't have time for. There just aren't enough hours in a day."

Cole talked about his career goals and his dreams. He spoke of the forty acres willed to him by his grandfather and how he'd once hoped to close himself off from the world by moving there.

"But you aren't going to now?" Robin asked.

"No. I no longer have any reason to hide. The house is nearly finished and I may still move there, but I'll maintain my work schedule." He stared down into his coffee. "I was approached last week about running for the state senate."

Robin's heart swelled with pride. "Are you going to do it?"

"No. I'm not the right man for politics. I'll support someone else, but a political career doesn't interest me. It never has, although I'll admit I'm flattered."

A band started playing then, and several couples took to the dance floor.

"Shall we?" Cole asked, nodding in that direction.

"Oh, Cole, I don't know. The last time I danced was at my cousin's wedding ten years ago. I'm afraid I'll step all over your feet."

"I'm game if you are."

She was reluctant but agreed to try. They stood, and she moved naturally into his embrace, as if they'd been partners for years. Robin's eyes slowly closed when Cole folded her in his arms, and in that moment she experienced a surge of joy that startled her with its intensity.

The dance ended, but they didn't leave the floor.

"Have I told you how lovely you are?" Cole asked, his mouth close to her ear.

Grinning, Robin nodded. "Twice. Once when you picked me up at the house and once during the meal. I know you're exaggerating, but..." She shrugged, then added, "When I'm with you, I feel beautiful."

"I don't think a woman's ever paid me a higher compliment."

She raised her eyes and was shocked by the powerful emotions in his.

"Do you mind if we leave now?" he asked suddenly.

"No, of course not, if that's what you want."

He frowned. "If it was up to me I'd spend the rest of the night here with you in my arms, but I have this sudden need to kiss you, and if I do it here and do it properly we're going to attract a lot of attention."

Cole quickly paid the bill and he hurried Robin to the car. The minute they were settled inside, he reached for her. He did as he'd promised, kissing her until she was breathless. Her arms clung to him as his mouth sought hers once more.

"At least I'm not making you cry this time," he said softly.

"That still embarrasses me," she told him. "It's never happened before. I still don't understand it. I don't know if I ever will."

"I don't think I'll ever forget it."

"Please do."

"No," he said, shaking his head. "It touched me in a way I can't explain. It helped me realize I was going to love you. After Jennifer and Bobby, I doubted there was any love left in me. You taught me otherwise. Jeff taught me otherwise. My heart is full and has been almost from the time we met." He took her hand and pressed her palm to his heart. "Do you feel it?"

Robin nodded. "It's beating so hard," she whispered.

"That's because I'm nervous."

"Nervous? About what?"

Cole slid a hand into his pocket and brought out a small black velvet box.

Robin's heart started to pound in double time. "Cole?" she said anxiously, not sure what she should think or how she should act.

"I love you, Robin." His voice was hoarse. "I knew it the moment I heard your voice when I called from Seattle. And every moment since has convinced me how right this is." He opened the box and revealed the largest diamond Robin had ever seen. Slowly he raised his eyes to hers. "I'm asking you to be my wife."

Nine

"You mean this whole evening…you arranged this whole evening because you intended to ask me to marry you?" Robin asked, pressing the tips of her fingers to her trembling lips. Despite her fears a gentle gladness suffused her heart.

"Surely it isn't that much of a surprise?" he said. "I've never made an effort to hide how I feel about you or how much I enjoy Jeff."

Contrary to what Cole might think, his proposal *did* come as a surprise. "I…I don't know what to say."

"A simple yes would suit me," Cole urged warmly.

"But… Oh, Cole, it would be so easy to marry you, so easy to join my life and Jeff's to yours and never look back. But I don't know if it would be right for us or for you. There's so much to consider, so many factors to weigh, in a decision this important. I'd like nothing better than to just say yes, but I can't."

"Are you asking for time?" Cole's eyes seemed to penetrate hers, even in the dark.

"Please." For now, that seemed the simplest thing to say, although her hesitation was based on something much deeper. Cole had rediscovered a peace within himself since meeting her and Jeff; he'd told her so that very afternoon. She was tempted to say yes, to turn away from her doubts and agree to marry him. Cole had been so good for Jeff, so wonderful to her.

"I hate to disappoint you," she murmured sadly.

"I know exactly what you're thinking, exactly how you're feeling."

"You do?" Somehow she doubted it. But knowing she couldn't delay it any longer, she jumped in with both feet. "I was...just thinking about what you told me this afternoon. How you'd recently dealt with the loss of Jennifer and Bobby. While you were talking, I couldn't help feeling your exhilaration. You've obviously found a newborn sense of freedom. I think the question you need to ask yourself is if this rebirth you've experienced is what prompted the idea of marrying again."

"No," he said flatly. "Falling in love with you did."

"Oh, Cole," she whispered. "It must seem like fate to

have Jeff and me move in next door, and it gets more complicated with Jeff being the same age as Bobby...."

"Maybe it does all appear too convenient, but if I was
just looking for a woman and a child, then Heather Lawrence would've filled the bill. It's you I fell in love with."

"But how can you be so sure?" she countered quickly.
"We barely know each other."

Cole smiled at her doubts. "The first time we kissed
was enough to convince me I was going to love you. It
was the Friday night after I returned from Seattle, remember?"

Robin nodded, wincing a little.

"I was so stunned by the effect that kiss had on me, I
avoided you for an entire week afterward. If you want the
truth, I was terrified. You'll have to remember, up until
that time I was convinced I was incapable of ever falling
in love again. One kiss, and I felt jolted to the core. You hit
me hard, Robin, and I needed time to step back and ana-
lyze what was happening. That's the reason I don't have
any qualms about giving you however long you need to
sort out what you're feeling. I want you to be very sure."

Robin released a pent-up sigh. Cole folded her in his
arms and his chin brushed against her hair while his
hands roved in wide circles across her back. The action
was soothing and gentle. She was beginning to feel more
confident in his love, but she had to be careful. She

wanted him to love her, because she was so much in love with him.

Cole tucked a finger under her chin and lifted her face to his. As their eyes met, he slanted his mouth over hers in a wildly possessive kiss, a kiss filled with undisguised need.

When he broke away, Robin was trembling. She buried her face in his neck and drew several deep breaths.

"If you're going to take some time to think about things," Cole whispered against her hair, "then I wanted to give you something else to think about."

"Have you had a chance to check those figures on—" Angela began, then stopped abruptly, waving her hand in front of Robin's face.

"A chance to check what figures?" Robin asked, making a determined effort to focus. She knew she'd been acting like a sleepwalker most of the morning, but she couldn't stop thinking about Cole's proposal.

"What's with you today?" Angela demanded. "Every time I look over here, I find you staring into space with this perplexed expression on your face."

"I was…just thinking," Robin muttered.

"About what?"

"Nothing."

"Come on, girl, you know better than that. You can't fool me." Angela leaned against the edge of Robin's desk and crossed her arms, taking her usual aggressive stance. "I've known you far too long. From everything you *haven't* said, I'd guess your handsome neighbor's involved. What's he done now?"

"Cole? What makes you ask anything so ridiculous?"

Angela frowned, shaking her head. Then she stretched out her hands and made a come-hither motion. "Tell Mama everything," she intoned. "You might as well get it over with and tell me now, because you know that sooner or later I'm going to drag it out of you. What kind of friend would I be if I didn't extract your deepest darkest secrets?"

"He took me to dinner," Robin admitted, knowing that Angela was right. Sooner or later, she'd wheedle it out of her.

"Where'd he take you?"

She shrugged, wanting to keep that to herself. "It was outside the city."

"*Where* outside the city?" Angela pressed.

"Heavens, I don't know. Somewhere along the coast on Highway 101."

Angela uncrossed her arms and started pacing. "It wasn't the Cliffhouse, was it?"

"I...I think it might have been," Robin murmured, concentrating on the task in front of her. The one she should've finished hours earlier. The one she couldn't seem to focus on, even now.

"Aha!" Angela cried, pointing her index finger at the ceiling, like a detective in a comic spoof.

"What?" Robin cried.

"If Cole took you to the Cliffhouse, he did it for a reason."

"Of course he did. The food was fabulous. By the way, you were right about Frank, he's exceptionally nice," Robin said in an effort to interrupt her friend's line of thought.

"You already told me what you think of Frank, remember?" Angela said. "Cole took you to dinner at the Cliffhouse," she repeated slowly, as though reviewing a vital clue in a murder mystery.

"To be honest, I think his choice of restaurant had something to do with Frank," Robin inserted, tossing her sleuth friend a red herring.

"So Cole was jealous?"

"Not exactly," Robin said, leaning back in her chair. "Well, maybe a little," she amended, knowing Angela would never believe her if she denied it completely. "I mean, Cole did invite me to dinner as soon as he learned I was dining with Frank, so I guess you could say he was a *little* jealous. But not much. Cole's not the jealous type— he told me that himself."

"I see." Angela was frowning as she walked back to her desk. Her look remained thoughtful for the rest of the morning, although she didn't question Robin again. But when they left for lunch, she showed a renewed interest in the subject of Cole.

"How's Jeff?" she began as they stood in line in the employees cafeteria.

"Fine," Robin said as she reached for a plastic tray.

"That's all you're going to say?"

"What more do you want to know?"

"I ask about Jeff once a week or so, then sit back and listen for the next fifteen minutes while you tell me about the latest craziness," Angela said heatedly. "It never fails. You've told me about him running away with a frying pan and an atlas. You've bragged about what a fabulous pitcher he's turning out to be, and you've given me a multitude of details about every game he's played. After you tell me all about his athletic ability, you generally mention how good he is with animals and all the tricks he's taught Blackie in the past week."

Robin tried to respond but Angela ignored her and kept talking. "Today I innocently ask how Jeff is, and what do I get? *Fine.* All right, Robin, tell me what happened with Cole Camden before I go crazy trying to figure it out."

"It's something I need to figure out myself," Robin said. She paused to study the salads before selecting a mound of cottage cheese and setting it on her tray.

"What are you doing now?" Angela cried, throwing her arms in the air. "You hate cottage cheese. You never eat it unless you're upset and looking for ways to punish yourself." She took the small bowl from Robin's tray and replaced it with a fresh fruit salad, shaking her head the entire time.

The problem with Angela was that she knew Robin all too well.

They progressed a little farther down the line. Robin stood in front of the entrées, but before she chose one, she glanced at her friend. "You want to pick one of these for me, too?" she asked dryly.

"Yes, I do, before you end up requesting liver and onions."

Angela picked the lasagne, thick with melted cheese and spicy tomato sauce. "If you're looking for ways to punish yourself, girl, there are tastier methods."

Despite her thoughtful mood, Robin smiled.

Once they'd paid for their lunches, Angela led her to a window table that offered a certain amount of privacy. Robin busied herself arranging her dishes and set the tray aside.

Angela sat directly across from her, elbows braced on either side of her lunch. "Are you sure there isn't anything else you'd care to tell me?"

"About what?"

"About you and Cole, of course. I can't remember the last time I saw you like this. It's as if…as if you're trapped in some kind of maze and can't find your way out."

The description was so apt that Robin felt a tingling

sensation along her spine. She did feel hopelessly lost. Her mind was cluttered, her emotions confused. She had one foot in the present, one in the past, and didn't know which way to turn.

"I talked to Frank on Sunday afternoon," Angela continued, dipping her fork into a crisp green salad. "He said he enjoyed the evening you spent with him, but doubted you'd be seeing each other again because it's obvious to him that you're in love with Cole Camden. In fact, Frank said you talked about little else the entire evening."

"He said all that?"

Angela nodded. "He's right, isn't he? You are in love with Cole, aren't you?"

"I...I don't know."

"What do you mean you don't know?" Angela persisted. "It's written all over you. You've got that glazed look and you walk around in a trance, practically bumping into walls."

"You make it sound like I need an ambulance."

"Or a doctor," Angela whispered, leaning across the table. "Or maybe a lawyer... That's it!" she said loudly enough to attract the attention of several people at nearby tables. "Cole took you to bed, and now you're so confused you don't know what to do. I told you I'd stumble on the answer sooner or later." Her eyes flashed triumphantly.

"That's not it," Robin declared, half rising from the table. She could feel the color crowding into her cheeks as she glanced around the cafeteria. When she sat back down, she covered her face with both hands. "If you must know, Cole asked me to marry him."

A moment of shocked silence followed before Angela shrieked with pure delight. "That's fabulous! Wonderful! Good grief, what's wrong with you? You should be in seventh heaven. It isn't every day a handsome, wealthy, wonderful man proposes to you. I hope you leapt at the chance." She hesitated, suddenly still. "Robin? You *did* tell him you'd marry him, didn't you?"

Robin swallowed and shook her head. "No. I asked him for some time to think about things."

"Think about things?" Angela squealed. "What's there to think about? He's rich. He's handsome. He's in love with you and crazy about Jeff. What more could you possibly want?"

Tears brimmed in Robin's eyes as she looked up to meet her friend's avid gaze. "I'm afraid he's more in love with the idea of having a family than he is with me."

"Is Cole coming?" Jeff asked, working the stiffness out of his baseball mitt by slamming his fist into the middle of it several times.

"I don't know," Robin said, glancing at their neighbor's house as they walked to the car. "I haven't talked to him in the last few days."

"You're not mad at him, are you?"

"Of course not," Robin said, sliding into the driver's seat of her compact. "We've both been busy."

Jeff fingered the bill of his baseball cap, then set the cap on his head. "I saw him yesterday and told him about the game, and he said he might come. I hope he does."

Secretly Robin hoped Cole would be there, too. Over the past five days, she'd missed talking to him. She hadn't come to any decision, but he hadn't pressed her to make one, willing to offer her all the time she needed. Robin hadn't realized how accustomed she'd grown to his presence. How much she needed to see him and talk to him. Exchange smiles and glances. Touch him…

When she was married to Lenny, they were two people very much in love, two people who'd linked their lives to form one whole. But Lenny had been taken from her, and for a long time afterward Robin had felt only half alive.

All week she'd swayed back and forth over Cole's proposal, wondering if she should ignore her doubts. Wondering if she *could* ignore them. Sleepless nights hadn't yielded the answer. Neither had long solitary walks in Balboa Park while Jeff practiced with his baseball team.

"Cole said—" Jeff started to say, then stopped abruptly as his hands flew to his head. A panicky look broke out on his face and he stared at Robin.

"What's wrong? Did you forget something?"

"My lucky hat!" Jeff cried. "It's on my dresser. We have to go back."

"For a baseball cap?" Robin didn't disguise how silly she considered that idea. "You're wearing a baseball cap. What's wrong with that one?"

"It won't work. You have to understand, Mom, it's my *lucky* hat. I've been wearing it ever since we played our first game. I had that very same hat on when I hit my first two home runs. I can't play without it," he explained frantically. "We have to go back. Hurry, or we'll be late for the game. Turn here," he insisted, pointing at the closest intersection.

"Jeff," she said, trying to reason with her son. "It isn't the hat that makes you play well."

"I knew you were going to say something like that," he muttered, "and even if it's true, I want to be on the safe side, just in case. We've got to go back and get that hat!"

Knowing it would only waste valuable time to argue, Robin did as he requested. After all, his whole career as a major-league pitcher hung in the balance!

She was smiling as she entered her driveway. Sitting in the car while Jeff ran inside for his lucky cap, Robin glanced over at Cole's place. His car was gone. It'd been gone since early that morning, and she suspected he was at the property, working on his house. Jeff would be disappointed about Cole missing his game, but he'd understand.

Jeff came barreling out of the house, slamming the front door. He leapt into the car and fastened his seat belt. "Come on, Mom," he said anxiously, "let's get this show on the road." As if *she'd* caused the delay, Robin thought to herself, amused by her son's sudden impatience.

By the time they arrived at Balboa Park, the car park was filled to overflowing. Robin was fortunate enough to find a space on the street, a minor miracle in itself. Perhaps there was something to this magic-cap business after all.

Jeff ran across the grass, hurrying toward his teammates, leaving Robin to fend for herself, which was fine. He had his precious cap and was content.

The bleachers were crowded with parents. Robin found a seat close to the top and had just settled in place when she saw Cole making his way toward her. Her heart did an immediate flip-flop and it wasn't until he sat next to her that she was able to speak.

"I thought you were working up on the property this weekend."

"And miss seeing Jeff pitch? Wild horses couldn't have kept me away." He was smiling at her with that cocky heart-stopping smile of his.

"How have you been?" she asked. She couldn't keep her eyes off him. He looked too good to be true, and his dark gaze was filled with warmth and tenderness. How could she help getting lost in eyes that generous? It seemed impossible to resist him any longer.

"I've missed you like crazy," he whispered, and the humor seemed to drain out of him as his eyes searched hers. "I didn't think it was possible to feel this alone. Not anymore."

"I've missed you, too."

He seemed to relax once she'd said that. "Thank you," he said quietly. "Have you been thinking about what I said last weekend?"

She bowed her head. "I haven't thought of anything else."

"Then you've made up your mind?"

"No." She kept her face lowered, not wanting him to see her confusion.

He tilted her chin with one finger, forcing her to meet his eyes. "I promised myself I wouldn't ask you and then I couldn't seem to stop myself. I won't again."

She offered him a weak smile, and Cole looked around him, clearly wanting to kiss her, but not in front of such a large gathering. The funny part was, Robin didn't care about being seen. She was so hungry for the reassurance of his touch, it didn't matter to her that they were in the middle of a crowded park.

"I see Jeff's wearing his lucky hat," Cole said, clasping her hand and giving her fingers a comforting squeeze.

"You know about that?"

"Of course. Jeff tells me everything."

"He panicked when he realized he was wearing the wrong one, and I had to make a U-turn in the middle of the street because he'd left the guaranteed-to-pitch-well baseball cap on his dresser."

"You can't blame him. The luck has lasted through five games now."

"I wonder if it'll last until he reaches the pros," Robin said, sharing a smile with him.

"You're doing all right?" Cole asked unexpectedly.

She nodded, although it wasn't entirely true. Now that she was with Cole, every doubt she'd struggled with all week vanished like fog under an afternoon sun. Only when they were apart was she confronted by her fears.

"After Jeff's finished here, let's do something together," Cole suggested. "The three of us."

She nodded, unable to refuse him anything.

"Come to think of it, didn't I promise Jeff lunch? I seem to recall making a rash pledge to buy him fish and chips because we were leaving him with Heather and Kelly when we went to dinner last week."

Robin grinned. "It seems to me you're remembering that correctly," she said.

They went to a cheerful little fish-and-chip restaurant down by the Wharf. The weather had been chilly all morning, but the sun was out in full force by early afternoon. Jeff was excited about his team's latest win and attributed it to the luck brought to them by his cap.

After a leisurely lunch, the three of them strolled along the busy waterfront. Robin bought a loaf of fresh sourdough bread and a small bouquet of spring flowers. Jeff found a plastic snake he couldn't live without and paid for it with his allowance.

"Just wait till Jimmy Wallach sees this!" he crowed.

"I'm more curious to see how Kelly Lawrence reacts," Robin said.

"Oh, Kelly likes snakes," Jeff told them cheerfully. "Jimmy was over one day and I thought I'd scare Kelly with a live garden snake, but Jimmy was the one who started screaming. Kelly said snakes were just another of God's creatures and there was nothing to be afraid of. Isn't it just like a girl to get religious about a snake?"

Jeff raced down the sidewalk while Cole and Robin stood at the end of the pier, the bread and flowers at their feet.

"You look tired," Cole said, as his fingers gently touched her forehead.

"I'm fine," she insisted, gazing out at the cool green waters of San Francisco Bay. But Cole was right; she hadn't been sleeping well.

"I see so much of myself in you," Cole said softly.

His words surprised her. "How's that?"

"The pain mostly. How many years has Lenny been dead?"

"Ten. In some ways I'm still grieving him." She couldn't be less than honest with Cole.

"You're not sure if you can love another man, are you?

At least not with the same intensity that you loved Jeff's father."

"That's not it at all. I…I just don't know if I can stop loving him."

Cole went very still. "I never intended to take Lenny away from you or Jeff. He's part of your past, an important part. Being married to Lenny, giving birth to Jeff, contributed to making you what you are." He paused, and they both remained silent.

"Bobby had been buried for six years before I had the courage to face the future. I hung on to my grief, carried it with me everywhere I went, dragging it like a heavy piece of luggage I couldn't travel without."

"I'm not that way about Lenny," she said, ready to argue, not heatedly or vehemently, but logically, because what he was saying simply wasn't true. She mourned her dead husband, felt his absence, but she hadn't allowed this sense of loss to destroy her life.

"Perhaps you aren't grieving as deeply as you once were," Cole amended. "But I wonder if you've really laid your husband to rest."

"Of course I have," she answered with a nod of her head, not wanting to talk about Lenny.

"I don't mean to sound unsympathetic," Cole said, his tone compassionate. "I understand, believe me I do. Emotional pain is familiar territory for us both. It seems to me that those of us who sustain this kind of grief are afraid of what lies beyond."

"You're exaggerating, Cole."

"Maybe," he agreed. "You're a lovely woman, Robin. Witty. Intelligent. Outgoing. I'm sure one of the first questions anyone asks you is how long it's been since your husband died. And I'll bet when you tell them, they seem surprised."

That was true, and Robin wondered how Cole had guessed.

"Most young widows remarry."

"Are you suggesting that because I didn't immediately fling myself back into matrimonial bliss I'm a candidate for therapy? Come on, Cole, even you must realize how ridiculous that is."

"Even me?" he asked, chuckling.

Jeff came loping toward them, his face flushed with excitement. "They're filming a movie," he cried, pointing toward a congested area farther down the pier. "There's cameras and actors and everything. Can I go watch some more?"

Robin nodded. "Just don't get in anyone's way."

"I won't. Promise. Here, Mom, hold my snake." He entrusted her with his precious package before racing back down the pier.

"He's a fine boy, Robin."

"He loves you already. You and Blackie."

"And how does his mother feel?"

The knot in her throat thickened. "She loves you, too."

Cole grinned. "She just isn't sure if she can let go of her dead husband to take on a live one. Am I right?"

His words hit their mark. "I don't know," she admitted. "Maybe it's because I'm afraid you want to marry me because Jeff reminds you of Bobby. Or because you've created a fantasy wife and think I'll fit the role."

Her words seemed to shock him. "No. You've got that all wrong. Jeff is a wonderful plus in this relationship, but it's *you* I fell in love with. It's you I want to grow old with. You, and you alone, not some ideal. If you want to know the truth, I think you're stirring up all this turmoil because you're afraid of ever marrying again. The little world you've made is tidy and safe. But is this what Lenny would've wanted for you?" He gripped her firmly by the shoulders. "If Lenny were standing beside you right now and you could ask him about marrying me, what would he say?"

"I...don't understand."

"If you could seek Lenny's advice, what would he tell you? Would he say, 'Robin, look at this guy. He's in love with you. He thinks the world of Jeff, and he's ready to embark on a new life. This is an opportunity too good to pass up. Don't be a fool. Marry him.'?"

"That sounds like something my friend Angela would say."

"I'm going to like this friend of yours—just as long as she doesn't try to set you up with any more of her divorced cousins," Cole said, laughing. His eyes grew warm as he gazed at her, and she suspected he was longing to take her in his arms and kiss her doubts away. But he didn't. Instead, he looked over his shoulder and sighed. "I think I'll go see what Jeff's up to. I'll leave you to yourself for a few minutes. I don't mean to pressure you, but I do want you to think about what I said."

"You aren't pressuring me," she whispered, staring out over the water.

Cole left her then, and her hands clutched the steel railing as she raised her eyes to the sky. "Oh, Lenny," she whispered. "What should I do?"

Ten

"Cole wants me to ask your advice." Robin continued to look up at the cloudless blue sky. "Oh, Lenny, I honestly don't know what's right for Jeff and me anymore. I love Cole. I love you. But at the same time I can't help wondering about Cole's motives...."

Robin paused, waiting. Not that she expected an answer. Lenny couldn't give her one. He never did; he never would. But unlike the other times she'd spoken to him, she needed a response, even though expecting one was totally illogical.

With every breath she took, Robin knew that, but the futility of it hit her, anyway. Her frustration was so hard and unexpectedly powerful that it felt like a body blow.

Robin closed her eyes, hoping the heat of the sun would take away this bitter ache, this dreadful loneliness.

She felt so empty. Hollow all the way through.

Her fists were clenched at her sides as tears fell from her eyes. Embarrassed, she glanced around, grateful that the film crew had attracted most of the sightseers. No one was around to witness her distress.

Anger, which for so many years had lain dormant inside her, gushed forth in an avalanche of grief and pain. The tears continued to spill down her cheeks. Her lips quivered. Her shoulders shook. Her hands trembled. It was as if the emotion was pounding against her chest and she was powerless to do anything but stand there and bear it.

Anger consumed her now. Consumed her because she hadn't allowed it to when Lenny was killed. It had been more important to put on a brave front. More important to hold herself together for Jeff and for Lenny's parents. More important to deal with the present than the past.

Lenny had died and Robin was furious with him for leaving her alone with a child to raise. Leaving her alone to deal with filing taxes and taking out the garbage and repairing leaking pipes. All these years she'd managed on her own. And she'd bottled the anger up inside, afraid of ever letting it go.

"Robin."

Cole's voice, soft and urgent, reached out from behind

her. At the sound, she turned and walked into his arms, sobbing, needing his comfort and his love in equal measure. Needing him as she'd never needed anyone before.

She didn't know how long he held her. He was whispering soothing words to her. Gentle words. But she heard none of them over the sound of her own suffering.

Once she started crying, Robin couldn't seem to stop. It was as if a dam had burst inside her and the anguish, stored for too many years, came pouring out.

Cole's arms were securely wrapped around her, shielding her. She longed to control this outburst, longed to explain, but every time she tried to speak her sobbing only grew worse.

"Let it out," he whispered. "You don't have to say anything. I understand."

"He doesn't answer," she sobbed. "I asked him… Lenny never answers me…because he can't. He left me…"

"He didn't want to die," Cole told her.

"But he did…he did."

Cole didn't argue with her. He simply held her, stroking the back of her head as though reassuring a small child.

It took several minutes for Robin to compose herself enough to go on. "Part of me realizes that Lenny didn't want to leave me, didn't want to die. But he did and I'm so angry at him."

"That anger is what makes us human," Cole said. He

continued to comfort her and, gradually, bit by bit, Robin felt her composure slip back into place.

She sensed Jeff's presence even before he spoke.

"What wrong with my mom?" he asked Cole.

"She's dealing with some emotional pain," Cole explained, speaking as one adult to another.

"Is she going to be all right?"

Robin hadn't wanted her son to see her crying and made a concerted effort to break away from Cole, to reassure Jeff herself. Cole loosened his hold, but kept his arm around her shoulders.

"I'm fine, Jeff. Really."

"She doesn't look so good."

Her son had developed the irritating habit of talking to Cole and not to her when she was upset. They'd done it that day her son had run away to the fort. Jeff and Cole had carried on an entire conversation about her while she was in their midst then, too.

Cole led her to a bench and they all sat down.

Jeff plopped down next to her and reached for her hand, patting it several times. Leaning toward Cole, he said earnestly, "Chocolate might help. One time Mom told me there wasn't anything in this world chocolate couldn't cure."

She'd actually said that? Robin started to smile. Wrapping her arms around her son, she hugged him close, loving him so much her heart seemed about to burst.

Jeff wasn't all that keen on being cuddled, especially in public, but although he squirmed he put up with his mother's sudden need to hold him.

When she'd finished, Jeff rolled his eyes and once more directed his comments to Cole. "She gets weird like this every once in a while. Remember what happened that day I ran away?"

"I remember," Cole said, and Robin smiled at the trace of amusement she heard in his voice.

"Will you stop excluding me from this conversation? I'm going to be all right. I just had this…urge to cry, but don't worry, it's passed."

"See what I mean?" Jeff muttered to Cole.

"But Jeff's right," Robin said, ignoring her son's comment. "Something chocolaty would definitely help."

"You'll be okay by yourself for a couple of minutes?" Cole asked.

"I'll be fine. I…don't know exactly what came over me, but I'm going to be just fine."

"I know you are." He kissed her, his lips gentle against her cheek.

The two of them left and once more Robin was alone. She didn't really understand why the pain and anger had hit her so hard now, after all this time. Except that it had something to do with Cole. But the last place she would ever have expected to give in to her grief was on Fisherman's Wharf with half of San Francisco looking on.

Jeff returned less than a minute later, running to her side with a double-decker chocolate ice cream cone. "Cole's bringing two more for him and me," he explained. "I told the guy it was an emergency and he gave me this one right away."

"That was nice of you," Robin said, wondering what the vendor must have thought. Smiling, she ran her tongue over the ice cream, savoring the cold chocolate. As profoundly as she'd wept, she felt almost giddy with relief now, repressing the impulse to throw back her head and laugh.

Cole arrived, and with Jeff on her left and Cole on her right she sat on the concrete bench and ate her ice cream cone.

"I told you this would work," Jeff told Cole smugly.

"And to think I scoffed at your lucky baseball cap," she teased, feeling much better.

When they finished the cones, Cole gathered up their packages and led them back to where he'd parked his car.

Blackie was there to greet them the instant they returned to Orchard Street. Jeff ran into the backyard to play with the dog, and Cole walked Robin to her door. He accepted her offer of coffee.

"I'm probably going to be leaving soon for my property," he said, watching her closely. He sat down at the table, his hands cupping the mug as though to warm them. "Will you be all right?"

Robin nodded. She walked over and stood beside him and pressed a hand to his strong jaw. "I realize you delayed going up there today because of Jeff and his baseball game. We're both grateful."

Cole placed his hand over hers and harshly expelled his breath. "I feel responsible for what you went through there on the pier. I should never have said what I did. I'm sorry, Robin, it wasn't any of my business."

"You only said what I needed to hear."

He smiled. "If I did, it was because of what happened to me in Seattle. It's quite a coincidence that both of us would come to grips with our pain while standing on a pier—me in Seattle, you here in San Francisco. I went home with this incredible sense of release. For the first time since Bobby and Jennifer's deaths, I surrendered my grief. In a way it was as though I reached up and God reached down and together we came to an understanding."

That so completely described what Robin had been feeling that for a long moment she couldn't say anything. What Cole had said earlier about carrying the pain, dragging it everywhere, was right on the mark, too. He understood; he'd done the same thing himself. A surge of love swelled within her.

"I know you don't want to hear this," he was saying. "I honestly don't mean to pressure you. But once I returned from Seattle and realized I was falling in love with you I started thinking about having another baby." He hesitated and took a gulp of his coffee. Then he stood up abruptly, nearly knocking the chair backward. "I'd better go before I say or do something else I shouldn't."

Robin followed him into the entryway, not wanting him to leave, but not quite ready to give him what he needed.

He paused at the screen door and his eyes immediately found hers. He couldn't seem to keep himself from touching her, brushing an auburn curl from her cheek. His knuckles grazed her skin lightly, and Robin's eyes closed of their own accord at the sensation that shot through her. Her heart was full, and she seemed to have all the answers now—except to the one question that was the most important in her life. And Jeff's.

"I'll see you sometime next week," Cole said roughly, pulling his hand away. Without another word, he walked out the door, pausing at the top of the porch steps.

He called for his dog and in response both Blackie and Jeff came running.

"You're not leaving, are you?" Jeff asked breathlessly.

"I'm taking Blackie for the rest of the weekend. You think you can get along without him till Monday, sport?"

Jeff shrugged and stuck his fingers in the hip pockets of his blue jeans. "I suppose. Where are you taking him?"

"To my property." Cole didn't turn toward Robin.

It was as if he had to ignore her in order to walk away from her.

"Oh, yeah!" Jeff said enthusiastically. "I remember you said something about it once. You're building a house, aren't you?"

"Remodelling one. My grandfather lived there as a boy and he left it to me, only it's been a lot of years since any-one's cared for that old house properly and there's plenty of work that needs to be done."

"I'll work for you," Jeff piped up eagerly. He made a fist and flexed his arm, revealing the meager muscles. "I know it doesn't look like much, but I'm strong. Ask anyone."

Cole tested Jeff's muscles, pretending to be impressed. "Yes, I can tell you're strong, and I'm sure I couldn't ask for a harder worker." Jeff beamed until Cole added regret-fully, "I'll take you up there another time, sport."

Jeff's face fell.

Before she even realized what she was doing, Robin moved onto the porch. "Cole."

He turned to face her, but the movement seemed reluc-tant.

Perhaps it was because she didn't want to be separated from him any more than he wanted to be away from her. Perhaps it was the thought of Jeff's disappointment when he'd already had so many other disappointments in his life. Perhaps it was this newborn sense of freedom she was just beginning to experience.

She stepped toward Cole. "Could Jeff and I go up to the property with you?"

Jeff didn't wait for Cole to answer before leaping excitedly into the air. "Hey, Mom, that's a great idea! Really great. Can we, Cole? Blackie and I can help you, and Mom can… Well, she can do things like make us some grub and bring us lemonade and other stuff women do when their men are working."

"I'll have you both know I pound a mean hammer," Robin felt obliged to inform them. If she was going to Cole's farm, she fully intended to do her share.

Cole looked perplexed for a moment, as if he wasn't sure he'd heard her correctly. "I'd love to have you come— if you're sure that's what you want."

Robin just nodded. All she knew was that she couldn't bear to be separated from him any longer.

"Be warned—the house is only half done. The plumbing isn't in yet."

"We'll manage, won't we, Jeff?"

"Yeah," Jeff said eagerly. "Anyway, boys got it easy."

Cole laughed. "How long will it take you to pack?"

"We're ready now, aren't we, Blackie?" Jeff almost jitterbugged across the front lawn in his enthusiasm.

"Give me a few minutes to throw some things together," Robin said, grinning. Jeff was smiling, too, from ear to ear, as he dashed past her into the house and up the stairs.

Cole's eyes held Robin's in silent communication— until Jeff came bursting out of the house, dragging his sheets and quilt with him, straight from his bed.

"Jeff," she cried, aghast, "what are you doing?"

"I took everything off my bed. I can go without plumbing, but I need my sleep." He piled the bedding at their feet. "You two can go back to looking at each other. I'll get everything else we need."

"Jeff," Robin groaned, casting Cole an apologetic glance. "I'll pack my own things, thank you."

"You want me to get your sheets, too?" he called from inside the house.

"No." She scooped up the bedding and hurried into the house, taking the stairs two at a time. She discovered Jeff sitting on the edge of her bed, his expression pensive.

"What's wrong?"

"Are you ever going to marry Cole?" her son asked.

At the unexpectedness of the question, Robin's heart flew to her throat, then slid back into place. Briefly she wondered if Cole had brought up the subject with her son, but instinctively knew he hadn't. "W-what makes you ask that?"

He shrugged. "Lots of things. Every time I turn around you two are staring at each other. Either that or kissing. I try to pretend I don't notice, but it's getting as bad as some of those movies you like. And when you were crying on the pier, I saw something. Cole had his arms around you and he was looking real sad. Like…like he wished he could do the crying for you. It's the same look Grandpa sometimes gives Grandma when he figures out that she's upset, and she doesn't even have to talk. Do you know what I mean?"

"I think so," Robin said, casually walking over to her dresser drawer and taking out a couple of old sweatshirts. "And what would you think if I said I was considering marrying Cole?"

Robin expected shouts of glee and wild shrieks, but instead her son crossed his arms over his chest and moved his mouth in odd ways, stretching it to one side and then the other. "You're serious, aren't you?"

"Yes." She folded and refolded one of the sweatshirts, her heart pounding in anticipation. "It would mean a lot of changes for all of us."

"How many other people are involved in this?"

Robin hesitated, not understanding Jeff's concern. "What do you mean?"

"Will I get an extra set of grandparents in this deal?"

"Uh…probably. I haven't talked to Cole about that yet, but I assume so."

"That means extra gifts on my birthday and at Christmas. I say we should go for it."

"Jeffrey Leonard Masterson, you shock me!"

He shrugged. "That's how a kid thinks."

Robin shook her head in dismay at her son's suddenly materialistic attitude toward her possible marriage. She was still frowning as she stepped outside.

Cole was in his garage, loading up the trunk of his SUV when Robin joined him. She handed him one small suitcase and a bag of groceries she'd packed at the last minute.

Cole stowed them away, carefully avoiding her eyes. "I guess you said something to Jeff about us?" She could hear amusement in his voice.

"Yes. How'd you know?"

"He brought down a paper bag full of clothes and asked what kind of presents he could expect from my parents at Christmas. He also asked if there were any aunts or uncles in the deal." Robin's embarrassment must have showed, because Cole started chuckling.

"That boy's got a mercenary streak in him I knew nothing about," she muttered.

Cole was still grinning. "You ready?"

She nodded, drawing an unsteady breath, eager for this adventure to begin. Jeff and Blackie were already in the backseat when Robin slipped into the front to wait for Cole.

"Are we going to sing camp songs?" Jeff asked, leaning forward. He didn't wait for a response, but immediately launched into the timeless ditty about bottles of beer on the wall. He sang ninety-nine verses of that, then performed a series of other songs until they left the freeway and wound up on a narrow country road with almost no traffic.

Jeff had tired of singing by then. "Knock knock," he called out.

"Who's there?" Robin said, falling in with his game.

"Eisenhower."

"Eisenhower who?"

Jeff snickered. "Eisenhower late, how about you?" With that, the ten-year-old broke into belly-gripping guffaws, as if he should be receiving awards for his ability to tell jokes.

Cole's mouth was twitching and Robin had to admit she was amused, too.

"The turnoff for the ranch is about a mile up the road," Cole explained. "Now remember, this is going to be a lot like camping. It's still pretty primitive."

"You don't need to worry," Robin said, smiling at him.

A couple of minutes later, Cole slowed, about to turn down the long driveway. It was then that Robin saw the sign. Her heart jumped into her throat and her hands started to shake.

"Stop!" she screamed. "Stop!"

Cole slammed on the brakes, catapulting them forward. "Robin, what is it?"

Robin threw open the front door and leapt out of the car, running to the middle of the road. She stared at the one word on the sign even as the tears filled her eyes.

Cole's farm was named *Paradise*.

Eleven

"Robin, I don't understand," Cole said for the third time, his dark eyes worried.

"I bet my allowance she's crying again," Jeff muttered, poking his head out the side window. "Something weird's going on with my mother. She's been acting goofy all day. Why do you think it is?"

"I'm not really sure," Cole said as he continued to study Robin.

For her part, Robin couldn't take her eyes off the sign. Jeff was right about her crying; the tears streamed unrestrained down her face. But these were tears of joy. Tears of gratitude. Tears of acknowledgment. It was exactly as Cole had described. She'd reached up and God had reached down and together they'd come to an understand-ing. She'd finally resolved her dilemma.

Unable to stop herself, Robin hurled her arms around Cole's neck. Her hands roamed his face. His wonderful, wonderful face.

Because her eyes were blurred with emotion, she couldn't accurately read Cole's expression, but it didn't matter. Her heart spilled over with love for him.

"Robin…"

She didn't let him finish, but began spreading a long series of kisses across his face, starting with his eyelids. "I love you, I love you," she repeated between kisses, moving from his cheek to his nose and downward.

Cole put his arms around her waist and pulled her closer. Robin was half-aware of the car door slamming and Jeff marching up the road to join them.

"Are you two getting all mushy on me again?"

Robin barely heard her son. Her mouth had unerringly found Cole's.

The unexpected sharp sound of a hand clap brought her out of her dream world. The kiss ended, and her eyes im-mediately went to Jeff, who was looking very much like a pint-size adult. His face and eyes were stern.

"Do the two of you know where you're standing?" Jeff demanded as though he'd recently been hired by the state police to make sure this type of thing didn't happen.

"There are proper places to kiss, but the middle of the road isn't one of them."

"He's right," Cole said, his eyes devouring Robin. He clearly didn't want to release her and did so with a reluctance that tugged at her heart.

"Come with me," Jeff said, taking his mother by the hand and leading her back to the car. He paused in front of the door and frowned. "Maybe she has a fever."

"Robin," Cole said, grasping her hand, "can you explain now?"

She nodded. "It's the sign—Paradise. Tell me about it. Tell me why your grandfather named his place Paradise."

"I'm not sure," Cole said, puzzled. "He lived here his whole life and always said this land was all he'd ever needed. From what I remember, he once told me he thought of this place as the Garden of Eden. I can only assume that's why he named it Paradise."

Robin nodded, unsurprised by his explanation. "When Lenny and I were first married, we talked...we dreamed about someday buying some land and raising animals. Enough land for Jeff to have a pony and for me to have a huge garden. We decided this land would be our own piece of heaven on earth and...from that we came up with the idea of naming it Paradise."

Cole shook his head slowly, and she could tell he didn't completely understand.

"This afternoon, when I was standing on Fisherman's

Wharf, you suggested I talk over my feelings about our getting married with Lenny."

"What I suggested," Cole reminded her, "was that you *imagine* what he'd say to advise you. I certainly didn't expect you to really communicate with him."

"I know this won't make any sense to you, but I've talked to Lenny lots of times over the years. This afternoon, what hit me so hard was the fact that Lenny would never answer me. That realization was what finally forced me to deal with the pain. To forgive Lenny for dying."

Jeff was looking at her in confusion, his mouth open and eyes wide.

"Here you were wanting to marry me and I didn't know what to do. I had trouble believing your proposal was prompted by anything more than the desire to replace the family you'd lost. I do love you, and I desperately wanted to believe you loved me—and Jeff. But I wasn't sure...."

"And you're sure now?"

She nodded enthusiastically. "Yes. With all my heart, I'm confident that marrying you would be the right thing for all of us."

"Of course we're going to marry Cole!" Jeff cried. "Good grief, all you had to do was ask me and I would've told you. We belong together."

"Yes, we do, don't we?" Robin whispered. "Cole," she

said, taking both his hands with her own. "I'd consider it a very great honor to become your wife."

"Jeff?" Cole said, tearing his eyes away from Robin.

The boy's face shone and his eyes sparkled. "I'd consider it a very great honor to become your son."

Cole brushed his lips across Robin's and then reached for Jeff, hauling him into his arms and squeezing him tight. Blackie started barking then, wanting out of the car. Robin quickly moved to open the passenger door, and the black Lab leapt out. She crouched down and wrapped her arms around his thick neck, hugging him. "You're going to have a whole family now, Blackie," she said happily.

Two hours later, just at dusk, Robin was standing in the middle of the yard. She'd loved everything about Paradise, just as she'd known she would. The house and property were nothing like the place she and Lenny had dreamed about, but she hadn't expected them to be. The four-bedroom house was much larger than anything they'd ever hoped to own. The land was covered with Ponderosa pine, and the rocky ground was more suitable to grazing a few sheep or cattle than planting crops.

Cole was showing Jeff the barn, and Robin had intended to join them, but the evening was redolent with a sweet-smelling breeze and she'd stopped to breathe in the fresh cool air. She folded her arms and stood there, smiling into the clear sky. A multitude of twinkling stars were just beginning to reveal themselves.

Cole walked quietly up behind her, and slipped his arms around her waist, pulling her against him. "Have I told you how much I love you?"

"In the last fifteen minutes? No, you haven't."

"Then allow me to correct that situation." He nibbled the back of her neck gently. "I love you to distraction."

"I love you, too."

He sighed then and whispered hoarsely, "It was a difficult decision to marry me, wasn't it?"

Robin agreed with a nod.

"Had I given you so many reasons to doubt me?"

"No," she said quickly, turning in his arms. She pressed her palms against his jaw. "I had to be sure in my heart that you weren't trying to replace the son you'd lost with Jeff. And I had to be equally certain you loved me for myself and not because I was Jeff's mother and we came as a package deal."

He shook his head decisively. "Jeff's a great kid, don't get me wrong, but there's never been any question in my mind about how I felt. The first time we met, you hit me square between the eyes. I didn't mean to fall in love again. I didn't even want to."

"I don't think I did, either," Robin confessed.

"Past experience taught us both that loving someone only causes pain. I loved Jennifer, but I could never make her happy. When we divorced I accepted my role in the breakup."

"But she had a drinking problem, Cole. You can't blame yourself."

"I don't, not entirely, but I accept a portion of the blame for what went wrong. It tore me apart to see Bobby caught in the middle, and in an effort to minimize the pain I didn't fight for custody. He was an innocent victim of the divorce, and I didn't want him to suffer any further distress. I was willing to do anything I could to spare him. Later, when I realized how serious Jennifer's problem with alcohol had become, I tried to obtain custody, but before I could get the courts to move on it, the accident happened. Afterward, I was left facing the guilt of having waited too long.

"The thought of ever marrying again, having children again, terrified me. I couldn't imagine making myself vulnerable a second time." He paused, and a slow, gentle smile spread across his face, smoothing away the tension. "All of that changed when I met you. It was as if life was offering me another chance. And I knew I had to grab hold of it with both hands or live with regret forever."

"Oh, brother," Jeff said as he dashed into the yard. "Are you two at it again?"

"We're talking," Robin explained.

"Your mouths are too close together for talking." He strolled past them, Blackie trotting at his side. "I don't suppose you thought about making me anything to eat, did you, Mom?"

"I made sandwiches."

"Great. Are there enough for Blackie to have one?"

"I think so. There's juice and some corn chips in the kitchen, too."

"Great," Jeff repeated, hurrying into the house.

"Are you hungry?" Robin asked Cole.

"Yes," he stated emphatically, "but my appetite doesn't seem to be for food. How long will you keep me waiting to make you my wife?"

"I'll have to call my parents and my brother so we can arrange everything. It's important to me that we have a church wedding. It doesn't have to be fancy, but I'd like to invite a handful of good friends and—"

"How long?"

"To make the arrangements? I'm not sure. Three, possibly four months to do it properly."

"One month," Cole said.

"What do you mean, one month?"

"I'm giving you exactly thirty days to arrange whatever you want, but that's as long as I'm willing to wait."

"Cole—"

He swept her into his arms then and his mouth claimed hers in a fury of desire. Robin found herself trembling and she clutched his shirt, her fingers bunching the material as she strove to regain her equilibrium.

"Cole..." She felt chilled and feverish at the same time. Needy, yet wealthy beyond her wildest dreams.

"One month?" he repeated.

"One month," she agreed, pressing her face against his broad warm chest. They'd both loved, profoundly, and lost what they'd valued most. For years, in their own ways, they'd sealed themselves off from others, because no one else could understand their pain. Then they'd discovered each other, and nothing would ever be the same again. Their love was the mature love that came when one had suffered and lost and been left to rebuild a shattered life. A love that was stronger than either could have hoped for.

"Do you see what I was telling you?" Jeff muttered to Blackie, sitting on the back porch steps. "I suppose we're going to have to put up with this for a while."

Blackie munched on a corn chip, apparently more interested in sharing Jeff's meal than listening to his comments.

"I can deal with it, if you can," Jeff continued. "I suspect I'll be getting at least one brother out of this deal, and if we're lucky maybe two. A sister would be all right, too, I guess—" he sighed deeply "—but I'll have to think about that. Girls can be a real headache, if you know what I mean."

The dog wagged his tail as Jeff slipped him another corn chip. "And you know what, Blackie? It's gonna be

Father's Day soon. My very first. And I've already got a card picked out. It's got a picture of a father, a mother and a boy with a baseball cap. And there's a dog on it that looks just like you!"

* * * * *

Is there ever such a thing as the perfect match?

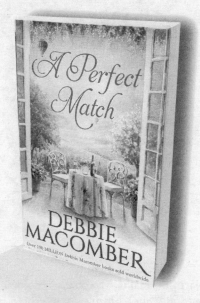

Could they really be the perfect match?

Both Tanner and Joanna are determined to resist marriage, but they haven't anticipated their daughters' desire to make them a family…

Make time for friends
Make time for Debbie Macomber

Finding love was never easy...

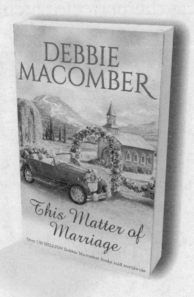

The alarm on Hallie McCarthy's biological clock is buzzing. She's hitting the big three-0 and there's no prospect of marriage, no man in sight. But Hallie's got a plan. She's giving herself a year to meet her very own Mr Right...

Except all her dates are disasters. Too bad she can't just fall for her good-looking neighbour, Steve Marris—who's definitely *not* her type.

www.mirabooks.co.uk

*Taking a chance on love would
be worth the risk...*

Chase Goodman has three weeks to find a bride,
so he takes out an advert: Bride Wanted.
Except when Chase ends up rescuing Lesley
Campbell, he unexpectedly falls head over heels.
Too bad Lesley is the only woman he's met
who isn't looking for a husband...

**Over 150 MILLION Debbie Macomber
books sold worldwide**

Take a trip to
Cedar Cove

DEBBIE MACOMBER
16 Lighthouse Road

DEBBIE MACOMBER
204 Rosewood Lane

DEBBIE MACOMBER
311 Pelican Court

DEBBIE MACOMBER
44 Cranberry Point

DEBBIE MACOMBER
50 Harbor Street

DEBBIE MACOMBER
6 Rainier Drive

Make time for friends. Make time for

DEBBIE MACOMBER

Take a trip to
Cedar Cove

Make time for friends. Make time for

DEBBIE MACOMBER

Welcome to
Blossom Street